WORLDS APART

WORLDS APART

Valerie Maskell

This first world edition published in Great Britain 1998 by
SEVERN HOUSE PUBLISHERS LTD of
9–15 High Street, Sutton, Surrey SM1 1DF.
This title first published in the U.S.A. 1998 by
SEVERN HOUSE PUBLISHERS INC of
595 Madison Avenue, New York, N.Y. 10022.

British Library Cataloguing in Publication Data

Maskell,   Valerie

Worlds apart
1.   Mothers and daughters - Fiction
I.   Title
823.9'14 [F]

ISBN 0 7278 5317 1

Typeset by Hewer Text Composition Services Limited,
Edinburgh, Scotland.
Printed and bound in Great Britain by
MPG Books Ltd, Bodmin, Cornwall.

Chapter One

ACROSS St Andrew's Lawns, the wide green space that stretched from the cliff-top promenade to the road that ran past the hotel, two young girls were making swift if jerky progress, slightly sideways, and occasionally tossing their heads. Any onlooker used to the ways of children would have realised at once that they were being horses. And that at the same time they were being riders. Any others would have wondered if they were crippled or mentally deficient.

Reaching the evergreen dusty hedge that bordered the side of the green parallel to the road, they drew rein, dismounted, and threw themselves down on the warm grass. Josephine Livingstone and Bronwen Harries remained in the characters of Pearl Black, film star, and her boyfriend Robert Freedom.

"Comet's such a marvellous horse, but I'm afraid I can't keep him. I shall give him back to you."

"I bought him for you, Robert. I don't want him back. I've got Star. I don't want any other horse but Star."

Jo stretched her tanned arms over her head. In her mind the black horse galloped powerfully away across a field, his coat gleaming and his mane and tail streaming artistically in the wind. Bronwen, a stocky roundfaced child with straight mousy hair said, "But you see, I won't be able to ride him much longer. I've got infantile paralysis. I'll have to be in a wheelchair."

1

"Then I shall give up my career and push you about."

"I cannot allow you to give up your career for me. Anyway, she wouldn't."

"Of course she would. If she loved him."

"She might in a book, not in real life. Anyway, I don't want to be Robert any more. I want to be Pearl."

"We can't change over in the middle like that. And you can't be Pearl. I'm Pearl. You could be my sister if you like, my sister Claudette."

"Who will you be then?"

"I'll go on being Pearl."

"There's nothing in it if one of us isn't a man. I don't see why it's always me."

"It's nearly six. You'll have to go soon."

They wrangled amicably as they crossed the road to St Andrew's Hotel and went up the marble steps under the striped awning. It was the best hotel in Culvergate and Josephine's father Clive Livingstone was the Manager. That is, he was known as the Manager and was paid for being the Manager, he walked to the bank each day with the takings and was unfailingly pleasant to the guests, while Beatrice his wife ran the hotel.

At that moment she was in the bedroom she shared with him, dressing for dinner. She had been ten minutes, no more, in the bath, and now she briskly chose a clinging black crêpe dinner gown, combed her hair carefully, put on some expensive make-up and scent, and was ready in under half an hour. She would inspect the dining room, check for late arrivals at reception, go out onto the long verandahs on each side of the main entrance, now almost deserted as the guests changed into their evening clothes, and make certain that all was perfect. Her staff believed that she could spot a cigarette end at a hundred yards. Any areas of neglect would result in the culprit being sent for and reprimanded, possibly even sacked. She would encourage Mr Charles, the head waiter, who was efficient but anxious, and tell the page-boy to use a clothes brush on his tightly buttoned,

2

dark red uniform, and remind a waitress to wash her hair that night, without fail. Moving around the sumptuously furnished lounge she would gracefully welcome newcomers, and regret with others the necessity for their imminent departure. They all felt honoured when Mrs Livingstone approached. Damn it all, she *was* the St Andrews. A wonderful woman. No wonder so many people came year after year to spend their summer holidays, and often their Christmases as well.

The style of the hotel was vaguely baronial. In the wide foyer Turkish rugs, brightly red and green, were laid on the dark, polished-wood floor. They matched the carpet on the imposing staircase that rose opposite the glass swing doors of the main entrance. The newel post was heavily carved, and supported an imitation flambeau with a flame-shaped electric light. Similar illuminations were supported by four bronze statuettes, and there was a central candelabra. Everything that could shine, shone; the brass stair-rods, the glass, the olde oak side tables, the buttons on the page-boy's uniform. The atmosphere of quiet, controlled bustle, the superfical calm masking the panic in the kitchens, the tension behind the desk, the anxiety in the dining room. Self-satisfaction had no place among the staff of the St Andrews. Beatrice liked to keep them all on edge, slightly nervous. In spite of all this, or perhaps because of all this, they were proud to work at the best hotel in Culvergate, and taking the air on the promenade in the late evening, would look across at its lighted windows with pride. This was a place for rich, successful men and rich, pampered women with children who had nannies to look after them, and the ordinary people who stayed in the boarding houses and smaller private hotels, or even the less prestigious large ones, could only pass by envying them.

Jo and Bronwen lingered in the foyer, engaging the page-boy in light conversation, so that Beatrice found them there when she came out of the lift. She looked at them critically, noting that Bronwen was plain while her daughter was quite pretty, though in a rather ordinary way, with fair straight hair, and blue eyes.

They looked hot and untidy and she dismissed them quickly to the office.

"Daddy's there. You and he can take Bronwen back to school."

Bronwen's father was in what he rather grandly called 'Communications', generally working in some far-flung part of the Empire, where he required the presence of his wife, so that their only child was doomed to spend the holidays on the school premises. This was not such a dreadful fate as it might have been. There were four other girls in similar circumstances, and the school nurse remained in residence to supervise them. Most of the time was spent on the sands, where the school hut was available for changing into and out of swimming costumes, for making tea, and sheltering when it rained. Once or twice during the seven weeks summer break the Principal, Miss Rosemarie Wells, would take them out to a suitable evening entertainment. But the other girls were either older or younger than Bronwen, no one else in her form was a holiday boarder, so she was allowed to accept occasional invitations from Josephine. Beatrice permitted the invitations because she wanted to get to know Miss Wells, who was a successful woman, at the head of an important business, as she was herself. Most women, those who spent all day running their homes and doing charity work, she found dull.

Clive Livingstone was indeed in the office, considering a pre-dinner whisky and soda, though it was a bit early. He was not doing anything because there was nothing for him to do. He had wandered about, trying to look important, for most of the day, but the only time he actually attempted to deal with anything – a complaint about a back room when a front one had been promised – he was told that Mrs Livingstone already had the matter in hand. He had no objection to escorting the girls back along the front to the Princess May of Teck School for Girls. He was proud of his own child and rather sorry for Bronwen who couldn't help being a bit of a lump, and Miss Wells kept a very good dry sherry.

* * *

The May of Teck, as it was known locally, occupied three large Victorian houses, terraced but of varying designs, that bordered a square, the north side of which was open to the promenade and the sea, Culvergate being perched on the northern shore of east Kent. In the centre of the square were four hard tennis courts of which the school had exclusive use between one-thirty and three-thirty every weekday afternoon. Rosemarie Wells did not undeceive prospective parents when they assumed that the courts belonged to the school.

Clive led the girls straight up the steps to the main entrance and rang the bell. Unaccompanied the girls would have gone round the back way, but they stood in the porch, waiting for the door to be opened, and were admitted by Miss Wells herself.

Rosemarie Wells, having inherited a boys' school from her father, had turned it into a girls' school and cast herself perfectly in the role of Headmistress and Principal. She was not a graduate, indeed she had not been to university, but that did not matter, being Rosemarie Wells was enough. She had long ceased to put after her name the letters authorised by her success in an obscure correspondence course. Tall, heavy, slow-moving, and the epitome of dignity, she wore a silk dress, a shirtwaist striped in blue and brown, and a rope of pearls was draped over her very full bosom. Her wavy brown hair was rather dowdily rolled up at the nape of her neck . . . dowdily because it suited the part. Her face and features were slightly on the large side, but they were regular, and handsome. She had well-shaped, firm lips, entirely suitable to her position, but her nostrils appeared slightly distended, giving her a sensuous look which Clive had noticed the first time they met.

Dismissing the children, she suggested that Clive might have time for a sherry and led him up the wide main staircase, and along the landing to her private sitting room in the house at the south end of the building, furthest from the sea. It was large, light and beautiful, with long windows curtained in turqoise brocade, chintz upholstery and some rather heavy mahogany. Several large watercolours adorned the walls and silver-framed photographs crowded a side table. A gilt-framed mirror filled the space between the windows. Old-fashioned it might be but the room had a lived-in look – knitting, books, magazines, paperwork lay about and soft music came from a new-looking wireless set. Clive liked the atmosphere. It reminded him of his old home with his parents, a pleasant place where you could be peaceful and not worry if the newspaper slipped off your knee onto the floor when you dozed off.

Accepting a large sherry, he leaned back against the flowered cushions. It struck him that the headmistress must lead a rather lonely life in the school holidays, and possibly in the term-time as well. He was glad he was not in a hurry. He and Beatrice usually dined at seven-thirty.

"Rather looks as though things are hotting up," he remarked by way of opening the conversation. He was referring to the political situation in Europe.

"What will you do if it comes to a war? I suppose the hotel will have to close?"

"I don't think it will come to that. It's all a bluff if you ask me . . . d'you know," he leaned forward excitedly, "I was talking to one of our guests a day or two ago, interesting chap, travels a lot. Well, he was in Germany only last March and would you believe it, his brakes failed going down a hill and he crashed straight into the side of a tank, part of a procession that was going on. 'Course, he thought his number was up, but no! The tank crumpled up like tissue paper. Tissue paper! It was made of plywood! They're bluffing, you see, putting on a show to frighten us into giving them their own way. The last thing they want is a war."

Miss Wells, who had heard such stories before, received this as seriously as she could, thinking that it was a pity such a handsome and charming man could also be so incredibly stupid. She said, "Well, I do hope you're right. Though as a parent you'll probably be glad to know that I have plans to move the school to North Wales if the worst comes to the worst."

"Good idea. Good idea. Get the children out of the way," said Clive, not realising immediately that Miss Wells would be out of the way herself, as well.

"If Germany were to invade France, you'd have to close the hotel then."

"Well, I suppose we would. After all, there wouldn't be many visitors, would there, with Jerry just over the channel? There could be air raids. This place was hit in the last lot, you know. But it won't come to that. In six months' time we'll be wondering why we all got so excited."

He smiled at her comfortingly and cheerfully, and she decided to be comforted and cheered, just for the moment. They chatted on, the content of their talk having little meaning, yet serving to build up a pleasant sense of companionship.

She asked after Beatrice whom, as the mother of a pupil, she had met several times.

"Busy," said Clive rather sadly. "Immersed in the Hotel. Of course, I'm immersed in it too, but you have to keep a sense of proportion. Life goes on."

"Yes, indeed," answered Rosemarie vaguely, wondering what she supposed herself to mean.

Clive rose, placing his empty glass on the little tray on the table.

"You must join us for dinner one evening. Beatie would be pleased."

"That would be delightful. Sometimes I yearn for a little adult conversation at meals!"

Both during the term and in the holidays, Rosemarie ate in the dining room with the girls, a hundred of them or five. She rang a bell by the fireplace.

"By the way, my name is Rosemarie. It's absurd isn't it, but I should so like you and your wife to call me by it, away from the school."

7

"What's absurd about it? A beautiful name for a beautiful woman!"

What a damned silly thing to say. But it was true, he had just noticed that Rosemarie Wells, middle-aged Headmistress, was beautiful. Fortunately she did not seem to have taken offence, merely smiling a little, her eyes downcast.

He was rather silent on the way home with his young daughter, quite failing to listen to her chatter, to which he usually made an effort to pay attention. He was wondering what the full-bosomed, monumentally dignified principal of his daughter's school would be like in bed.

When they reached the St Andrew's guests were beginning to filter into the restaurant. He sent Josephine upstairs to tidy herself – in the holidays she ate with her parents in the evening, at their table in a corner between the kitchen and the entrance – then he went along to the office in search of his wife. Finding her there, perched on the desk, wearing her glasses and reading some papers, he kissed her carelessly, on the side of her forehead.

"Mind my hair," she murmured absently, patting it back into place. "Do go and change Clive, its gone quarter past. What HAVE you been doing?"

"I had a sherry at the school, with your friend Miss Wells. She says we're to call her Rosemarie."

"Really? She's not my friend, I hardly know her. But still, we could ask her to dinner some time . . . D'you think she'd come?"

"Probably. She's a bit intimidating. Always makes me feel as if I'm on the carpet."

"Yes, I suppose she is. Wonder if she's ever had a lover? That enormous bust would get in the way a bit."

He had noticed before that Beatrice had an uncanny way of voicing his own thoughts. He decided to go and dress before he was tempted to sail too close to the wind. He took the lift to the second floor, walked to the end of the corridor and through the door marked Private. Jo had turned on the

8

wireless in the sitting room and an American crooner's voice filled the apartment. Irritably he went in to turn it down. This room, though similarly designated a sitting room was as different as possible from the one at the May of Teck. The previous spring, after nine successful years at the hotel, Beatrice had discarded the furniture supplied to them by the proprietors, which was similar to that in the rest of the building, and selected square armchairs covered in grey velvet, with a settee to match, a square black table with chromium legs, and frameless mirrors. She got rid of the darkened oil paintings leaving the newly silver-grey walls bare, and changed the patterned rugs for a plain dark grey carpet fitted to the room in the new fashion. The owners would not allow her to remove the oak fire surround, so she had recklessly had it painted to match the walls and installed a modern gas fire with a curved grid that was supposed when alight to resemble burning coal, and did not. Some nameless silver flowers, their long stems curving gracefully from a black vase, completed the effect. The black, grey and silver room was extremely smart and about as inviting, Clive thought, as an operating theatre. He changed into his dinner jacket while his daughter put on a rather childish cream tussore, which she hated. After all, she would be twelve in two months' time. She had various striped or flowered dresses which were considered suitable but they all seemed to be in the wash, have buttons missing, or need ironing. She would complain to Patty, the maid only a few years older than herself whose duties included cleaning the private rooms and seeing to the family laundry. Thursday was Patty's evening off and she would probably be going out with her young man who worked at a local garage. If not she might spend the evening in her room, reading *True Confessions* or *Film Weekly*.

Patty's room was an unusual one. Reached by a narrow flight of stairs from the third floor it was a circular space contained by the glass dome that ornamented the roof. There was just room for a bed and a chest of drawers and it was either extremely cold or far too hot, but Patty liked it because it was the first room she had ever had to herself, and it had a wonderful view out to sea. There was no wardrobe and she kept her pink net and taffeta dance frock in a box under her bed. Jo thought that she might keep Patty company in her sky-filled room for part of the evening, with a back number of *True Confessions* and some sweets. But she would complain first. She knew that staff must not be allowed to get away with anything.

Rosemarie joined the five holiday boarders and Nurse for supper in the dining room. They sat together at a long table in the bay window overlooking the square to eat macaroni cheese and stewed apples with custard. The big room with nine more tables covered in white American cloth, ten brown bentwood chairs pushed in round each one, was shadowy in the middle, brightening a little towards the flat window at the back, with its less salubrious view of the asphalted playground. There were flowers and table napkins, refinements that did not appear during the term, and conversation was encouraged. Rosemarie made considerable efforts to give the place a more homely atmosphere during the holidays. The small sixth-form classroom which boasted two easy chairs, the only ones available for girls, was open to all as a common room, a wireless set was allowed and they could wear their own clothes: shorts and jumpers, brightly patterned cotton dresses, trousers even, wide cut with turn-ups, which they called slacks. Most of the rules, such as 'No talking in the corridors' and 'Lights out at 8 p.m. for Juniors and 9 p.m. for Seniors' were relaxed, but still the place was bleak. The walls, dark brown below and cream above the dado, the floors covered with dark brown linoleum, with grey haircord carpet on the stairs, the curtains of plain porridge coloured cretonne, had all been there since the May of Teck had been a boys' school. Money for renewal was somehow never available. And Rosemarie put education before decoration. The wage bill for her graduate teachers, like the cost of textbooks and writing materials, was high.

The school nurse, seated at the opposite end of the table, was quite a young woman, and prettyish. Rosemarie wondered if she was altogether a good influence. Alright when Matron was in residence perhaps but a bit too much brother-and-bob with the older girls when left to her own devices. Still she was engaged to a doctor, and hers was only a temporary appointment.

The two youngest girls, Bunty Browning and Mollie Jackson caused her no real anxiety, apart from Mollie's being delicate and suffering intermittently from asthma. But the rather silent, rarely smiling Bronwen was a bit of a worry. She was not an attractive child. Her short mousy hair parted on the side hung lank and unbecoming on either side of her rather expressionless face, and her large grey eyes with their stubby lashes had a watchful look. And Nurse had complained that she had been frightening the younger girls with tales of earthquakes and man-eating tigers set in the very outposts of the Empire inhabited by their parents. Now, apparently, she was Josephine Livingstone's best friend, and Rosemarie did not care for that either. Josephine seemed to her a rather lonely little thing, deprived as she was of a normal home life, the sort that might be too easily influenced into some kind of naughtiness, but as at the moment it was not obvious what form this naughtiness might take she allowed the friendship, which she could quite easily have broken up by moving one of the children up or down a class, to continue.

The two sixth-formers constituted a problem. Joan Forster and Dora Browning, who was Bunty's sister, had been best friends for a year or more, sharing a desk, walking side by side in the long crocodile to the games field, together whenever the opportunity arose. Sitting in the evenings they unobtrusively held hands, walking in the playground they linked arms or half-embraced. At the beginning of each term they asked to be allowed to share a bedroom – sixth-formers were only two to a room – and Matron had been instructed not to permit this. In term-time the school was a hotbed of passionate feelings, juniors with crushes on the seniors, seniors infatuated with this or that member of staff, but these two sixteen-year-olds had eyes only for each other. Then

11

there was the additional fact that Joan's parents, resident in Singapore, were in arrears with their fees. If Joan were to leave the school for any reason Rosemarie would obviously never receive the money that was owing. In any case, since the girl could not be thrown out onto the street or put unaccompanied on a boat for the Far East there was really nothing to be done. Despite the hovering fears of war the conversation was cheerful, even humorous. It was tacitly agreed that the younger girls were to be protected from anxiety, though the older ones would be invited into the sitting room to listen to the nine o'clock news. During the previous term Rosemarie had instituted a series of lessons called Current Events, designed to encourage the older girls to keep up to date with the international situation. The senior teachers took it in turns to give these lectures and by this means the headmistress hoped to give the students a wide, impartial outlook.

At the St Andrew's, though there was dancing after dinner, many of the guests crowded round the wireless set in the lounge, listened with serious faces and wondered whether they ought to cut short their holidays. Like illness, the prospect of war made one wish to be in one's own home.

Jo was a child with little appetite. She had picked at her hors-d'œvres, refused the fish and left most of her roast lamb. The ice cream she enjoyed. She ate in silence, only addressed by Clive, who encouraged her to eat and Beatrice, who told her to sit up straight, at long intervals, but she enjoyed the festive atmosphere of the dining room. A trio of musicians played on the tiny platform, and although it was broad daylight outside the electric flambeaux glowed, giving extra sparkle to the glass and silver. The men were smart in dinner jackets, the women in their clinging low-backed gowns were for the most part elegant, and even the children present were dressed up, though the younger ones had partaken of Nursery Supper earlier, afterwards being exiled to their rooms. Seeing a boy rather younger than her daughter looking bored and miserable, Beatrice decided that the two children should play table tennis together in the games room after the meal. Jo knew better than the protest but she was resentful, and played as badly as she could. Having lost the game she escaped. Meeting her father in the foyer she begged for some potato crisps and he fetched her two packets from the bar. She hugged him briefly and ran up the stairs – she was not allowed to use the lift – to share them with Patty. She was glad to hear that Patty's young man was working late. They sat on the bed in the sky-filled dome, which was still warm from the day's sunshine and ate crisps and read aloud bits out of *True Confessions* and were very companionable. This lurid periodical had a peculiar pungent smell which seemed to Jo to be the very odour of evil, though Patty said it was just the printer's ink. The fact that photographs rather than drawings were used to illustrate these very personal histories seemed to vouch for their truth. Only later, after she was in bed, did Jo ponder the meaning of the sensational headlines. WOULD MY TWINS BE BLACK? THE HEART-RENDING STORY OF A LIVERPOOL HOUSEWIFE, or MY BOSS'S EVIL POWER: WHAT HAPPENED TO A YOUNG DENTAL NURSE IN LINCOLNSHIRE.

As the sky darkened above and around them in their eyrie, dance music became audible from below, and out at sea the lightships flashed their lanterns on, and off, on, and off. Knowing that no one would bother to check on her presence in her bedroom until later Josephine ignored her official nine o'clock summer holiday bedtime, until Patty rose and removed the metal curlers from her straight dark hair. She slept with these intruments of torture in place each night, but by evening the rolled-up ends she so desired had returned to lankness and she was forced to put them in again for as long a period as possible if she intended going out during the evening.

"Why don't you have a perm?"

"My Ken doesn't like permed hair," said Patty with pride. "It goes all frizzy."

She smoothed back her fringe, securing it with a ready-made ribbon bow fixed to a clip, purchased from Woolworths. She rubbed Potter and Moores powder creme into her pale complexion and made a satisfyingly glamorous mouth with bright red lipstick. Unfortunately the film-star effect of these measures was somewhat diminished by the old navy-blue mac which, originally second-hand, she had previously worn to school.

"You'd better go down," she said, trying to get a full length view of herself in her small mirror. "Your Mum wouldn't half create if she knew you was up here."

"She won't know," said Jo who wanted to stay behind with *True Confessions*. "Anyway, it's generally Dad who comes up in the evening, and he wouldn't say anything."

"He might not say anything to you, but if he told your Mum she'd probably give me my cards."

"What cards?"

"Insurance cards, of course. Give me the sack."

"That wouldn't be fair."

Patty laughed sardonically, as she drew the thin curtains round the encircling glass and Jo felt she had said something childish. Though surely her mother would not be unfair?

"I've got to go, or Ken'll think I've let him down. Come on." Reluctantly Josephine descended the steep flight of stairs which led directly from the dome, followed by Patty. In her own room she withdrew from under the mattress her latest literary acquisition, one of the *Schoolgirl's Library* series. The little books with their crude black and yellow paper covers, were favourites of hers and Bronwen's. They cost fourpence each and so were easily affordable to one with sixpence a week pocket money. They were concealed because both girls, while enjoying their sensationalism, knew perfectly well that their cheapness, ugliness and poor quality print would hardly recommend them to parents or teachers. The one in which Josephine soon became absorbed concerned the daring exploits of Valerie Drew, Schoolgirl Detective in Secret. Rapidly identifying with this slim blonde heroine only a couple

14

of years older than herself Jo hardly had time to cram it under her pillow, switch off her lamp and pretend to be asleep when she heard her father enter the private apartment and open her bedroom door softly. Satisfied that all was well, he tiptoed away, leaving his daughter to brood over the dullness of her own life compared to that of Valerie Drew, not to mention the heroines of *True Confessions*.

Chapter Two

WHEN the school assembled on the second Wednesday of the autumn term Rosemarie offered up prayers of thankfulness for peace. She told the girls how Mr Neville Chamberlain had returned from Munich having out of this nettle danger plucked this flower safety. She spoke briefly of the tragedy that had been so narrowly avoided, and announced that a special celebratory School Social would take place on the following Saturday evening. If she detected a faint groan from the resident staff she ignored it. Socials were no fun for her either, doomed as she was to playing the piano for most of the time. The occasion would consist of dancing and games in the gymnasium, with lemonade and biscuits at half time, and coffee for the staff. Everyone wore some form of party dress for these events, thinness of material being for some reason the most important requirement. Even in winter the revellers would shiver in art silk print dresses, despite the woolly vests that seemed so determined to make their presence visible at the neck. This evening Rosemarie would wear her ankle-length voile, artistically patterned in shades of rose and mauve, originally purchased for Sports Day two years before.

Socials were arranged not merely for the enjoyment and relaxation of the pupils, but to instil into them the way of civilised society, though success in both these areas was decidedly limited. For the staff they were a tiresome encroachment on their free time, and most of the senior girls emulated this attitude.

Jo, who had heard about Mr Chamberlain on the wireless earlier that morning, found she was slightly disappointed. Talk of the closing of the St Andrews Hotel had given rise in her to hopes that she and her parents might move to a private house, with a garden, where she could have a dog, and her mother would never tell her to go away because she was busy.

Jo was quite proud of Beatrice's elegant and youthful appearance, pleased with her obvious power and importance and yet she often wished for the sort of maternal figure depicted in the comics she had read when younger. These ladies were invariably to be found in the kitchen, always wore aprons and were constantly involved with the well-being of their families. Rupert's mother was a good example, excepting, or course, that she was a bear. Jo could not help hoping that, once released from the hotel, Beatrice would turn into one of these mothers. It was too late, she supposed vaguely, for her parents to have more children. And even if it were not, they would be too young to be companionable. Perhaps if this different way of life were to come about her father could be persuaded to adopt a sister for her, one who would fit neatly into the pattern of her life and take the place of the imaginary sibling who was her frequent companion.

She would have been surprised to learn that her headmistress shared, up to a point and not without a degree of shame, her feelings of disappointment. Rosemarie had been running the school, with considerable academic success, and sometimes a little financial success as well, for just over fifteen years. It had grown from five pupils in the first term to one hundred and twenty-eight in the current one, which was its forty-sixth. And it had begun to bore her a little. Most of all she was bored with Socials.

In her sitting room she slipped a glass of sherry to fortify herself for the celebration ahead. On her piano a pile of sheet music lay ready for her to take upstairs to the gym, where there was a 'baby grand'. She liked to surprise the girls with the up-to-dateness of her repertoire and had been practising 'Top Hat' and other hits from current films. A gramophone would have been adequate for the dancing but playing herself gave her more control and was rather better than making conversation with the teachers for two and a half hours. She would have a half-hour break during which everyone would join in games organised by Miss Colman, the games mistress. There would be games at the beginning, too, to break up the age groups and get things going. Most of the seniors were in love with Collie, as she was privately known and would put on a show of enthusiasm for her sake.

Standing at the window she saw a car stop outside the main entrance to her left. A child, Josephine Livingstone, jumped out and ran along to the side entrance. The driver opened the window and called to her, "Like my new acquisition?" He was seated in a gleaming new black Hillman Minx. Rosemarie waved in a friendly way, but since she could hardly carry on a conversation at this distance she drew back. After all, had she not the previous term severely reprimanded Pauline Streatfield for calling out to the fishmonger's boy from her classroom window? On the other hand she not did not wish to offend the father of a pupil. So she went downstairs and opened the front door.

At first she thought she had made a mistake. The man climbing the front steps was in the uniform of an army officer – smart, well-cut service dress. He removed his peaked cap as he approached and it was indeed Clive Livingstone, with the three pips of a captain on each shoulder. He was quickly admitted, and she led him in to the conveniently situated 'visitors' room'. Immediately to the left of the front door and used exclusively for interviewing the parents of pupils and prospective pupils, it was elegantly if uncomfortably furnished with inherited furniture, and was always in readiness for its appointed task. Now, since the corridors were full of girls and staff on the way up to the evening's gaieties, it was a useful bolt-hole.

There was one framed photograph, on a side table. It showed a very good-looking young man dressed like Clive in the uniform of an army officer. The collar of his greatcoat was turned up and his cap was worn at a rakish angle. If the opportunity arose, Rosemarie would admit to parents that he had been her cousin and fiancé, whom she had lost in 1918. This was perfectly true, although she had lost him not to death but to a girl called Muriel Evans. And he had been rather less than her fiancé, though rather more than her cousin.

So it was with a sense of inevitability that she turned to face Clive Livingstone.

"I've joined the Territorials," he said. "Felt I had to do something." He did not add that this was a short cut to getting a commission which might prove elusive if he waited to be conscripted. And conscription was in the air, so he did not regret his decision. Especially not when he saw Rosemarie's expression.

In her flowered voile she seemed softer, more approachable, though at the same time her dangling jade earrings gave her a worldly look.

He had meant to make some vague comment about his daughter's progress. Instead he took Rosemarie's hand and said, "You know what I want to say, but we can't talk here."

"I'm going up to town tomorrow. The lounge of the Cumberland Hotel at four o'clock."

Rosemarie, hearing her own words, was astonished, but found she had no desire to withdraw her suggestion. Clive was astonished as well. He'd expected to woo her, to court and persuade her over a fairly long period, during which he could at any point change his mind. He felt almost cheated, as though he had been preparing to climb a tree to pluck some delicious, perhaps slightly overripe fruit, and now the prize had dropped neatly into his hand as he stood on the ground . . . But he said he would be at the Cumberland on the Sunday, and kissed her very gently on the lips, once, before unobtrusively taking his leave.

Bronwen said to Jo, "Your father's in the visitors' room with Miss Wells."

"No, he's not. He had to go to a meeting."

"Well, he was. I saw him go in. What have you been doing?"

"I haven't been doing anything. Have I?" She racked her brains for possible misdemeanours to which the headmistress might wish to draw her father's attention, adding, "I did tell Mary Wilson that Miss Craig had B.O. You don't think she could have told her, do you?"

"Shouldn't think so. Anyway, its true. Perhaps Miss Wells and your Dad are having an affair."

"What d'you mean, an affair?"

"A love affair, stupid."

"Don't be silly."

"You're the one that's silly. I expect he was putting his hand up her skirt."

"Of course he wasn't. I'm going to join in the game. Come on."

"You're a baby. You don't know anything, do you?" But Bronwen followed Jo to join the group around Miss Colman. Jo moved round to the other side. There were times when she almost didn't like having Bronwen Harries for a friend. She said such awful things that no one else would ever think of. Some of them were funny and some sort of exciting, but she didn't want her to talk about Daddy like that.

Later in the evening, when Rosemarie was playing the piano, Jo looked at her carefully. She knew about divorce and people who wanted to get rid of their husbands or wives so that they could marry someone else, but it was not conceivable that her father should prefer the dowdy, heavy Miss Wells to the slender, youthful Beatrice who looked quite like a film star when she had her evening dress on. Except that Mum was busy so much of the time. She'd seen her father's expression when he was reproved for touching his wife's hair, or joined her in the private sitting room to find that she was on the point of leaving. And Dad was so nice and kind, she wondered why her mother did not love him more. She considered momentarily the idea of her parents divorcing, with Miss Wells becoming her stepmother, but the ideal was so ludicrous it nearly made her laugh out

21

loud. Supposing she hugged you to her chest! Jo felt herself blush at the thought. It would certainly be better to keep her own flat-chested, undemonstrative mother.

By nine o'clock quite a festive atmosphere pervaded the gymnasium. The vaulting horse and other equipment had been pushed into a side room, and although the ribstalls still lined the walls and the ropes dangled in a rather sinister way from the ceiling, the place was really quite cheerful. A big vase of flowers stood in front of the velvet curtains that concealed the tiny stage, there was a buzz of chatter every time the music stopped and all the lights were on though it was not yet dark outside. Jo had danced twice with Joan Forster, with whom she had fallen in love during the school production of *The Beaux Stratagem* in the previous term. Unfortunately as rehearsals proceeded Miss Purvis, the English teacher, had been forced by Rosemarie to cut more and still more lines on the grounds of impropriety, with the result that the plot had been quite impossible to follow; but in spite of this Joan, who was tall and buxom, had made a dashing Archer, whose androgynous appeal had devastated a considerable number of younger girls. Most of them had recovered from this affliction by the end of the summer holidays, but Jo still presented bunches of violets bought with her pocket money, sat next to her when the rare opportunity offered, and daydreamed about being marooned with her on a desert island. To brush past Joan in the corridor, to receive a careless smile, provided a moment to treasure all day, while to be sent on an errand, to fetch plimsolls or tennis racket was the height of bliss. Her imagination never went beyond these delights, yet she thought she would never love anyone as much as she loved Joan Forster. They had danced two waltzes together, the first being the result of a lucky chance in the Paul Jones, and the second she had plucked up courage to request. Apart from the difficulty caused by the difference in height these dances had been quite a success, since they had been taught by the same teacher – ballroom dancing was an extra, half a guinea per term, on Fridays after school. Now the evening was almost over she felt confident enough to approach her beloved again. Joan, magnificent in a red and white printed rayon with a flared skirt and daringly low neck, was sitting among her friends. When Rosemarie started the last waltz Jo nerved herself to join the group of older girls. She stood in front of Joan waiting for her to finish her conversation, which took an uncomfortably long time. In fact she considered walking away, but thought that she would look even sillier and more conspicious if she did. So she waited miserably embarrassed, until Joan turned her head.

"Could we . . . have this dance?"

It came out in a silly sort of whisper. Joan rose, and for one second she was overjoyed. But Joan turned to her friend Mavis Welsh, pulling her in to the dance, saying as she did so "Oh, do go away, you little pest. I've had two dances with you already."

She said something to Mavis and they both giggled as they waltzed away. Jo felt the colour rush to her face and tears fill her eyes. She turned and sauntered as casually as she could across to where the girls from her own form had congregated at intervals during the evening, but they were all dancing except Elsa Parrish, a girl from a poorer background than the others. Her dress looked as if it had been handed down from her elder sister, or bought to allow for growth, for though already well worn it was still too long and the supposed-to-be-puffed sleeves hung dismally. Her hair was lank and she had a slightly sour, unwashed smell which worried Rosemarie and made other girls reluctant to sit next to her. She greeted Jo eagerly.

"We could dance," she said, "it's the last Waltz."

"I don't want to dance with you," said Jo, as rudely as she could. This made her feel better at first, and then later on, much worse. They stood side by side watching the dancers, until Rosemary crashed out the introduction to "Auld Lang Syne" when they were forced to join in the circle, crossing their arms and holding each other's hands until the wretched thing was over.

*   *   *

23

At nine-thirty when the Social was ending Beatrice left the manager's office at St Andrews for her customary tour of the public rooms. The cocktail bar, the card room, the lounge, the verandahs, the restaurant, the ballroom if it was in use. She visited them all each evening, even during the off-season. Sometimes she found reasons for anxiety, negligence by a member of staff, a guest drinking too much or making a nuisance of himself, or not up to to standard sartorially. Women guests, she found, were rarely guilty of these misdemeanours. In any case she felt capable of dealing with any crisis, even those in the kitchen which were frequent.

Tonight she felt she had been reprieved. She walked along the carpeted corridor, across the foyer and past the reception desk to the restaurant, where there was a dinner-dance in progress. The hotel not being full, she had given orders for a space in the centre of the room to be cleared for dancing, instead of using the ballroom, which would have been sparsely filled. The atmosphere was lively. At the removal of the threat of war, people were ready to chat to strangers, sharing their relief and plans for the future. The men, naturally, were all in dinner jackets, the women in full-length gowns of clinging crêpe, pleated and draped silk, or stiff, gleaming taffeta. The colours glowed and mingled under the moving lights directed onto the dance floor. Beatrice was wearing her newest, black of course, but with a very low back indeed. Usually she was ready to talk at this time, to join in conversations, to sympathise with even the least justified complaint, but tonight she just wanted to look. To look and listen and savour the joy of being exactly where she wanted to be, of doing exactly what she wanted to do. The crowded dance floor, the peace and quiet in the card room, the welcoming dignity of the foyer, the romantically lamplit verandahs, they were all hers. Her achievement and pride. A well-run, first-class hotel. And now she would not have to leave it, close it down, become an army wife somewhere, go mad with boredom. If Clive had been tedious before, he showed signs of being even worse now he had joined the Territorials. In the hotel it didn't matter, she was busy, there was space. But in an officer's quarter somewhere, among other military families, it simply didn't bear thinking about. Now that fear was removed she could look forward happily. Especially now that he had a new toy, his first car, as well as the Territorial Army to occupy his time.

As she returned to the foyer her husband and child came up the steps. She must tell him to go and take off that silly-looking uniform, quite out of place in the hotel. Josephine looked glum for a child who was supposed to have been enjoying herself. As she met them a rather gushing middle-aged woman with rigid iron-grey waves of hair and a rather too-youthful evening gown of cerise tulle, hurried up to them.

"Oh, Mrs Livingstone, I've been hoping to catch you . . . and is this your dear little girl? What a pretty dress!" She bent down quite unnecessarily to address Jo, putting on a specially coy, teasing voice. "I think you've been out to a party! Did you have a lovely time?"

Jo, standing close to her father, stared at the carpet, finding nothing to say. The woman continued to Beatrice. "How lucky you are, my dear! A handsome husband, and a lovely little girl."

Jo began to trace the pattern on the carpet with the toe of her silver, one-strap shoe.

Beatrice looked down at her child.

"Funny little thing. Not a bit like me. I've given up trying to understand her. Did you want me for anything special, Mrs Carpenter?"

"Oh, well, I know it may not seem very important . . ." The woman launched apologetically into a very minor complaint, and Clive took Jo away. As they went up in the lift he felt displeased with his wife. Nobody likes to be described to a stranger as a 'funny little thing'. He remembered visiting Beatrice in the nursing home where Jo had been born. 'Funny little thing' was what she had called her then. Adding that she was more like a monkey than anything, and referring to her as

25

'the monkey' until her own mother had reprimanded her. She was not interested in children, and had not wanted any of her own. Josephine represented a momentary lapse very early in the married life of her parents.

Beatrice had cared for the baby quite conscientiously, according to the current ideas of child-rearing. Feeding her at set hours, leaving her to cry, were accepted as being good for babies, but you were supposed to talk to them, and this Beatrice found more difficult. When Clive applied for, and to her immense surprise was offered, the managership of the St Andrews, a nanny was found, an unqualified but loving young woman, who stayed until Jo started at a local kindergarten. It was Clive who usually found himself free to take and fetch her from school, to tuck her in at night when the maid responsible had put her to bed. Beatrice, having at first shared and eventually taken over the managership of the hotel, was always too busy. But she was so good at the job. The guests were happy, the owners delighted, the staff hardworking and reasonably content, and Clive, who was reduced to wandering about trying to look as if he was about to do something, told himself that he was a lucky man. But he did not believe that Jo was a lucky little girl.

"What is it, pet?" he said as they entered the private apartment. "Has something upset you?"

Jo shook her head fiercely, and broke away to run into her own room. Clive sighed. There was no doubt that his wife was a rotten apology for a mother. He decided to mention the matter to Rosemarie, though it was doubtful if she would want him to talk about his daughter in the lounge of the Cumberland Hotel at four o'clock the next day. He was glad she had chosen a Sunday, otherwise who would meet Jo from school? As it was all he had to do was to say that he was required to spend the day on Army business. Rosemarie! There was a woman who ought to have married and had kids! What a criminal waste of that vast, maternal bosom! It would certainly be different from sleeping with Beatrice. Rosemarie would take up a lot more of the bed, for a start. He smiled inwardly at this joke and thought it was a pity he couldn't share it with his daughter, who so sadly needed a joke to cheer her up. He decided to go down and fetch her a packet of crisps from the bar.

Chapter Three

PATTY and Jo left the hotel by the staff entrance at four o'clock on the following Wednesday. Jo was happily excited. For months she had listened to stories of Patty's home and family, the four older brothers, the married sister, the young twins and the sister with a baby, and had angled for an invitation. Beatrice was actively discouraging; Clive didn't think it could do much harm; Patty was doubtful, though her Mum was reported as saying that Jo would be welcome. Jo thought Patty's mother sounded nice, so they were on the way. At the May of Teck, lessons ended at twelve-forty-five on Wednesdays, and it was Patty's half day, too. She had two a week and a whole day only once a month, but she had returned to the St Andrews especially to fetch Jo. After tea they would go to the first house at the Regal Cinema, in the square, and see *Snow White and the Seven Dwarfs*, and Jo would be home before nine o'clock. Patty promised Jo that they would have tubs of ice cream in the interval, while the organ played and the coloured lights showed up the complicated drapery of curtains around the screen, but just before they set out Clive handed his daughter half-a-crown with the words "That will pay for your seats, and you can treat Patty to an ice cream." He wondered why Patty looked disappointed, though Jo guessed that Patty wanted to pay for the ice cream herself.

Jo felt quite nervous as they approached the home of the Mason family. They were at the back of the town, as far as possible from the sea, in a street of tall, narrow, Victorian houses that had seen better days. Jo asked the number and on being told ran ahead and was halfway up the steps before she saw that Patty was waiting by a gate from which another narrower flight of steps led downwards into a dank concrete-floored space.

"This is the way. We don't never use the front door."

At another time Jo would painstakingly and without giving offence, have corrected Patty's grammar, but the moment seemed inopportune. She returned and followed Patty down to the 'area'. Patty opened a door and called out, "Mum! We're here."

She led Jo directly into the huge kitchen, where once a Victorian cook had ruled with a rod of iron. The old range was still present and still used, though now supplemented by a gas cooker. The huge dresser at the far end was piled high, not only with crockery but with with brushes, combs, a straw hat, a small enamel chamber pot and a fruitcake. In the middle was a huge deal table at which sat a young red-haired woman wearing a lot of make-up. She was feeding a fat, pale baby with a bottle which seemed to contain tea. She looked what Jo knew her mother would have called 'common', and later on Jo decided that this was due to her eyebrows, which appeared to have been completely removed and then drawn on, very thin and arched, with black crayon. This was obviously Ada, the sister with the baby. Patty's mother was there too. The first thing you noticed about her was her hair, because it was red like Ada's, almost shoulder length, but straight and secured with a slide. She was wearing a clean, flowered, crossover overall, with a blouse underneath, but no skirt, because Jo could not help noticing the bare veiny thighs when the front edges of the overall gaped apart which they did a lot of the time. Her arms, protruding from the too-tight short sleeves of the blouse were red to the elbows, and then very white. She had a high colour, but no make-up at all.

"Here she is then, well, come along in, dearie, We've heard a lot about you from Pat. I've just made a pot of tea."

Ada looked at Jo without saying anything and to cover her embarrassment Jo went round to admire the baby, which she did not like the look of at all. Babies that stayed in the hotel were clean and curled and frilled and cuddly, and smelt gorgeous. This one did not. She was glad to take the cup of tea which Patty's mother placed, saucerless on the table for her but there was far too much sugar in it and the lack of a saucer made her uncomfortable. In fact she was feeling more and more out of place. The clock on the cluttered mantelshelf over the range told her it was barely twenty past four – over an hour before they could depart to the pictures. The fact that nothing to eat was produced with the tea was perhaps a blessing. The atmosphere, strongly tainted with baby, the washing boiling on the range, the cabbage cooked the day before and the kippers they'd all had for breakfast, was not conducive to appetite. Jo decided that 'Tea' must have meant simply tea.

Jo wondered how they could possibly pass the time. She had not realised that Patty's family would be not only poor, but common. Only poor people wore overalls all day, and no skirt. Only poor people had babies who smelt, and drank tea without using saucers. Only common people wore too much make-up on their faces and grubby down-at-heel bedroom slippers on their feet, like Ada. Jo saw that her ideas were all wrong. Knowing Patty's family lived in a big but shabby house, and were always, from what Patty said, laughing and jolly, she had visualised something more like the idealised homes of the fiction she read, often concerning households that had seen better days. In these spacious homes the china did not match, but was thin and pretty just the same, the tablecloth was pristine, if darned, the rugs and curtains shabby but clean, and the whole place light and smelling of fresh air. But these were lived in by families that had come down in the world, whereas Patty's family had not yet begun to go up, in spite of Patty's father doing quite well as a master builder. Jo sat awkwardly at the table, trying to drink her tea, and wondering what to say. After a while there were voices and hurrying feet on the area steps and June and Ronnie came in, grubby from playing on a piece of waste ground. The twins

31

were about Jo's age, and although they went quiet on seeing the visitor there was hope for some conversation when the subject of film stars arose. When they found that Jo had never seen Tom Mix and did not like Westerns, even this fascinating topic failed them.

Two of the older brothers appeared next, home from work. They were happily discussing the football match they hoped to attend on the following Saturday afternoon, which eased things along somehow until their mother reprimanded them for talking about something that could not interest the guest, whereupon they too fell silent. It was a little easier during the meal that in the end followed, though Jo refused jelly because she had never seen jelly in a pudding basin. Jellies of her acquaintance were either glistening, battlemented castles or set in shallow glasses and decorated with whipped cream. The basin was crazed with frequent immersion in boiling water, and she thought it might not be clean.

"Do have some, Jo, my Mum done it specially," whispered Patty, so of course she gave in. The loaf was on the table and Patty's Mum clutched it to her bosom and sawed slices off in a very dangerous way. Having seen its proximity to the baby's enamel chamber pot, Jo was able to refuse the fruit cake with considerable determination.

Before they left to go to the cinema Patty took her to the outside lavatory. It was clean, but the toilet paper was rough and crinkled, and there were also squares of newspaper on a hook. There was nowhere to wash your hands and Jo did not like to wash them afterwards in the kitchen. She noticed that Patty did not bother either. Perhaps none of them did. She hoped she would not get some dreadful disease; her own mother had definitely stated that this was a possibility in such circumstances, but there was no help for it.

They walked down the hill and through the square to the cinema, and joined the queue for the ninepennies. Both were regular film-goers, though Jo usually patronised the Astoria which was nearer to the St Andrews. She was allowed to go with a friend, on Saturday afternoons, providing the film being shown had a U certificate. Otherwise, of course, children were not allowed in. It was quite cold, waiting in the queue. Jo had on her beige summer coat, and Patty was wearing the jacket of her best navy coat and skirt over a too-summery pink and white cotton dress. Jo deplored this. You couldn't wear a costume jacket other than with its natural partner, a skirt of the same material, and she meant to explain this sometime, though not today. She always felt it incumbent on her to educate Patty who usually accepted Jo's recommendations without resentment. Patty had put on more lipstick, before setting out, and more "Poudre de Tokalon", and just a dash of "Evening in Paris." Soon Jo understood why. As the matinee audience poured out and they moved towards the box office they were joined by Patty's young man, from the garage – Ken. Jo, having never seen him before, was surprised to find that he was much shorter and thinner than she had imagined. Younger, too, and he had a boil on his neck. He had fair curly hair, cut painfully short at the back and sides and was wearing a white shirt, with the collar open outside his navy-blue jacket, and grey trousers. Obviously this was a planned meeting. He was about to accompany them into the cinema. Jo felt cheated. This was to have been her treat, with someone whose company she enjoyed. Now Patty would talk to him instead. And what about paying? Should she offer to pay for him as well? That would amount to . . . two shillings and threepence, after which she would not have enough for the ices. Patty's young man produced half a crown for the tickets, and would not even let Jo pay for herself. This made her thoroughly miserable. She was rich, well, fairly rich, anyway, and they were poor, common people, and favours could not be accepted from them. She also felt obscurely that she had lost her rights in Patty. The organ was playing and the lights were up so they easily found their seats. Patty sat between Ken and Jo, with Jo feeling unnecessary and out of place. Everything had gone wrong. She managed to enjoy most of the programme but sometime before the main feature came to an end she started to want to go to the Ladies. She could have told Patty, who would have gone with her, but she somehow couldn't do that with Ken there, especially as by that time he and Patty were holding hands. So she spent the rest of the evening in acute discomfort and when they were all three within a hundred yards of the St Andrews she suddenly ran ahead into the hotel without saying goodnight. Almost in tears she dashed into the guests' cloakroom on the ground floor, which she was not allowed to use, and had never seen a more beautiful sight than the gleaming white porcelain.

Later that evening, when Clive asked her if she had enjoyed herself she mumbled, "It was alright," and refused to say more. Beatrice said she had always known it would be a mistake.

But she did not say this until later that evening, when she and Clive were alone. They had entertained a guest to dinner. Beatrice, naturally unaware that her husband and Rosemarie Wells had met in the Cumberland Hotel on the previous Sunday, had decided that her daughter's absence with Patty provided an ideal opportunity to extend her social life to include Jo's headmistress. The hotel was less than full, everything was running smoothly, and she proposed that after dinner in the restaurant they should repair to the private sitting room for coffee and liqueurs. Should they, she asked herself, invite one or two more guests? They had business aquaintances, there were people she liked, but there never seemed to be time for more than superficial relationships, even if she really wanted them. Her life was busy and challenging, there was the opportunity to dress up and to be admired, every evening. Until recently she had not wanted more, but now it occurred to her that here was another woman on her own level of ambition and confidence. Most of the middle-class women she knew controlled a household, a maid or two, but she and Rosemarie both had the responsibility of huge establishments. She looked forward to talking to her and decided to invite no one else. She would suggest to Clive that he drove their guest home, but he was being slightly less than cooperative.

"Are you sure you want her to come? She might be boring. It is our evening off, after all."

"It will be nice to have someone different to talk to. And we shan't have the bother of Jo."

"Jo's not a bother."

"You know what I mean. Rosemarie wouldn't want kids around. Especially kids from her own school."

"I suppose not. Well, I'll probably leave you to it after dinner, and go down and have a hand of bridge. There's sure to be somebody wanting to make up a four."

"You'll do no such thing. What would she think if you rushed off as soon as dinner was over?"

Clive did not doubt that Rosemarie would be considerably relieved if she did not have to make polite conversation with her new lover once dinner was over, but he could hardly put this into words. In fact there was a great deal that he could not put into words, even to himself.

On the previous Saturday he had left the school in a state bordering shock; his impulsive phrase "We can't talk here" had been taken up with such swiftness and decision – the sort of swiftness and decision which his wife would undoubtedly admire. But he had not intended anything decisive to happen so soon. A flirtation, perhaps, something that would give a bit of a kick to the daily round, the common task, as it were. Then perhaps, one day, if she was willing, and the opportunity arose naturally . . . he had not seen himself lying to Beatrice and taking a slow Sunday train up to town the next morning.

If Rosemarie had experienced any doubts she had ignored them. During the previous week the apparent imminence of war had cleared her mind to a remarkable degree. She had begun to ask herself what she wanted from life, if she had changed, whether being headmistress of her own quite prestigious school was sufficiently fulfilling. When her cousin had departed with his bride she had faced the fact that for her generation of women there was a shortage of possible husbands. Untrained but gifted, she had taught the youngest boys in her father's school and become interested in education, developed ideas about the position of women in a male-dominated society. As headmistress of the May of Teck she had instilled into her girls the belief that women could do and be whatever they chose, that marriage was not the only, or even the best option. She had invited them to admire her own independence, but her loneliness she had not admitted, even to herself. She had put on weight, become both intellectually and physically an imposing figure, acquiring an undoubted air of majesty which suited her status but kept at a distance the very few eligible men she met. Then at forty-one, during the long solitary weeks of that war-clouded summer holiday, she had faced the probability of a lonely middle age and had begun to remember her lover. Not that she had ever quite forgotten him, but she had managed to avoid dwelling on what might have been, and disciplined herself not to recall the hours they had spent in bed in her room on the top floor. Now, with the sun shining outside, the school as quiet as the grave, her own childhood friend having left after her brief yearly visit, her usual occupations palled. Her piano stood reproachfully unopened, her books were boring, the watercolours she painted were inept, her embroidery a mess, and between her and these pastimes came the long-repressed memories of her cousin Dennis, who, being an orphan, had spent his leaves at the school. And when it came to embarkation leave, well . . . The afternoons, the nights, the passion she had felt for him, the physical joy they had shared. He hadn't minded her plumpness; caressing her heavy breasts he had said she was a real girl. For two weeks, and then later for a few brief periods, she had been a real girl, but to no one had she ever been a real woman. It wasn't fair.

Rosemarie looked at herself in the gilt-framed mirror between the long windows. She'd meant to have the room redecorated this summer but a number of the girls' beds needed replacing. The mirror had been there ever since she could remember. It had reflected her in her cousin's arms . . .

"Why shouldn't I be a real woman?" she asked her reflection.

She liked Clive. Liked the look of him. He was tall, well-set up, she approved of the kindly affectionate tone he used to his young daughter, and the responsible way in which he personally returned Bron to the fold after her visits. She'd become aware of his admiration, and decided to encourage him. He was married, yes, but there were not enough men to go round. There had to be some sharing. It was quite simple. So when he had said "We can't talk here" she had been ready with her plan.

He'd looked surprised and had said, "I say, are you sure?" but agreed to meet her. But she'd been afraid he wouldn't come. She had reached the Cumberland, the new and glamorous hotel at Marble Arch where she had stayed once or twice before, and booked a double room for herself and her husband Captain Livingstone. Though the management of the hotel would discourage unmarried couples she did not believe they would doubt her, with her heaviness and her dowdiness, her majestic poise. They did not. She'd found a table in the lounge where they were serving tea, told the waiter she would wait for her husband and sat alone for over twenty minutes, before Clive, in uniform as she had half expected he might be, appeared in the entrance she was anxiously watching. After tea and toasted scones, they had ascended to the seventh floor, found room 731 and spent three surprisingly satisfactory hours before Clive left to catch the last train back to Culvergate.

Naturally they both tried to suppress the memory of those hours as they enjoyed the hors-d'œuvre, and the soup, the fish and the roast lamb, and the crème brûlée, but it was not easy for either of them. Beatrice was a bit disappointed in Rosemarie. She was really very heavy-going. As they mounted in the lift towards

37

the private sitting room nobody seemed to be able to think of anything to say. Beatrice, seldom at a loss, tried to find some compliment regarding her guest's evening gown. It was black lace, dreadfully matronly, and certainly not new. The double row of small graduated pearls and the drop earrings really didn't help at all. You'd have thought she'd have had her hair done, too, for this evening. It wasn't likely that she went out to dinner very often, after all. She considered her own appearance with satisfaction. Her husband was staring fixedly at the indicator, as if uncertain when they would reach their own floor. Well, one would hardly have expected him to stare at dowdy middle-aged Rosemarie but still, an admiring glance or two in her own direction would have been nice.

Clive was thinking how extraordinary it was that a fat matronly lady in black lace and pearls, the accepted uniform really of fat matronly ladies, should for him have such an abundance of 'it'. He knew it was damn silly, of course, but he could hardly keep his hands off her.

Jo was in bed, having washed minimally at the basin in the corner of her room, and been visited by her father, who had fetched her milk and biscuits from the kitchenette. He was worried about her, she didn't seem to have enjoyed herself at all, and he'd have liked to tell Beatrice, but with Rosemarie there he could not do so. When coffee had been brought up to them he poured out cherry brandy with a hand that was, what with one thing and another, slightly unsteady, and excused himself in order to go and look in on his daughter. As he left the room he heard his wife saying, "Clive's such a wonderful father. Just as well really because I'm afraid I'm not at all the maternal type," and he wondered why people always said "I'm afraid", when they were really rather proud of something. They said, "I'm afraid I'm rather particular," or "I'm afraid I have a very small appetite." A few days earlier a woman guest had said to him, "I'm afraid I can't stand violence," as though every one else enjoyed it. He certainly did not enjoy violence himself;

38

and as he walked along the passage, he asked himself why in that case he had joined the Terriers, and why he'd been just a bit disappointed, if he was honest, when the threat of war was apparently removed? He would have liked to hear Rosemarie's reply but failed to do so. She said, "I suppose I am a mother manquée."

Beatrice, not understanding, said vaguely, "Oh, I'm sure you are not."

Rosemarie said, "I do like to feel I am a mother to my girls," knowing while she spoke that this was absurd, that her relationship to the children and adolescents in her care was not in the least like that of a mother.

"But you would not really prefer to be the mother of a family, would you? I mean you don't have to wash them, or see to their clothes, or look after them when they're ill. You have a career, your life is interesting. I remember that speech you made at the last prizegiving . . . I found it quite inspiring. It was so much what I've always felt myself, that women are wasted half the time, that they waste themselves . . ."

"Did I say that? I wouldn't want to suggest that running a home and bringing up a family wasn't worthwhile . . ."

"No, you didn't quite say that, but you implied that there are better ways of spending your life, and I think you are right."

Conversation proceeded fluently enough and Rosemarie enjoyed the evening, amused by the slightly bizarre situation. Certainly she seemed to have an admirer in the wife of her lover, who was obviously ambitious. Yet Rosemarie, in spite of her championship of independent women, had never quite managed to convince herself that running the school was more satisfying than marrying Dennis and bringing up his children would have been. Often she felt she knew far too little about her household . . . finding a child weeping in the cloakroom, her face buried in someone's coat, hearing giggles that were stifled at her approach, or a voice from a staff bedroom saying, "I'm sick of girls; if I see another girl I shall scream," or, as had happened that morning, finding a scrap of paper on the floor and reading the pencilled words "I love Miss Whitehouse."

Miss Whitehouse held the title of Senior Mistress. Tall with thick, dark, bobbed hair and an elegantly casual style, she taught geography throughout the school, as well as senior maths, and was Rosemarie's right-hand woman. The school would not have run smoothly without Miss Whitehouse, and yet . . . Rosemarie had her doubts. As she went up to bed after Clive had driven her the short distance back to the school, a number of small worries returned to her. She thought it was hard to know what was best sometimes.

Chapter Four

HALF-TERM came in November, and Jo and Bronwen arranged to spend it together. They were pleased and excited by the prospect of greater freedom, available to them because Bronwen had recently become a daygirl. Her father had retired early, returned to England and bought a house not too far from the St Andrews. So now they could be real, full-time, best friends. The whole business had been accomplished with remarkable expedition, neither Rosemarie nor Bronwen being informed until it was almost a fait accompli.

Bronwen was of course delighted, and Rosemarie not exactly ill-pleased. While the change entailed a certain financial loss she was at least partially free of responsibility for this strange child. She intended to mention to Clive that she did not consider Bronwen a desirable friend for Jo, but somehow when they were together she never felt like bringing up the subject.

They had been together on two occasions since that first time at the Cumberland. Exploring in his new Hillman Minx Clive had found a charming country tearoom which offered, as well as cream teas with home-made scones, very comfortable overnight accommodation. It was inland, about eighteen miles from Culvergate near the village of Wenham, and here, as Captain and Mrs Livingstone, they stayed on alternate Sunday nights. In the interests of discretion Rosemarie took the train to Warne Bay, having admitted casually to the presence of an invalid aunt in that area, where she was picked up at the station by Clive, after which they drove the remaining few miles. Beatrice was reasonably tolerant of the frequent duties required of officers in the Territorials. It was a bit risky, but it was worth it. They were enjoying themselves.

As Rosemarie packed a small suitcase for her third visit to the Hunter's Moon with, among other things, a black chiffon nightgown trimmed with ecru lace – Terry's had ordered it in 'outsize' especially for her – Jo and Bronwen were in Bron's bedroom in her parents neat new semi-detached home, planning their day. Half-term holidays at the May of Teck were not unduly prolonged. Lessons had ceased on the Friday at four o'clock, and would be resumed on the Tuesday, but still, a whole Saturday of freedom was an unusual pleasure. It would be the pictures in the afternoon, definitely. The newest Ginger Rogers film was on at the Astoria and they wouldn't have missed it for worlds. But some entertainment must be devised for the morning. The day was bright and Bronwen's mother, a thin woman with skin prematurely aged by the tropics, unaccustomed to domestic responsibility, had told them they ought to go out. They put on their coats ... Bronwen had only her dark green school uniform but Jo had a new camel hair overcoat, with a belt, in which she felt really grown-up if rather too warm on a mild autumn day. Unfortunately the hat Beatrice had chosen to go with it was a round-brimmed, brown velour, up-at-the-back-down-at-the-front, juvenile style which Jo was determined never to wear.

They set off down a road of recently built houses which led to the front. There were many different styles of architecture, mock-Tudor, art deco, pseudo-Spanish, nearly all semi-detached, and some with green-tiled roofs which they both admired. One or two houses were finished but empty, with the doors wedged open so that prospective buyers could look round. These Jo and Bronwen explored thoroughly, considering which bedrooms they would choose for their personal occupation. And when this palled they decided to play an exciting game invented by Bronwen and referred to as the 'Calling for Peggy game'.

With care, they would decide on an occupied house. The rules of selection were vague. Cars parked outside usually meant there was a man at home, which Jo preferred to avoid, and they liked a place with an air of prosperity. Apart from that, as they walked towards the sea, something about a front garden or an inviting porch would say 'This is The One'. On this occasion it was a detached residence which attracted their attention. One of the oldest in the neighbourhood, it already had a Virginia creeper, still with some brilliant red leaves unshed, scrambling up its red-brick walls. Dormer windows projected from the roof, and the front gate that led into the well-grown garden was of wrought iron. The name 'Crowsteps' was painted on a neat board fixed to the low wall beside the gate. It was all very traditional and cosy. A safe-looking house. They went up the path and knocked boldly with the carefully 'antiqued' metal knocker. They had to knock again before a very small elderly woman opened the door.

"We said we'd call for Peggy."

Bronwen spoke up clearly, the old woman looked as though she might be deaf.

"Who?"

"Peggy. She said we were to call round." Bronwen here became inspired. "She said we could play in the garden. Isn't she here?"

The old lady looked nervous.

Jo said, "Come on, Bron, we must have got the wrong house."

"No, there's no one called Peggy lives here." The old woman seemed bewildered. Then she said. "I'm Mrs Price. This house belongs to my daughter. I suppose you can play in the garden if you want to. Go round the side. And don't go into the greenhouse."

For a terrifying moment Jo thought that Bronwen was about to accept this invitation. She said, "Bron, COME ON!"

Turning away Bronwen said politely, "Thank you very much but we'd better find Peggy. You see, we promised."

"That's right. Always keep a promise. Here." Mrs Price felt in the pocket of her cardigan and brought out two wrapped sweets, which were gracefully accepted.

As the door closed their giggles burst out uncontrollably; they staggered out onto the pavement, helpless with laughter. Bronwen held out the two ancient toffees, that smelt of mothballs and had unidentifiable crumbs adhering to them.

"Throw them away" said Jo.

"Perhaps they're poison. D'you think she was a witch?"

"There's no such thing. But she didn't look rich enough to own that house, did she? Supposing we had gone to play in the garden?"

"I bet she was a white slaver. In disguise. The kind that come up to you on stations and give you an injection and you wake up in a harem somewhere."

"She didn't look like a white slaver to me."

"Well, she'd try not to, I suppose. I wouldn't mind being in a harem anyway. The chief's favourite wife. And all the other wives would have to obey my least command."

"You might not be his favourite."

"I would be. Shall we have another go?"

Bronwen had turned a corner and run ahead. As Jo caught up with her she turned into the gate of a large white flat-roofed house, the front door of which was a sunburst of wrought iron over frosted glass.

"This is the sort of house I want," she said as she rang the bell. Jo stayed at the gate and was relieved when she saw a servant in a butcher-blue dress with a starched white cap and apron in the doorway.

To Bronwen's "We've called for Peggy. Would you tell her please," the girl said curtly, "There's no Peggy here, you've got the wrong house. It's a pity you kids haven't got nothing better to do," and shut the door smartly.

"You went there last week," said Jo as Bronwen rejoined her.

44

"No I didn't, that was the one across the road."

But it was an unsatisfactory experience. There was no fun to be got out of annoying a maid. Maids didn't count.

"Let's do something else now." For Jo to 'Call for Peggy' more than once or twice was to tempt Providence.

"You're afraid."

"No, I'm not."

"See that house over there? Go and do that one, on your own. I dare you?"

"Not on my own."

"You can't refuse a dare."

"It's not a very nice house."

"What's wrong with it?"

There did not seem to be much wrong with it. It was one of a pair, rather bare-looking in their newness, with neatly curtained windows and a shiny chromium knocker.

"Come on, then."

Once again Bronwen led the way, but reaching the door she drew back, saying, "It's your turn. I'm going to be deaf and dumb."

There was no bell, and Jo's knock was somewhat half-hearted. They waited.

"There's no one in."

Jo turned away, relieved. She had accepted the dare and was let off lightly.

"Yes, there is. Listen."

A series of heavy thumps became audible. Bronwen grasped Jo firmly by the belt of her new coat, while with her other hand she banged hard with the knocker.

After a moment the door was opened by a man. Youngish, tall, pale skinned, with thinning hair and round-lensed spectacles, he was wearing a diamond-patterned sweater over a striped shirt, and flannel trousers.

Jo did not like the look of him. She tried to think of an alternative question, one that would release her from the

45

situation without delay. Bronwen nudged her sharply and made an inarticulate noise.

Thus prompted she whispered nervously, "Can Peggy come out? We said we'd call . . ." then as the man continued to stare at her silently, she added, "but perhaps we've got the wrong house."

At the far end of the narrow hall a door stood open. A woman's voice called, "Who's that, Barrie? Who've you got there?"

The man turned his head.

"It's alright, Mother. It's only some kids."

"If Peggy doesn't live here . . ." said Jo desperately. She could see into the hall now. It was untidy, there were piles of books on the floor, newspapers stacked on a small table with a red rubber hot water bottle on the top of the pile, cardigans and a shirt hung over the banisters.

"Well, find out what they want. Bring them in. Bring them in, Barrie."

The man opened the door wide and Bronwen stepped inside, followed unwillingly by Jo. It did not occur to her simply to turn round and walk away. She could not let Bronwen down, she could not be rude to the man. She heard the door close at her back and the stuffy, sickly smell of the place enclosed her.

"In there."

Bron, not speaking, confidently led the way into the back room, which Jo was disturbed to see was not furnished as a dining room or lounge as were the downstairs rooms of the houses she knew. It was plainly a bedroom. In the inner corner a high single bed was untidily made. An electric fire glowed in the fireplace, on the far side of which a huge unwieldy-looking wheelchair contained the fattest woman they had ever seen, weaning a grubby dressing gown, unfastened over an equally grubby nightdress.

"Come along in, dear, it's not often anyone comes to see me." She broke off to address the man, irritably. "I told you Barry, I'm too near the fire. I'm scorching my dressing gown." And certainly a smell of burning cloth was adding itself to the mingled, unpleasant odours that permeated the air of the room. Barrie heaved the chair round with difficulty, which explained the thumps they had heard previously.

"I'm Mrs Bates and this is my son Barrie. Now I'm too far away, I'm in the draught from the windows. Just three inches towards the fireplace, Barrie, three inches, no more . . . For heaven's sake, I can't see the girls now, you know I can't turn my head. Alright, that'll have to do, I suppose, just heave me up a bit, and I'll have another pillow off the bed."

Barrie grabbed a pillow and stuffed it down behind her, but before doing so he stood holding it for a second and it crossed Jo's mind that he would have liked to suffocate the woman. Catching his eye, Jo looked down at the carpet, feeling that she had read his mind, fearful that he had read hers.

"Come this way a bit, I can't see you. Who sent you? Are you Girl Guides? Come over here and let me look at you. You're not shy, are you? Come and let me have a look at you."

Jo looked at Bronwen, who was still wearing her blank deaf-and-dumb expression and was no help at all. She advanced a step or two towards the chair, uncomfortably aware that the man had moved over to the door and was effectively blocking their escape route.

"We were looking for Peggy, but—"

"Well, there's no Peggy here, I'm afraid. We wish there was, don't we, Barrie? Perhaps she'd help you get straight. Do you know that we've lived here five months and we're not straight yet? That's because he goes out. Goes out and leaves me alone. All alone, in the evenings. Do you know Peggy's surname? We've got the telephone book. Is she on the phone? Barrie, pass me the telephone book."

"No, please, it doesn't matter." Jo looked pleadingly at Bronwen, who almost always took the lead. Why wasn't she getting them both out of this horrible house, away from these horrible people?

47

"Now, what's the surname? And your friend's father, do you know his initial?"

"No, I don't know . . . it's quite alright, I expect we shall meet her coming up the road—"

"Just sit down a minute, while I find the number. Does your friend know the name?"

Jo obediently sat down on the edge of an upright chair. The upholstered seat looked unclean, and she tried unsuccessfully to perch on the wooden frame, without coming into contact with the stained, fawn-coloured material. Bronwen continued stolidly to play her part.

"She's lost her voice," muttered Jo, thinking this minor affliction sounded more believable than Bron's chosen disability.

"Oh, would she like a cup of tea? Tea's very good for the throat. You could make some tea, couldn't you, Barrie?" Turning her head and shoulders with some difficulty, the woman looked at Bronwen. "Why don't you go and help Barrie make the tea while we try to find your friend's number?"

For once Bronwen seemed uncertain of what to do, which was frightening. Jo stood up. Vague warnings from her mother, the rules that prevented her from mixing with hotel guests other than under supervision, the out-of-bounds nature of the lift suddenly clicked into a recognition of the fact that she and Bronwen must not be separated.

"We've got to go now," she said. "My father's waiting at the top of the road in his car."

The man quite meekly stood aside and Jo, followed by Bronwen, reached the front door. She tried to open it but the patent lock was tricky. The man reached over her shoulders, imprisoning her while he dealt with the recalcitrant latch.

"She's an invalid," he said. "Doesn't get much company. Everything has to be done in that room. Everything. And there's no one but me."

Jo's desire to escape increased. Was he really trying to get the door open? But he opened it and in a moment they were in full

48

retreat, without the formality of a goodbye. Jo remembered this later and hoped they hadn't seemed impolite. Bron thought it didn't matter. The top of the road seemed like safety, but when they looked back they could see Barrie was standing at his front gate, watching. They did not stop running until they were among the shoppers in the main road. This time they did not giggle, they did not fall about, propping one another up, spluttering with mirth. When eventually they slowed down they walked along sedately, not speaking. It was some minutes before Bron said, "What a horrible man."

Jo answered, "She was horrible too."

Bron said, "Everything. In that one room." And Jo told her to shut up.

Beatrice had been shopping. When Jo reported her return her mother was in the office wearing a suit in a newly fashionable colour, a rather gingery brown called London Tan, that was exactly right for the season. The jacket had wide stitched lapels and link buttons at the waist, the skirt was calf-length and very straight and she had on a dashing little bottle-green hat, a Robin Hood style with a long feather. Beatrice had walked up St Andrew's Road to Eastonville's shopping centre, a broad street running parallel to the promenade. She crossed over to Terry's, and entered the portals of the store with just the frisson of pleasure that its owners would have hoped for. At the cosmetic counter with its display of French perfume, she paused to consider Schiaparelli's 'Shocking' and one or two others, but made no purchase. Arriving in the lingerie department on the first floor she looked round for an assistant. Garments of the type she required were displayed here and there but she wished to be served. And quickly. She drummed her fingers irritably on the plate glass of the counter. The buyer, recognising her at once, hurried across, apologising for the lack of attention which had kept Beatrice waiting all of thirty seconds, and to make up for it she opened drawer after drawer, shaking out nightdress after nightdress, fold after fold of peach satin, pure white silk, ice-blue crêpe de Chine. Beatrice fingered the materials, finding this likely to be scratchy, that too prone to creasing, the colours too juvenile.

"At my age," she said, "you have to be sophisticated." She smiled. "It's our only hope."

"Oh, Mrs Livingstone. I'm sure you could wear anything, with your figure!"

But Miss Harness, the lingerie buyer now held up a delicious confection in black chiffon, with narrow ribbon shoulder straps, heavily trimmed with ecru lace around the hem and at the top. It was very pretty, and certainly it was what they both thought of as sophisticated. The right size too. Small Womens. Beatrice bought it.

"Will you take it, Madame, or shall we send it to the hotel?"

"Oh, send it, will you?"

"It won't be till Monday I'm afraid. Will that be alright?"

"I suppose so. Alright. Monday." Beatrice spoke grudgingly, though actually Monday suited her very well. "Put it on the account."

"Of course, Madame."

"And put in three pairs of stockings will you? Size nine, silk. Aristoc. Not too pale. I must hurry."

Unencumbered, Beatrice left the department. Reaching the ground floor she paused at the perfumery counter to buy the Schiaparelli 'Shocking'.

Jo was particularly quiet during lunch, but neither of her parents noticed this, both being pre-occupied. In fact they were rather quiet themselves. Beatrice broke a silence to say, "You'll be off soon, then?"

She excused Jo from the table and poured coffee for herself and Clive. They chose to drink it in the restaurant, rather than in their own sitting room. It wasn't worth the bother of going upstairs. Guests would take theirs in the lounge, but to join them would have been to sacrifice even the minimal privacy afforded by their corner table.

"Yes. Must be off by two-fifteen. It's an exercise. Home about ten on Monday."

"I didn't realise you'd be away at night, when you started this Territorial thing."

"It's only once a fortnight. At the moment." He added this because it looked as though the Territorial Army, if not Rosemarie, was soon going to demand a good deal more of his time. It was a good thing that Beatrice was too busy to attend the coffee parties arranged by other Territorial wives. Were she to do so she would soon find out that Clive's absence at weekends were not entirely due to TA activities. It was chancy, in any case. He knew that some of his fellow officers made a habit of meeting in the Men Only bar, The Knights Rest, but she was unlikely to go there during the evening.

At the Princess May of Teck School for Young Ladies Rosemarie sat at the head of a table with Miss Triggs, Handwork and Sewing at the opposite end and four senior girls on either side. The room was less than half full. A number of pupils had departed for their half-term exeats on the previous evening, some more had left that morning, and more would be collected that afternoon. Most of the staff would go as well, and Rosemarie would be left, apart from Bronwen, with the same four girls who had stayed at school for the summer, plus two new girls, who had arrived, somewhat inconveniently, a few days earlier. They were Jewish sisters from Germany whose father was hoping to transfer his business to England. But supposing he failed to do so? Judging from what she read in the newspapers it did not seem likely that he could succeed. He had claimed to have influential friends, but would they not be afraid to help a Jew now that Jews were being deprived of their possessions, deported, and beaten up? Supposing, eventually, there was a war? Would she be saddled

51

with them indefinitely without hope of the bills being paid? But looking at the pale-skinned, dark-eyed children, politely answering questions in careful English, Rosemarie could not regret her decision to take them.

Matron was of course in residence, and Miss Whitehouse would take over while Rosemarie visited her invalid aunt in Warne Bay on the Sunday. Joan Forster, eating the cold meat and jacket potato which they always had for dinner on Saturdays, found her headmistress in an extraordinarily good mood, and conversation easier than usual. Rosemarie was making an effort to keep the stream of light chat flowing. Whenever it flagged her mind returned unbidden to the past and future delights of the bedroom at the Hunter's Moon. Clive standing shameless before her because she had said she wished to see him entirely naked, though to begin with he had turned his back when slipping out of his pyjama trousers. Joan was looking at her enquiringly and Rosemarie realised that she had not heard a word of her last sentence because behind her own attentive expression lurked a picture of her lover's penis. Feeling herself blushing she remarked on the heat in the room which obviously baffled the girl still more, as it was rather chilly. Fortunately they were then asked to choose between rice pudding and stewed figs and custard, and when each one at the table had made her choice and the results had been translated into "Nine rice and three figs and custard, please," she was able to introduce a new subject quite easily.

That afternoon Jo and Bronwen went to the pictures, as planned and were cheered by Ginger Rogers and Fred Astaire. That, they believed, was real grown-up life – smoking and dancing and wearing lipstick and falling in love. Not wheelchairs, and vaguely threatening situations and everything in one room.

Bronwen invited Jo to tea, but Jo refused. Still slightly unsettled, she wished to return to the safety of her own home, far from ideal as it was. Bronwen sulked.

"I could come out tomorrow," Jo spoke placatingly.

"There's nothing to do on a Sunday."

"We could think of a new game."

"There isn't anything new."

"There must be. We could be detectives like in Valerie Drew. You know. Schoolgirl detectives in secret." Just the sort of thing Bron would like, Jo thought, but she was disappointed.

"There's nothing to detect."

Bronwen was enjoying her sulk and did not want to give it up.

"There's always something. We could be a proper agency, make reports and things."

"We'd have to get notebooks. And printed paper."

"What do we need printed paper for?"

"They always have it. And I haven't got a notebook."

"We can buy notebooks. And I'll get some paper from Dad. We can cut off the top and put the name underneath. Livingstone and Harries Private Investigators. Discretion assured. Like in Valerie Drew."

"What's the point?" Bronwen was still unwilling to relinquish her bad mood. "When we've found something out, who shall we tell?"

"I don't know. It all depends." Jo was becoming aggrieved. "I thought it would be fun, that's all. You think of something then."

"Oh alright, I don't mind being detectives, I suppose."

"It doesn't matter."

"It was your idea, and now you don't want to. I wish you'd make up your mind. I could call for Betty Wilcox instead. She said I could go round any time."

The spectre of being Best Friendless rose before Jo. She said, "I suppose I could come to tea if you like. Only I'll have to phone and tell my mother. Will your Dad take me home? My Dad's away in the Army, and I'm not allowed to walk when its dark."

After this capitulation Jo's suggestions were more favourably received and when the Harries family dropped her outside the St Andrew's that evening she was a director of the Jobron Detective Agency, Discretion Assured.

Beatrice and Jo dined at their usual table, Clive's place being taken by his mother-in-law. Beatrice had changed into one of her long black gowns, and Jo into a rather summery print with a dirndl skirt. Mrs Hewitt wore wine-coloured marocain, with a cowl neck and long sleeves. Beatrice had assisted her in the purchase of this dress and had succeeded in checking the old lady's preference for sequins, beading, and brocade. Clive had departed for his Territorial camp. Only one night was to be spent under canvas in a field seven or eight miles away, but Clive did not propose to return until Monday morning. The prospect of the weekend filled him with pleasure. As a Captain in the Army, even the part-time Army, he could be sure of respect, or at least a show of it. And he was good at obeying orders, he liked to be told what to do. He enjoyed passing orders on, too, knowing they would be obeyed, and, if they turned out to be ill-advised, the responsibility would not be his. Major Upcott would have to carry the can.

Beatrice saw no harm in his playing soldiers really. It kept him out of her way. Now he'd given up making any pretence of being involved in the management of the St Andrew's they were really getting on very well. Of course, she needed him. Head Office, although they understood the position, would never give the management of such an important hotel to a woman on her own. For this reason she had begun to think that his flagging interest in her own slender if not actually thin body needed reviving. After all, he'd been very keen on all that at one time. Of course Clive would never be unfaithful, he simply wasn't enterprising enough and he knew she wouldn't stand for it. But still, no harm in a bit of married bliss to reinforce their partnership. She had a hair appointment on Monday morning, and would have a manicure as well, and see that the menu included his favourite dishes. A pity it couldn't be tonight, the Saturday dinner dances always engendered a romantic atmosphere, but never mind.

Jo looked up from the slice of ham from which she had been carefully removing the fat,

"Mummy, can I have some paper from the office?" Beatrice asked what it was for.

"To draw on."

"Haven't you got a drawing book?"

"No."

"Why not buy one with your pocket money?" Jo received two half-crowns on the first of each month.

"I've only got fourpence left, and I want that for Mars bars." Mrs Hewitt opened her purse.

"There you are, you can get one on Monday."

"Thank you, Gran. But could I have some paper to be going on with, please Mum?"

"Don't call me Mum. I'll see if I can find some scrap for you."

Beatrice sighed meaningfully. How would Jo learn the value of money if her grandmother was constantly giving her handfuls of change? She'd been quite different when her own daughters were young, it had been like getting blood out of a stone in those days. The scrap paper was eventually forthcoming, but it had some sort of price list on one side – useless for Jo's purpose. On the way upstairs she slipped into the seldom-used writing room and appropriated some of the hotel notepaper from the writing desk. Six sheets was the maximum she dared to take, but it would do till Dad came back. Of course she would not tell him what it was for. The detective agency would obviously be another secret game. In her bedroom she carefully trimmed off the heading and replaced it in neat capitals with JOBRON DETECTIVE AGENCY. On the left she wrote Discretion Assured and on the right, under the heading Directors she put her own name and then Bron's. Then she counted the money her grandmother had given her. It amounted to one shilling and seven pence. Plenty for some sweets as well as two notebooks. Bron, she hoped, would be pleased.

Sunday afternoon they spent setting up the office of the detective agency in a corner of Jo's bedroom, happily anticipating the unravelling of mysteries, and the unmasking of criminals which they would undertake. They dwelt on the official gratitude they would earn and the headlines which would make them famous. SCHOOLGIRLS LEAD POLICE TO STOLEN PROPERTY or SPY CAUGHT BY GIRL DETECTIVES. These were Jo's contributions. Bronwen's were more picturesque, based on *News of the World* captions, this Sunday paper being the favourite of her mother's recently installed cook-general. PRISONER OF ESCAPED MANIAC RESCUED and HOTEL STRANGLER CAUGHT, were her favourites. Jo did not like HOTEL STRAN-GLER very much but Bronwen said it could easily happen. After all, any hotel was full of strangers and you didn't know all their life histories, did you? Bronwen would have pursued this theme, but Jo was noisily turning out her cupboard. Eventually she found her old scrap book, which would do for press cuttings, she said. Her grandmother had a press-cutting book, kept from the days when she had been the star of the local Operatic Society. When Bronwen seemed inclined to return to the subject of the hotel strangler Jo suggested they should start practising being detectives. The St Andrew's was no more than half full and Beatrice was not about so when Bron suggested that they sit in the almost empty forbidden lounge for a while Jo hardly protested. They listened, while pretending to read, to a conversation about gardening, after which they followed the two middle-aged men concerned down to the promenade and back. It was boring, they agreed, but good practice, and Mr Willis, a stockbroker from Croydon and Mr Barnes, a veterinary surgeon from East Grinstead, had definitely not realised that they were being followed.

Chapter Five

CLIVE had a satisfactory weekend. The manoeuvres on which his battalion was engaged went really well, his side taking most of the 'enemy' prisoner. Major Upcott patted him on the back and said he could always rely on Livingstone to 'play it by the book'. Initiative, he said was all very well, but you couldn't have every Tom Dick and Harry doing the thinking. Clive was not sure whether this last remark had been meant for his ears, but anyway, Upcott had been pleased and that was all that mattered.

As he waited outside Warne Bay station for Rosemarie he thought he was a very fortunate man. There was Beatrice, as glamorous a woman as you could find, and really keen on running the hotel, which he'd found, to be perfectly honest, a bit of a bore, and there was his mistress, the sensuous, curvaceous, handsome Rosemarie. Head of a reputable school. His mistress. The very word excited him. Chaps like Guy Upcott and Will Fitzgerald had mistresses, the whole town knew about them; not men like himself, steady fellows with strong-minded wives. They'd never believe that he and Rosemarie . . . why if anyone who did not know them were asked to guess which was the mistress and which the wife they would undoubtedly put their money on Beatrice for the illicit love. Rosemarie looked far too imposing and dignified for the role, though he could think of moments when dignity had not exactly been her strong point . . . the funny thing was she liked it, wanted it, and Beatrice didn't seem to, not since the beginning. And he wasn't a bad looking chap, after all, he thought, catching sight of himself in his driving mirror. Then he began to think about

Jo who had, when he'd grown his moustache, said he looked like David Niven. Well, she was too young to suspect anything yet, and by the time she was old enough Heaven knew where they would all be. A war was the most likely thing. So he might as well make hay while the sun shone. All very well for Beatrice, she was perfectly happy as she was, but he was a man. What did she expect? And anyway she had slimmed and dieted until she was more like a telegraph pole than a woman.

And supposing war did come? The hotel would be closed, the school would move to a safe area, and he would be absorbed into the real Army. In the Catering Corps in all probability. He wondered how Beatrice would take to living as an officer's wife. Jo, of course, would go with the school, with Rosemarie. So they wouldn't be losing touch and might even be able to meet, sometimes. Perhaps Bea would want to rent a house so that Jo could continue as a daygirl, and which would be somewhere for him to spend his leaves. Pretty dull for her, stuck in some remote part of England without friends and with nothing to do. No, he couldn't really imagine her doing that. But how would Jo take to being a boarder? Would it take her away from that kid Bronwen she was so friendly with? A kid that really gave him the creeps. She had a way of looking at you as though she knew far too much, which of course could not possibly be the case. Jo was innocent, compared to that one. He wanted her to stay innocent, for years yet. If Bronwen also went away with the school they would be thrown into each other's company even more. He definitely should have a word with Rosemarie. Finding the right moment was difficult, though, when most of their time together was spent in bed. He pictured her leaning bulkily back against the pillows, a narrow strap slipping off her well-upholstered white shoulder, her large breasts flopping sideways under her transparent nightgown. You couldn't discuss your daughter at such moments. Perhaps at breakfast . . . deep in thought he barely noticed the sound of a train arriving and departing on the far side of the little station. In summer this

London train would be crowded with returning trippers but in the November dusk only one woman came out through the main doors – a heavy woman in a rather long navy-blue coat, sensible shoes and a felt hat that shadowed her face. An uninteresting woman. She glanced round and began to walk in Clive's direction. He actually had time to wonder if she had mistaken his car for a taxi when the woman suddenly stopped being a nameless, dull stranger and became Rosemarie, his mistress. His love. That she should seem so different, even momentarily, was disturbing. As he leaned over to open the door for her he had a dreadful feeling that the whole thing was a mistake, that he had to take this woman to bed and make love to her, and he simply didn't want to. It was the hat. It must be the hat. It was a middle-aged hat. Yet he didn't feel much better when she complied with his request to take it off.

When they arrived at the Hunter's Moon the two proprietresses, Miss Caxton and Miss Simms were delighted to see them, business being slack at that time of year.

"Your usual room," they beamed. "You know the way. And there's plenty of hot water."

Their room was as olde worlde as the rest of the place. Massive oak beams crossed the ceiling, the oak door did not fit and the floor was uneven. There were flowery curtains and a huge brass bedstead with a feather-filled mattress. On the marble-topped washstand stood a flower-decorated china basin and a ewer full of cold water, but the rather less old world bathroom was next door, with, as had been claimed, plenty of hot water. He took a bath before dinner, though he had to dress again in his uniform. He could not be sure of bringing a sports jacket and flannels without Beatrice asking questions. Territorial weekends, she believed, lasted until the Monday morning. He didn't think the truth would be brought to her notice, even if the crowd visited the Men Only bar, the Knight's Rest; it was in the basement with a separate entrance and was rarely visited by Beatrice during opening hours. So he was quite safe. If only the picture of the navy-blue woman leaving the station would go away. It was not until they were seated opposite each other at a rather small table among the horse brasses, copper kettles and chintz hangings of the otherwise deserted tearoom, that he began to readjust. Rosemarie was wearing plum-coloured velvet with a very low V-neck, and her pearl drop earrings. She wore powder and lipstick, too, and had achieved just that amalgam of massive dignity and sexual attractiveness that he found so intriguing. The Fortress! He would soon be storming it again! He smiled and Rosemarie, who had been a little troubled by his unaccustomed silences, though she put them down to exhaustion, was able to relax, and to chat entertainingly throughout the delicious meal. They had pork chops, and all the trimmings, with apple tart and cream afterwards, and then cheese and biscuits. Rosemarie had a very hearty appetite and ate more than Clive.

Miss Caxton served a good breakfast the next morning, starting with porridge, continuing with bacon and eggs, and finishing off with toast and marmalade. They drank coffee. Miss Simms had knocked gently on their door at seven-fifteen, entering in answer to Clive's commanding "Come in", with the usual tray of tea, just in time to see Rosemarie lean dangerously out of the high bed and snatch up Clive's pyjama trousers which he had thrown out during the night. Beatrice was not to know that his fellow Territorials would see no need to take nightwear on their weekend exercises, but Clive liked to be seen wearing his pyjama jacket when Miss Simms brought the early morning tea. Though when she carefully set down the tray she always avoided glancing even for one moment at the occupants of the bed.

This morning when she had crept out they had a good giggle and felt grown-up, worldly-wise, and childish and naughty all at the same time. A delightful feeling. After all, thought Clive, a frustrated spinster like poor little Miss Simms, with her fluffy fading hair and spectacles . . . to such a one their activities would be a closed book. He said something of the sort to

Rosemarie who glanced at him sharply for a moment but said nothing.

They sat over breakfast with their cigarettes. Miss Whitehouse would be taking prayers, and reading the notices in Rosemarie's place, so she was in no particular hurry, and Clive was a little regretfully aware that the St Andrew's would start the week perfectly well without him. Only Jo would be likely to miss him, but it was a clear day. If Culvergate, eighteen miles to the north-east had similar weather she would not need a lift to school.

He allowed his hand to cover Rosemarie's as it lay on the table. It had been a very good night; Rosemarie's cousin had known a lot about making love; he read books, he was uninhibited and had an enthusiastic partner, more than willing to learn. Clive had discovered what he knew from other boys, an embarrassed housemaster at his very minor public school, and a young servant-girl at his grandparents' house who had fallen for his youthful good looks and led him shamelessly up the garden. Recalling the pleasures of the night he wondered if they had time to go back to bed for half an hour, ten minutes even. Five would be enough, the way he felt. Miss Caxton, with her nineteen-twenties fringe and projecting teeth approached them smiling.

"Everything alright? Good. It's such a pleasure to have you, Mrs Livingstone. And Captain Livingstone. Any time, you know. Just a quick telephone call and your room will be waiting." You'd almost think she knew. She hurried across to the uncarpeted oak staircase mounted a few steps and called, "Wendy! Wendeeee!"

It seemed that Miss Simms appeared at the head of the stairs. The brief conversation that followed was hushed, but not so hushed that Clive and Rosemarie could fail to hear most of it in the quiet of the closed tearoom.

Miss Caxton spoke again. "Darling. Darling, you know I

didn't mean what I said. Please forgive me and come down. Captain Livingstone wants his bill."

Miss Simms's words now sounded indistinguishably from the top of the stairs, and a moment later a door banged. The normally cheerful Miss Caxton heaved an unaccustomed sigh and disappeared.

"Sounds as though they've fallen out." Clive looked at his watch. "I hope she won't be too long."

"A lovers' tiff, that's all."

"Lovers. But . . . you mean . . . not really lovers . . ."

Rosemarie smiled in a rather irritatingly superior way.

"Why not? They're happy together. Why should they not do as they like? There aren't enough men to go round. Though they'd probably have chosen it anyway."

Clive was appalled. Confused, and appalled.

"Two women together, in bed? Those two, they wouldn't. It's . . . disgusting. I've heard about men, but . . . I never realised that women . . ."

This time Rosemarie laughed.

"I'm afraid they do. And in my position it's something I have to be aware of. I've got my doubts about my senior mistress, at the moment, and things like this can upset the whole establishment. I know, I've been through it before . . . the quarrels and the jealousy . . . three years ago I—"

Too late she realised that Clive was looking at her in horror. Idiot. She'd actually forgotten his daughter was a pupil at the school.

"Senior mistress? Does she teach Jo?"

Rosemarie was furious with herself. What had happened to her own normal discretion? Her silence on the subject of her work and all that it entailed? Last night had happened to it, of course, her guard was down and she must be careful.

"No, no. She doesn't take Jo's class at all." The lie was safe, she had not mentioned Miss Whitehouse by name.

"It's not the girls, it's other staff members . . ." But as she spoke she thought of Miss Colman, and the way a worshipping crowd of girls would gather round her at every opportunity. Yet she was irritated. If you couldn't talk freely to your lover, then who could you talk to? Clive was such a charming man, so gentle and considerate, so lovable. But so innocent, naive almost. Perhaps it wasn't surprising that his wife had become bored with him. As soon has this thought had passed through her mind she felt ashamed of her own disloyalty

"Well, I don't know. And you think these two here . . . I wonder if there's anywhere else . . ."

"Darling, don't be silly. What they do can't affect us." She hoped it couldn't. But Clive, who was normally very jovial with Miss Simms when she presented the account, today was only just on the polite side of brusqueness.

"Don't worry about them," she said, patting his arm as they drove towards Warne Bay station. "It takes all sorts to make a world."

"Yes, but when it's people you know . . . I mean, I suppose I knew that sort of thing went on, in clubs and things in places like Hamburg, but the Hunter's Moon . . ."

"Everyone isn't as lucky as we are," said Rosemarie soothingly.

When they drew up at the station she kissed him goodbye, pulled on the navy-blue hat, opened the door and with some difficulty left the car. It lurched significantly as her weight was removed, and what with that and the hat the middle-aged stranger took over again. Clive never left the car to see her off, there was no point in making himself more visible than he had to, so Rosemarie heaved her small suitcase off the back seat and in her long navy coat and depressing hat disappeared into the booking office.

Clive did not feel right until he was almost in sight of the hotel. Fifteen miles of dwelling on the pleasures of the previous night were only just enough to reinstate his picture of himself as a man of the world. A man of the world who was having a passionate affair with a glorious woman, under the roof of two innocent and envious spinster ladies. It wasn't easy, but he did it. What with one thing and another, he did not meet his wife until lunchtime, after he had, for form's sake, checked the bookings for the coming week, and made sure the equipment in the billiard room was in order. Then, having also had a drink with a couple of friends in the Knight's Rest, it all seemed so long ago that he didn't even feel pleasantly guilty.

By the time he went up to say goodnight to Jo he was perfectly happy, feeling thoroughly in command of his situation and cheerfully looking forward to a meeting of Territorial officers on the Wednesday evening. One liked having something definite to do. To his surprise, it being nearly nine, Jo was not in bed. She was in her room, sitting at the square table which had once been in the living room of the apartment, doing her homework. Her small wireless set was playing Arthur Askey's signature tune. She looked up as her father entered.

"How's my girl? You shouldn't be doing homework at this time, surely?"

"I've got to get it done."

"What time did you start?"

"Hours ago. We're supposed to do four subjects, half an hour each, but everything takes much longer than half an hour. I've been doing this ever since eight o'clock, and I've still got my French."

"Perhaps I could help you with that. I used to be quite good at it."

"I've got to learn some verbs."

"Well, would you like a drink or something? I'll get Patty to bring you some Ovaltine. And couldn't you concentrate better without the wireless?"

"No, it helps me. Don't switch it off."

"Who teaches you Arithmetic and so on?"

"Miss Palmer. She's not too bad really."

"Is that the top mistress, whatever she's called?"

64

"Senior Mistress? No, that's Miss Whitehouse. She doesn't take us for Maths. Why?"

Palmer? He was fairly sure that Palmer was not the name mentioned by Rosemarie. That was a relief.

"Just getting them sorted out. You like school, do you? Get on with everybody?"

"It's OK."

"You like Miss Wells?"

"S'pose so. Don't see her much, except at prayers. Can I have some biscuits with the Ovaltine, Dad?"

"I expect so. And don't be too late to bed. Leave the French until morning."

"Oh, Dad, don't be so daft. There won't be time in the morning."

"There will if I take you to school in the car."

"It doesn't make that much difference." And she had arranged to meet Bronwen on the corner.

From the door Clive looked back at his blonde child, hunched over her work, counting on her fingers and sighing noisily. She looked lonely, though perhaps loneliness at home was better than boarding school. If a hotel could be home. He remembered his childhood home in the country outside the town. With his three sisters jumping on the furniture and leaving things about it had been shabby and untidy but comfortable. The bedrooms had been icy in winter but there would be huge fires downstairs. And there were the dogs. His father was not often there but his mother was about most of the time. And the girls. You could always find someone to talk to. Someone who would listen if you thought Father had been hard on you. And there was nowhere you couldn't go. In this huge place Jo was not allowed to wander freely about. She could use the games room, with permission, which was usually given when she asked for it, and of course took her meals in the restaurant, but she was not allowed in any of the other public rooms, or the lift. Clive had always thought that these were unnecessary restrictions, but remembering that morning's conversation with Rosemarie, he began to wonder. Were there a lot more funny people about than he had imagined? He thought he would suggest to Beatrice that she had another word with Jo on the subject of Not Speaking to Strange Men. And perhaps he ought to add Women. Inside or outside the hotel. What a responsibility a child was!

He went down to order the Ovaltine. He could have rung the bell in the sitting room, but why bring Patty upstairs twice? Walking to the lift he wondered what his wife was doing. Busy in the office, probably, and he thought he might go and find her, but then he decided that after all he'd look in The Knight's; there'd certainly be someone there that he knew, ready for a chat. You needed a bit of a chat at the end of the day. He imagined himself with Rosemarie, sitting opposite her at some fireside, but somehow the picture failed to come to life. Rosemarie was either immeasurably dignified, or quite the other thing, and neither mode of behaviour was what he wanted at that moment.

He ordered Jo's Ovaltine, and stayed in The Knight's Rest till closing time at ten-thirty. Ascending the stairs to the ground floor he met the receptionist coming to look for him.

"Mrs Livingstone asked me to tell you she'd gone up, Sir. She's got a bit of a headache. And would you do the round, she said?"

Clive said, "Of course", not adding that he usually did the round of the place at night, fastening windows, locking doors, making sure fires were safe, guests mostly in their rooms and the night porter on duty. This was one job, almost the only one, that he had not relinquished, though of course Bea performed this duty on his Territorial nights now.

It was like Bea to get this girl to remind him to do something he would have done in any case. What did she take him for?

Beatrice, going to the apartment soon after ten-thirty, saw a light under Jo's door and found her asleep with her French textbook open on the eiderdown. You wanted your child to get on but was the Wells woman trying to cram them too hard? Why hadn't Clive been up earlier and seen that Jo was settled down? She, Beatrice, could not do everything. She ran the business, engaged the staff, supervised the menus and ordering of supplies and kept an eye on the books, while he sauntered round trying to look important. She was not the maternal type, he'd known that when he married her. She wouldn't have had any children if she'd had her own way. Not that she'd be without Jo, really. No trouble on the whole, Well, she'd see she didn't get trapped into marriage at twenty-three. That was the thing she liked about the Princess May – the emphasis on preparing girls for careers. What couldn't she have achieved herself if she'd been given that sort of opportunity? But Jo, lying asleep, fragile and fair, with shadows visible under her dark eyelashes, did not look in the least like a potential career woman. Beatrice switched off the pink-shaded bedside lamp and left quietly.

Feeling irritated with her husband, she was not now very enthusiastic about the plan she had in mind. It had been borne in upon her during the last few weeks that Clive had quite ceased to make any demands on her. To begin with it had been a relief; she'd never really liked that sort of messing about, or the loss of control and the vulnerability it entailed. Clive had got his daughter, whom he seemed to like, and really she felt she had done all that could be expected of her in that line. Then she'd begun to worry. A chance word – if it had been a chance word – of her mother's had reminded her that men, if it wasn't available at home, would certainly find it elsewhere. Mrs Hewitt was a worldly sixty-year-old, who had, after the death of her husband, successfully supported three daughters, Beatrice being the youngest, until they were all married. The Japanese Tea Room was still a popular place and Mrs Hewitt had no intention of retiring. Her hair remained glossily black and she still wore the fringe that she had chosen for the Oriental look when she first opened the tearoom twenty years earlier.

It was the twin beds, installed by Beatrice when she had

refurnished the apartment, that had caused her mother to have misgivings. Beatrice had shown her the room proudly, the dressing table with the long triple mirror, the plain lilac walls, and the pale cyclamen bedspreads and fuchsia eiderdowns on the twin beds. She had expressed her disapproval at once, having learned something from her own sadly curtailed marriage. Beatrice had said, Nonsense, no one had a double bed these days, they were completely out of fashion. Civilised, modern people did not want to share beds all the time. She thought it unhygienic.

Now, over a year later, Beatrice remembered and wondered. Had Clive got a fancy woman somewhere? Suppose he wanted to leave her? Surely he'd never be such a fool! But then he might, and if he did Beatrice would more than likely lose her job. Her job and her home. The owners would never believe that a woman could run the St Andrews on her own.

Well, she didn't think Clive could have strayed very far yet, though of course he'd had chances, and he was quite good-looking; sometimes women who stayed at the hotel struck Beatrice as being on the lookout for a bit of fun, but he wouldn't be so stupid as that, would he? And they had no ordinary social life, though they knew people of course. The only woman they'd had anything to do with socially of late had been Rosemarie Wells and the idea of her as a paramour was laughable. Beatrice actually smiled as the idea crossed her mind.

But in spite of her dismissal of her mother's fears, Beatrice thought it would be wise to make herself attractive and available from time to time. After all, she had a lot to lose.

This enterprise was less easy than she had expected. Several times she had come in from the bathroom in her satin dressing gown that matched the eiderdowns, to find Clive fast asleep in his twin bed, and she herself was often too tired to bother, in any case. But for over two months now he had shown no interest, in fact he had even stopped talking about it. She was worried. Something must be done. So she had bought the black chiffon nightdress, the only one in stock at Terry's, invested in the Schiaparelli 'Shocking', and on this Monday evening when Clive had been absent for two nights went up earlier than usual. An hour later, with her preparations complete, she stood in front of her triple mirror, considering herself from all angles. Well, she had a slim figure which was what every woman wanted, though the black nightdress could have done with filling out a bit more. She'd had to diet quite drastically after Jo's birth, she'd put on so many pounds, but for some years now she'd been positively thin without making any effort at all. She put it down to work and worry and being on her feet most of the day. Skinny, her mother called her. Darling mother! The bodice of the nightdress was gathered alluringly, to accentuate the breasts, but on Beatrice the thin material sagged rather depressingly. Her dark hair was shampooed at Tessier's every other Monday afternoon, and set in careful undulations each side of a centre parting, with the ends rolled up neatly at the back. All the staff at Tessier's believed that to show an end of hair was as grossly indecent as having one's French knickers make a public descent. Beatrice wondered whether she should comb it through, give it a more natural look, but decided not to. She'd never get it right in the morning if she did that. She usually wore a hair net at night, quite a fine one in a colour to match her hair. Really, you could hardly see it. She put it on, and then took it off again. She dabbed some 'Shocking' behind her ears and in her elbows. It was a delicious, musky scent, different from any perfume she had ever tried. She thought it was bound to do the trick. Instead of creaming her face she put on a very little powder and lipstick, afterwards going to the sitting room to pour herself a gin and vermouth. She hoped it would put her in the right mood. Back in the bedroom she slipped off her satin robe. It was warm in the private apartment, which was centrally heated like the rest of the hotel. The radiators were big and ugly, but they worked. Kicking off her pink velvet slippers she reclined on top of the eiderdown so as to give Clive the full benefit.

When he came up she was lying there reading. This was usual.

She liked a good novel and had no time during the day. The gin and It had worked quite well and she looked forward to her husband's embraces with equanimity if not enthusiasm.

Clive was very tired, one way and another. He undressed, put on his blue poplin pyjamas.

"Aren't you having a bath?"

"Had one when I came in," mumbled Clive as he left the room. This was untrue. His most recent bath had taken place on the previous evening. He liked the Hunter's Moon bathroom, because although the fittings were modern it was unusually large, having once been a bedroom, and had an easy chair in a pink and white flowered cover that matched the curtains, and an old-fashioned cheval glass on a white-painted stand. A romantic bathroom.

He soon returned, and leaned over Beatrice to give her the usual peck on the cheek, or hair, or forehead, whichever was most accessible. On this occasion she put her hand on his arm, looking up at him with an apparently loving gaze but noting that at close quarters what looked from a little distance like a healthy flush was clearly revealed as broken veins.

The hand on his arm was unusual. Feeling some further gesture was called for he patted her shoulder and said kindly, "I should get into bed, dear, you'll get cold like that." He couldn't understand why she was lying on top of the eiderdown, anyway, unless she'd had her bath too hot, which she was normally careful not to do.

He turned thankfully away to his own bed, neatly turned down by Patty when she had removed the bedspreads for the night. He punched his pillow into the shape he liked, turned his back to the other bed and pulled up the white cotton sheet and the soft pale blankets almost over his head. Thus concealed, he could begin to relive the events of Sunday night even before Beatrice pulled the string attached to the shared reading-light fixed to the wall between the two beds. A stupid arrangement in any case, Clive had told her when shown the refurbished room a year earlier. A shared bed and independent bedside lamps would have made more sense. Well, he didn't mind the twin beds now, especially with Rosemarie, in fact they were a good thing on the whole, but the light was a nuisance. He was not given to reading in bed himself and was forced to put up with the glare until such time as Beatrice chose to extinguish it.

Tonight, too angry and disturbed to concentrate on her Sheila Kaye Smith she tugged so hard at the cord that it nearly came adrft. What sort of a man was her husband? Offer him a glamorously scented, alluringly gowned woman that most men would give anything to have in bed with them and what does he do? Goes to sleep! In his own bed. Of all the weedy, ungrateful cads you could be married to! Once again she ran over the list of favours she had done for him. Had she not taken over the running of the hotel, and done it far far better than he ever could? Organised and used her own impeccable taste in the redecorating and refurnishing of their private rooms and given him all the free time he wanted so that he could play about with the Territorials? Not to mention agreeing to the purchase of a car which she would never have time to drive herself. And last but not least she had in great danger and acute discomfort to say the least, borne his child. In fact, if it weren't for the anomalies of their position as regards the hotel owners, she ought to be divorcing him. For sheer, bloody-minded ingratitude . . . She also turned her back to the other bed, she also banged her pillow about, as noisily as she could. But they were both very tired; Beatrice and Clive in their separate beds and their separate lives, simultaneously fell asleep.

Chapter Six

"AND I am no more eighteen!"

The dumpy, grey-haired lady with the foreign accent smiled and patted Beatrice on the arm.

"So I say to myself I will come to the St Andrews for rest and recuperation. Just for a few days on my own. Dear Mrs Livingstone will be there to take care of me, and kind Mr Livingstone, also. And here I am. We must have a good talk later."

Beatrice turned to the head porter. "Vic, get Mrs Osterreicher's case taken up at once please. Would you like some tea sent to your room?"

"That is so kind! But no, I don't think so. I will have a little walk to the sea and blow away the cobwebs, and then I will take tea in your beautiful lounge, if that is convenient."

"Then I'll see you later. And we're all delighted that you are safely here."

Beatrice led the way to the lift, to which they were followed by the page-boy and the huge, bulging, old but expensive-looking leather suitcase, and then as the lift doors closed turned to see Jo lurking near Reception.

"Jo, how many times have I told you not to hang about down here?"

"Who was that?"

"A guest. Now go up and have your tea. I expect Daddy's there."

"Aren't you coming?" Clive always wanted to wait tea for his wife, which was tedious for Jo.

"Soon as I can. Now run along"

"She's not English, is she? That lady."

"No. She's German. Now go along."

German! This was extraordinary. Jo understood Germans to be the enemy, or at least the potential enemy. Christmas was over, and had been marred by much doom-laden talk of the where-shall-we-be-by-Christmas-next-year variety. Also Clive was spending more and more of his time with the Territorials, getting ready, he said, to fight the Germans. Now there was one in Room 106.

The hotel had been nearly full for the holiday and although these visitors had almost all departed, the dinner and dance for New Year's Eve was well booked in advance by local people. Jo was to stay up and attend, as a special treat. Rosemarie had been invited to share in the celebrations at the hosts' table. This had been Beatrice's idea. She still felt the need of a woman friend, someone on her own level, and Rosemarie remained the only candidate. Jo went up to tea as instructed to find only Patty in the private apartment, looking quite appealing in a new black dress, extra frilly white apron and organdie cap, which outfit had been her Christmas gift from the management. Jo had given her a necklace of red glass beads, sixpence from Woolworths, and received in return some Californian Poppy scent from the same establishment. Patty was ironing Beatrice's satin slips and French knickers on an ironing board in the kitchenette. The tea tray was on the low black and chromium table in the sitting room. Her father being absent Jo took a sandwich from the tray and joined Patty.

"Are there any nice Germans, d'you think, Patty?"

"My Dad says there are some that are alright, and he was in the War, so I expect he knows."

"But they're killing the Jews aren't they? We've got these two girls at school who are Jews and they think their father's been taken prisoner, because he hasn't written to them for ages, and he used to write every week." Jo bit thoughtfully into her sandwich.

"Don't make crumbs, Jo. You're not the one that'll have to sweep them up. And don't eat all the sandwiches before your Mum and Dad come up."

"There's a German staying here. A lady. She came before."

"Well, I shouldn't think your Mum would let her stay here if she was a real German."

"I've got to wear my green velvet tonight. Is it OK?"

"Don't ask me. I'm not your lady's maid."

"Well, the collar was half off last time I looked at it."

"Then it's still half off, I suppose. It's time you started looking after yourself a bit."

"I'm no good at sewing."

"Only because you don't want to be."

"Oh, don't be mean, Patty darling. Shall I go and get it?"

"I'll have a look at it later, if you behave yourself and don't make crumbs all over my clean floor."

"Oh, thanks Patty, you're an angel." Jo perched on the corner of the little table.

"Tell me about June and Ronnie."

The visit to Doughty Street had not been repeated. In fact for some time embarrassment had prevented Jo from even mentioning the brothers and sisters whom she had so longed to see in the flesh. But with the lapse of time this had faded, and now she could ask for news of Ada-and-the-baby and the twins with all her old interest.

"They got into trouble last week. Playing on a building site. June grazed her knee. And Ronnie cut his hand. Blood everywhere, there was. It'll be a wonder if he doesn't get lockjaw, cutting it there." She indicated on her own hand, stretching the skin between thumb and forefinger. "You always get lockjaw if you cut yourself there."

"What's lockjaw?"

"You go all stiff and you arch your back, and then you die."

"Patty! Ronnie won't get that, will he?"

"You never know." Patty spat lugubriously on the flat iron she had heated up on the gas ring. An electric model was available but she distrusted it.

"This German lady, could she be a spy, d'you think?"

"Is it that one that came before?"

"I think so, though her hair's grey now. She used to hug me a lot."

"You want to look out for that sort," said Patty mysteriously, after which she refused to commit herself further.

Beatrice and Clive came up for tea at that point and Clive wondered at the kitchen's providing five sandwiches for three people and said somebody needed ticking off. This did not go down well with his wife who took it as criticism and the atmosphere was distinctly strained until Clive said, "Was that Mrs Osterreicher I saw downstairs?" and Beatrice said yes it was and she had sent her two sons ahead away from the Nazis and then got all her household goods crated up and brought to England.

"And now she's tired out and has come down for a short rest. I am no more eighteen, she said, and of course, she isn't. It must have been a tremendous undertaking for a woman like her. And every moment she stayed there she was in danger of being arrested. It all sounds simply terrifying. She definitely thinks there's going to be a war. D'you want some more tea?"

Clive passed his cup, and Beatrice, who did not like chocolate cake said Jo could have her slice if she liked, and with the atmosphere of resentment lifted Jo accepted this offer and enjoyed the cake.

The evening started well. Rosemarie wore her dark red velvet, and some new drop earrings, French paste, a secret Christmas present from Clive. Their restrained sparkle brightened her eyes. Beatrice wore her present too, a marcasite watch set in a flower-shaped brooch. The centre of the flower was a tiny door which opened to reveal its face. It glittered expensively on Beatrice's clinging, cross-cut black gown. Jo wore her bottle green velvet with the lace collar. It wouldn't fit her for much longer, thought Beatrice. It was really a mistake to buy expensive clothes for kids, you never got your money's worth of wear. The green dress was only just long enough now, and you couldn't do much with velvet. If you tried having it let down the mark of the original hem would show. She had bought the dress for Jo at Terry's for the previous Christmas, but she had not worn it half a dozen times. That worked out at over ten shillings a wearing, if you thought about it. An absurd extravagance but then Jo paid for dressing. The darkly gleaming silk velvet made her look fairer and more fragile than usual. Even the little bow in her hair, presumably bought by Jo herself, was green velvet and quite a good match. She noticed that the bodice was getting tight across the chest. Jo's figure was developing, but she wouldn't be starting anything yet, would she? Beatrice herself had been twelve when she began menstruating. Well, sooner or later there would be all that to contend with. Beatrice looked forward to the time when Jo would be eighteen, when she would be more of a companion, and less of a trouble. Which reminded Beatrice that her own mother would be joining them for dinner also, something she had not known when inviting Rosemarie. Mrs Hewitt usually went to one of her other daughters on New Year's Eve. In the tarnished brocade which had been her evening dress for many years, with her slave bangles and her black fringe she would look thoroughly common, but there was nothing to be done about it.

Jo was not looking forward to the meal. She did not see why they had to have Miss Wells. Neither did Clive, who had been unaware of the invitiation until after Rosemarie, strangely to his mind, had accepted it. He would have to play a part and he was not, he believed, much of an actor.

77

But Rosemarie was a superb actress. Addressing him as Mr Livingstone until Beatrice requested her to call them Clive and Beatrice, she kept the social chat flowing. Jo, seated between her mother and her grandmother, was glad to be as far as possible from her headmistress. Mrs Hewitt, with Clive on her other side, took care to engage her granddaughter in conversation at intervals, though she would have not considered it good manners for Jo to join in the adult talk. Of course they discussed the international situation – that was inevitable. There were no more stories about cardboard tanks and calling Germany's bluff, now they all knew the reality of concentration camps and refugees.

Clive found it hard to make a sensible contribution. Rosemarie was seated next to him in still massive dignity, yet had changed from the woman she had been on that earlier occasion. Her restraint, her consciousness of being a headmistress, seemed imposed rather than natural. He felt that at any moment it might break down. This made him nervous and yet at the same time excited him. He felt he could not wait until the weekend to make love to her and was wondering if he could creep into the almost deserted school later that night. Just thinking of it was nearly too much for him, and he had to make sure that the white tablecloth was decently draped over his lap. She rather frequently managed to press his thigh with hers, or touch his shoulder. He was worried about the old lady. His wife's mother was a perspicacious old cow, he had always thought that. He hardly dared to address Rosemarie; instead he talked to Beatrice across the table and tried to cheer Jo, who was looking rather glum. Beatrice was not pleased with his behaviour and decided to tell him off, later in the evening, for his lack of attention to her guest. But the wine helped, and the good food, and then halfway through dinner Jo noticed to her delight, sitting at a far table, the Liddiard family. Beryl Liddiard was in Jo's form at the Princess May, and in fact they had been best friends for nearly two terms a year or so earlier. Then when Jo was absent with mumps Beryl had decided to be best friends with Mavis Kemp, instead. Jo had been deeply hurt by this, but soon after became best friends with Bronwen, who seemed to be the only person available. It was funny really, because she didn't actually like her all that much, yet at the same time she enjoyed her company. Anyway, there wasn't really anyone else.

But it was not Beryl whose presence delighted Jo. It was that of her two brothers, Noel and Peter. They were eighteen and nineteen years old, tall, both auburn-haired and very handsome. Beryl was small and dark like her father, while the boys resembled their mother. Mrs Liddiard was a large, handsome woman with strong features and a loud voice, while her husband was a small man with a monkeyish face, that was somehow attractive cast in a feminine mould on Beryl. One felt that in sorting out the Liddiards nature had at last managed to get it right.

The restaurant, still decorated with holly and ivy – no paperchains, which Beatrice considered vulgar – was warm and lively, and with the central space cleared for dancing, quite full. The Reg Winner Quintet occupied the tiny stage at the side of the room facing the sea, beyond which the space widened to contain a bar area, where tonight extra tables had been placed in case of last-minute bookings.

Beatrice intended to achieve a real party feeling, on this special night, rather different from the sophisticated atmosphere of the formal balls or the romantic intimacy of the Saturday dinner dances. To this end Clive would become Master of Ceremonies for the evening, there would be set dances like the St Bernard's waltz, or even the new Palais Glide, and one or two games and competitions for the children present, as well as the usual foxtrots and waltzes. Then as midnight approached the night porter, who fancied himself as an actor, would appear as Old Father Time, standing in a spotlight in the middle of the darkened room. As rapidly becoming more and more enfeebled, he faded away into the kitchen with the last strokes of Big Ben, amplified from the wireless, the spotlight would shift to the double entrance doors which would burst open to admit the golden-haired two-year-old son of a local greengrocer whose parents had free tickets for the occasion. He was of course dressed in white and his pram which was for some reason disguised as a sleigh was propelled by his equally golden-haired young mother, wearing Russian costume with a fur hat. His arrival was the signal for peals of bells, cheers, hugs and kisses and a rainstorm of balloons let down from the net which had held them close to the ceiling until that moment. The baby looked totally bewildered but at least did not cry until the band struck up Auld Lang Syne. Everyone rose and formed a huge circle, arms crossed and hands joined, and Jo was forced to grasp the right hand of her headmistress whose left was clutched by that of an elderly man whom Rosemarie had never previously met and certainly did not take to now that she had. Thus linked they all sang 'Should Auld Aquaintance be Forgot' for what seemed a very long time. Jo, sandwiched between Rosemarie and her grandmother, thought it was even worse than a school social. That done they all sat down; at every table somebody poured more wine, healths were drunk and good wishes exchanged. At the table near the door Beatrice was unfortunately inspired to tell the story of how six years earlier a smaller and chubbier Jo had been cast as the spirit of the New Year. In a white dress with a wreath of snowdrops on her head she had looked enchanting, and all she had to do was step forward and smile. Clive had ordered a basket of expensively forced spring flowers for her to carry. Somehow or other Jo and the basket had not been united until a few minutes before she was to make her appearance. The florist had been lavish in interpreting the order and the basket was on the large side and crammed with vegetation. Jo said it was too heavy, and her father removed some of the flowers. She said it was still too heavy and Clive, desperate and thanking God that Beatrice was otherwise engaged, removed some more. This went on until there were only three or four narcissi and a little greenery left. The bells began to peal and Jo recognizing her cue had stamped crossly into the ballroom, presenting the rejoicing diners with a mutinous looking six-year-old carrying an almost empty basket. What an omen for nineteen thirty-two, trilled Beatrice, who had been furious at the time. She laughed merrily while Jo cringed beside her.

"But actually it turned out to be a very good year for us, so perhaps we should have got her to do it again!"

'You're embarrassing the child," said Jo's grandmother, causing Rosemarie to look at her and make things worse.

Then Clive rose to announce a waltz, afterwards taking the floor with Beatrice to restart the dancing. They were excellent ballroom dancers, graceful, and well matched . . . it had been the common interest that had brought them together, and the guests, instead of rising to join in, sat watching them and clapped when they performed an intricate step – not a new one, they hadn't danced together very much lately – but impressive for all that. After they had circled the floor twice it filled rapidly, and Jo was left with the two women, her grandmother and her headmistress, in a mood that was not exactly celebratory. In fact, sitting at the table in her too-warm, too-childish velvet dress, she hated everything. She was also desperately tired in spite of having rested for an hour or so in the afternoon, and only pride prevented her from going to bed. Making a mumbled excuse she rose and went to the table near the stage where the various prizes for games and raffles had been set out. The St Andrews was known for the high quality and lavish number of prizes that were presented during this sort of evening, and the baskets of fruit, boxes of chocolates and other desirable objects always helped these occasions to go with a swing. More than anything Jo had needed an excuse to get away from the two women, but she approached the table with interest and was surprised to see that a trophy that particularly appealed to her had not yet been awarded. This was a small square powder compact made, it appeared, entirely of mirror-glass, finished with a silky pink tassel, and displayed in a small open box which was lined with dark blue, silver star-patterned paper. The little box appealed to Jo almost as much as the compact. As well as this there remained a bottle of whisky and a large fancy tin of chocolate biscuits.

Covetously gazing at the compact she realised that someone had joined her and went hot all over when she realised that it was Peter Liddiard, the younger of Beryl's two brothers. If only she didn't feel such a child in her puffed sleeves and lace collar. Beryl actually had a full-length dress in pale pink taffeta in which she looked at least fourteen. She felt even more childish when Peter Liddiard said kindly, "Hello. You go to my sister's school don't you? I bet you'd like that tin of chocolate biscuits."

Jo saw this as a confirmation of her own too-youthful appearance and said ungraciously, "Actually, I'd much rather win the compact."

Peter, apparently intent on making her feel worse than ever, then said, "I'd have thought you were a bit too young for that sort of thing, but still I suppose you could put it away for a year or two."

Before Jo had time to think of a suitably lofty response to this remark there was a roll of drums to invoke a moment's quiet, during which Clive announced that there were still prizes to be won and asked for ten gentlemen to take their partners for the next game, after which the compact and the whisky would be awarded to the winning couple, while the second couple would receive the magnificent tin of biscuits. And then to Jo's amazement her hand was taken by Peter Liddiard who said, "Now's your chance, Miss Livingstone. May I have the pleasure?"

Perhaps he was acting on an impulse of kindness, or had been brought up to do the gentlemanly thing, or simply wanted to join in the game; whatever his motivation, Jo was pleased. She had danced a waltz with her father once, and joined in the Palais Glide and the Lambeth Walk but this would be the first time ever that she had taken the floor with a really good-looking young man who was old enough to be grown-up, and young enough to be an object of interest to her own age group. It would be something to tell Bronwen, who was spending New Year's Eve tamely at home with her mother and father. They took their places in the line, and Clive, pleased to see his daughter enjoying herself, began to explain the rules of the game, punctuating his speech with a mildly suggestive joke or two. Then, before he had got very far, Peter leaned sideways down to Jo and muttered the word, "Winchester."

"What do you mean?" Baffled, afraid of letting him down she stared up at him.

"I've played this before."

Clive was looking at them and the boy straightened up, giving Jo's hand a conspiratorial squeeze. The next moment the male partners were made to line up at the opposite end of the room. There they were told that each one must think of the name of a town, to be whispered to Clive as he proceeded along the row of men with a pencil and notebook. The idea of the game was that, at the word 'Go', each man would make every effort to communicate his chosen name to his distant partner, who then had to run to Clive, and tell him what she believed her opposite number's choice to be.

Clive called "Ready, Steady, Go!" and pandemonium set in. With all the men shouting at once it was of course, difficult if not impossible to catch the actual words, and now Jo understood what Peter expected her to do. He expected her to cheat. So she cheated. It seemed there was nothing else she could do. If they did not win he would think she was a squeamish namby-pamby idiot, and she would be letting him down; he would never speak to her again. A split second after the shouting began, while the nine other female partners of varying age were straining their ears, and making things worse by yelling "Louder! Louder!" which was all part of the fun, Jo shot across the room to her father with the word Winchester on her lips and won the game, and the mirror-glass powder compact.

Clive looked a trifle suspicious when Peter led her up to accept the prizes, but he handed them over, and Peter put his arm round her shoulders as they walked away. Just before he delivered her politely to her grandmother he gave her a little squeeze.

"That's the way to do it. Go after what you want. Only don't be so quick off the mark next time. You were a bit obvious."

Jo put the compact down on the table, and to Mrs Hewitt's surprise, showed no further interest in it. Almost immediately she said she would go up to bed, and her grandmother, who thought she ought not to be wandering round on her own in that great place, after midnight, accompanied her up to the apartment. In her room, Jo hid the compact at the back of a drawer, without even removing it from the box. She would never use it. It was not really hers. How could Peter Liddiard, who seemed so nice, turn her into a cheat? And be one himself? Jo had never, ever, cheated at anything. It was the worst thing you could do, after stealing and murder. Everything she had ever read had instilled this belief into her. All the school stories, the Angela Brazil *Madcap of the Lower Fourth* variety, to the equally enjoyable Valerie Drew series made it crystal clear that cheats or sneaks were quite simply beyond the pale. She told herself as firmly as she could that it had not been her idea, or her fault. But the compact, at the back of the drawer, said otherwise. She could have refused, but then she would have seemed stupid and ungrateful and lost face for ever with Peter Liddiard. Only now of course she never wanted to see him again so it wouldn't have mattered.

Ashamed, bewildered, and tired out, she put her head under the bedclothes and went to sleep, while Mrs Hewitt switched on the light in the sitting room, and sat down to await her son-in-law, who was supposed to be driving her home to the flat over The Japanese Tearoom.

Later on, in the Hillman Minx, after Rosemarie had been dropped outside the Princess May, she commented on the oddity of her granddaughter's behaviour.

"She didn't seem at all pleased with her prize, did she?"

"She's a funny kid. Hard to know what she's thinking sometimes."

84

"You think she's quite happy, do you?"

"Lord, yes. As happy as a sandboy."

Clive swept briskly round into the main road and stopped outside the teashop. He offered to escort his mother-in-law up to her flat, but did not insist when she said it wasn't necessary. He intended to go straight back to the school to say a proper goodnight to Rosemarie, who would be waiting to open the door for him. Alone together for a brief moment when Beatrice was making the rounds of the tables, and Mrs Hewitt had gone up with Jo, they had made this arrangement.

Chapter Seven

AT THE beginning of every term Rosemarie interviewed each member of her staff, privately. Her father had always done this and she believed it to be a useful way of informing herself. She had arranged the interviews for the Saturday of the second week, early in February, to let everyone settle down a bit first.

The games mistress was the first on her list. Although there was a large desk in the room Rosemarie chose to seat her interviewees opposite her, beside the fire. She wanted them to chat naturally, and if possible, indiscreetly.

Miss Colman was wearing, as she usually did, a brief navy-blue gym tunic, with the badge of her training college on the chest, a white shirt underneath it, and long black stockings which evidently reached up to her neck. She had visited a hairdresser before the term began, and he had cut her crisply curling dark hair too short; it seemed to be shaved almost up to her ears, making her less attractive than usual. A faint black shadow adorned her upper lip. She was immensely fit and vital, and, it seemed, a stranger to uncertainty in any area of life.

They discussed the advantages of lacrosse over hockey, the matches to be played against other schools, and new equipment for the gym. They talked about remedial exercises for round-shouldered girls, and problem daygirls who tried to get out of games. The games periods were at two o'clock on the huge rented field at the back of the town, a good twenty minutes walk from the school. If you had dinner at home and went straight back to school afterwards instead of up to the playing field you could always say you had forgotten it was your day for games or your dinner had been late and you'd missed the bus. Miss Colman was baffled by this sort of behaviour – she could fully sympathise with anyone trying to skip Geography or Maths, but games! She loved teaching them almost as much as she loved playing them, shouting advice, blowing her whistle, running faster than any of the girls could run. Crying "Bully Off," or "Cradle the ball," or "Pass! PASS!" she was happy. Teaching the netball team to 'shoot' the ball successfully into the suspended net, demonstrating her own skill again and again, gave her an immense sense of achievement.

At the end of the session they would all return to the school on foot, hot, sweaty and tired, and go straight into class, which Miss Colman deplored. She had suggested that showers be installed for use after games, but apparently this was out of the question. Apart from the expense, Miss Wells believed there would a risk of the girls catching cold. Better to cool down gradually.

Teachers were expected to stick to the rota pinned to the door of the staff bathroom which allowed them two baths a week each but Miss Colman, once her charges were safely back in their classrooms, had a quick, illicit bath in the top floor bathroom furthest from anywhere the headmistress might be prowling. She intended to bring up the question of showers again during her interview.

Rosemarie expected this and had her refusal ready. She also meant to discuss the fact that she believed there had been too much 'emotion' in the school during the previous term, and she hoped that more physical activity, and an ever more packed timetable might help to keep these undesirable feelings down to a reasonable level. Too much to expect that no one would fall in love, no one would let down a best friend, that 'crushes' on teachers or older girls would become a thing of the past. The rule that forbade the presence of any girl in a dormitory or bedroom not her own must be determinedly enforced.

To some of the staff it was difficult to mention these things, but to Miss Colman it was quite easy, combining as she did, a comprehensive knowledge of physicality with a relentlessly 'healthy' outlook. Their discussion was unusually frank and free. It would not be desirable, suggested Rosemarie, for the girls to grow up with an antipathy to normal relationships. In an all-female establishment there were inherent dangers. Miss Colman understood her worries, and promised to do her best to exhaust the girls physically, leaving it to other teachers to keep them wholesomely occupied mentally. Then she told Rosemarie about the hiking holiday she hoped to arrange for herself at Easter. A mixed group of ramblers to which she belonged proposed to walk the Pennine Way. Sex, she seemed to suggest, was just another form of healthy, comradely exercise, best performed under canvas, as an expression of one's love of the open air and nature generally.

Rosemarie agreed vaguely and tried not to think about the small, closely curtained room at the Hunter's Moon, where fresh air and comradeship had no place at all.

Next on the list was the new French teacher, Miss Perkins. She was twenty-seven, had a good degree, and there was absolutely no danger of anyone's falling in love with her. Her lack of physical appeal had been among her qualifications in Rosemarie's eyes, when she had first interviewed her during the previous term, but now she wondered whether she had been wise. This young woman resembled a caricature of a school mistress. Rosemarie had more than once been handed confiscated comics or cheap periodicals cruelly illustrated with near-caricatures not only of fat girls called Bessie Bunter, but scraggy teachers with old-fashioned pince-nez perched on large bony noses. Their hair was always scraped back into a hard knot. If Winifred Perkins had made an effort to look like one of these drawings she could not have been more successful. Tall and gaunt, she had long straight hair of a not unpleasing light brown, but this was drawn severely off her face, plaited, and twisted into a heavy bun on the back of her head. She wore horn-rimmed spectacles, a droopy, mud-coloured cardigan, over a lace-knit beige jumper, and a sagging brown skirt. She seemed to suffer even more than most people from chilblains, and her bony nose was as red as her large-knuckled hands. She sat down in the chair Rosemarie indicated, remaining bolt upright on its edge, looking unhappy.

"Don't worry, Miss Perkins, this is just an informal chat, part of my routine at the beginning of term. Now, how are you settling down?"

"Quite well, I think." Miss Perkins realised she had spoken inaudibly, coughed, and tried again.

"Quite well, I think."

"Now, you are taking French right through the school, quite a full week. How are you finding the girls?"

"Very nice."

"Do they behave themselves? No passing notes, or talking in class?"

"Well, a little."

"You must come down on it at once. A warning and then ten minutes' detention."

Detention, when it amounted to thirty minutes, had to be worked off during the Wednesday half-holiday.

"I don't want . . . to be too strict . . . at first."

"Don't be afraid of being strict. In fact I would recommend that you *ARE* strict at first, and ease up a little, later on. The other way round is more difficult. If you try to become strict when you have been too easy, they will resent it."

"Yes, I see. Perhaps I had better try . . ."

"But most of our girls are well-behaved, just a little lively at times. Keep them interested, that's the secret. I hope you are making friends among the staff?"

"Oh, yes. They are all very nice."

Rosemarie continued to advise and encourage for ten minutes or so, eventually dismissing Miss Perkins with relief. She had, she thought, made a mistake. This woman would never control a class. They would despise her at once; her appearance and her lack of confidence would destroy the automatic respect they gave to authority. What had made her engage this girl? Her degree, of course, plus the fact that she seemed eager to have the job, even to come 'on trial' for a rather low wage. Her very lack of personality had been an added inducement. She would be joining a group already over-endowed with quirks, opinions, and self-assertion on the part of its members.

Rosemarie felt tired and irritated. She would have liked a sherry and a cigarette, but she had five more teachers to see before six o'clock, when she would share these pleasures with Miss Whitehouse, the senior mistress.

Miss Curnock, who taught Botany and Geography was a fair-haired woman of around thirty, with invisible eyebrows and eyelashes, and pale eyes. Surprisingly, at the end of the previous summer vacation, she had accepted a proposal of marriage. She was, it appeared, to become the second wife of the widowed rector in the village where her parents lived. The difference this prospect had brought about in her was striking. From being quiet, lacking in animation or interest in anything very much, she had returned to school at the start of the previous term glowing with a new vitality. From being merely thin, she had filled out sufficiently to be described as slender; she was talkative and more confident, laughed when anyone made a joke, and spent all her spare time sewing her trousseau. She entered the room smiling, and at once told Rosemarie that she would be leaving at the end of the term, and that her wedding would take place a month later.

Rosemarie looked grave. "I do hope you have thought this over carefully," she said, assuming her character of worldly-wise, kindly adviser which was one of her favourite roles. "Your fiancé is quite an elderly man, is he not?"

"James is fifty-eight." said Miss Curnock. "Hardly elderly. And he is amazingly young for his age."

"All the same . . . twenty-five years . . ."

"Twenty-three."

"You have a good career before you. It is something to be an independent woman," went on Rosemarie, rather half-heartedly. These were things that as a feminist and an employer she had to say, but looking at Sybil Curnock she knew they fell on stony ground.

"This is where I'm going to live . . ."

Rosemarie took the offered snapshot and saw a gracious Georgian house. Standing at the gate, just discernible, was a baldish, thin man in a clerical collar.

". . . and that's James. He really does need feeding up a bit, but he'll be alright when I get there."

"Are there any children?"

"Oh, yes, James has two grown-up sons but he's always wanted a daughter. He wants one exactly like me." Miss Curnock blushed virginally.

"I suppose it will be a quiet wedding."

"Well, I'm having a white dress, and veil, and my sister will be bridesmaid. James says I'm entitled to my special day, even if he is a widower. He's so understanding. Not that I would really have minded. I told him I didn't mind if the wedding was at eight o'clock on a Monday morning with two witnesses, just so long as he was there." She laughed happily.

"It looks a huge house. Quite a task to run that. And of course you will have other duties."

"All it needs is a little organisation. James doesn't want me to work too hard."

"Well. I shall be sorry to lose you."

Rosemarie asked herself why on earth she was trying to put the wretched woman off? She wasn't a career type at all. Could she conceivably be jealous? They had a brisk discussion of Miss Curnock's timetable, during which it was noticeable that she was less amenable than before to extra duties, and parted politely. Rosemarie, waiting for the next on her list thought of the beautiful rectory, and the ex-teacher bringing up her child or children, busy and happy, secure in the love of her balding husband. Of course it was quite likely to turn out badly, what with the difference in age and the grown-up sons, but still, after the interview with the bride-to-be, her own life seemed a little less satisfactory.

After Miss Curnock came Miss Card, Science, Chemistry and Physics, a sarcastic little woman whom Rosemarie did not quite like, although she was good at getting the girls through their public exams, and then Miss Denny who taught the youngest girls, and could have been taken for a pupil herself, with her wide grey eyes and unpermed short brown hair. Miss Denny did not like being away from home and counted the days till the end of term just as the girls did. It always took her some time to settle down but on this occasion she seemed happier. Was she making friends, Rosemarie asked her. Miss Denny admitted that Miss Whitehouse had been awfully kind, and really made all the difference now that she had got to know her. Rosemarie thought that someone nearer her own age – Miss Colman, perhaps – but Miss Colman it appeared had little free time, being ever ready to give extra gym or country dancing sessions to the fifth- and sixth-formers. Deciding to think these facts over later on, Rosemarie asked the usual questions, received reasonably satisfactory replies, and went on to interview Miss Barton and Miss Craig. Miss Barton, the junior Maths teacher was small and lively, with dark-rimmed spectacles that in no way detracted from her extrovert personality, and Miss Craig was a tall, dour Scots lady who taught German and Latin, older than the rest of the staff and with a fondness for her own company. She had a dry wit which she occasionally exhibited at the dining table or in class, too dry sometimes for the girls to understand. Some people thought she drank.

It was six-thirty by the time the senior mistress, Miss Whitehouse, entered the sitting room. Rosemarie made up the fire. The room looked inviting with the old brocade curtains drawn over the tall windows and the pier glass reflecting the glowing lamps which augmented the central light. Rosemarie relaxed, poured sherry and offered her cigarette box. She always treated the senior mistress as a colleague and an equal, though this evening at the back of her mind lurked a small, worrying figure. Miss Denny.

Phyllis Whitehouse took her seat with the confident air of a close friend, sinking down into the easy chair with the sigh of one who relaxes after a day of very hard work. It was true that she worked hard, even on Saturday which was half day for the girls she would have been teaching all the morning, then correcting exercises, and giving extra coaching during the afternoon. She had been on duty at teatime, eating slabs of bread and margarine spread with jam or Marmite, and drinking unsatisfactory tea out of one of the huge brown enamelled teapots, at the head of a long table. It was not her turn to be one of the fortunate few who each Saturday took tea in the staff room. As senior mistress she could have avoided tea duty on Saturday, but this was not her way.

She was tall, with bobbed dark hair, about forty years old and invariably wore a well-cut navy skirt, a white shirt blouse and sometimes a tie. Today she had compromised by wearing a cherry-coloured silk scarf tied in a floppy bow under her shirt collar. Crossing her legs, resting her elbow on the chair-arm, holding her cigarette in the air, she looked both graceful and dashing. In private, they were on first name terms.

"You've ploughed through that lot then," she said sympathetically. "Any worries?"

"I don't think so really," Rosemarie paused and sipped her sherry. "Miss Denny. Is she settling down better this term?"

"She'll do. She just needed taking out of herself."

"She said you had been kind."

"Did she?" Phyllis Whitehouse looked pleased, momentarily, then frowned and said, "I hear we're going to lose Sybil Curnock." The conversation followed the expected lines. Rosemarie did not say, as she might have done, perhaps ought to have done, "I do not trust you with Patricia Denny. She is young and lonely. You are mature and quite frankly you seem to me predatory." What she did say was, "Yes, at the end of term. I shall have to start advertising."

They went on to discuss the timetable, the very few difficult girls, the amount of preparation work the sixth form could be expected to do, and the suitability of *As You Like It* as a school play. They also considered Rosemarie's contingency plans in the event of war. After which they chatted about books and music while they finished their sherry, finally parting on excellent terms.

Beatrice was in her office checking the bookings. There were fewer than she would have liked, for Easter. This was obviously due to the political situation. It really was beginning to look as though things were boiling up over there. Well, they, the Germans, certainly couldn't be allowed to invade England. Some of the stories that Mrs Osterreicher, who was making quite frequent short visits because of a friend in a local nursing home, had told her, really were very upsetting. If they were true. Clive believed she exaggerated in order to gain sympathy, but her accounts of friends or friends' husbands who had received night-time calls from the Gestapo seemed to Beatrice only too plausible. She spoke of the woman with whom she was now sharing a flat, Trudi Myers. Her husband, a well-to-do Jewish furrier, had been taken from their home at three o'clock one morning, and a week later his wife and young son had been brought to England by Mrs Osterreicher, whose own sons were already safely installed. Business friends in Stafford had taken them in some months earlier. Beatrice could not see why she should invent any of this. Reluctantly she became convinced that their lives were going to change.

She decided to go up to the apartment and have a drink with Clive, and then remembered that it was Saturday, and he had, as usual, gone off somewhere in uniform. Jo was up there with that unattractive kid she was so fond of; what was her name? Blodwen . . . something Welsh. She rang the bell for whoever was on duty, and ordered a dry Martini and a packet of du Maurier from the bar, and the *Evening Standard*, copies of which were on sale in the foyer.

*   *   *

95

Jo and Bron were busy being detectives. At school they had distributed colourfully crayoned handbills to all of Form IIIA, and had received several commissions as well as a few sneers. These commissions were markedly uninspiring but they were trying to carry them out to the best of their ability. They had traced Frances Lewis's illicit copy of *Girl's Crystal* to the practice room where it had fallen behind the piano and proved to Daphne Morgan that her pet caterpillars were escaping, not being stolen. This had been self-evident from the first as no one but Daphne Morgan was interested in caterpillars. There were other investigations mostly concerning missing objects, and though they enjoyed questioning their clients about their movements and retracing them meticulously, the most exciting success was the recovery of Rene Alcock's shoe-bag from the bus station, which she could have thought of herself if she'd had any sense at all. They entered these cases in their records, marking each one 'Successfully Concluded', but they were out for bigger game. And that very evening, as they waited in the foyer for Bronwen's father to pick her up, bigger game, in the quite bulky form of Mrs Osterreicher, presented itself.

Sunday morning was really quite pleasant for February. Waking in a bell tent on his camp bed, acknowleging the delivery of shaving-water from his batman – in everyday life a fishmonger's assistant who even in uniform smelt slightly of his trade – Clive quite looked forward to the day of drill, target practice and so on. He had spent the previous Sunday night with Rosemarie and so was not due to meet her that evening, but the thought of returning to the hotel depressed him – he didn't feel like playing bridge, or chatting to the German woman or sitting in their bleak sitting room, where he would be alone except for Jo, and even she seemed to have homework or something that kept her in her bedroom most of the time. Bea could be quite good company when she was in a good mood but she never came up until nearly ten; heaven only knew what she did in the evenings, and then she always went down again last thing, even when he was there to see that the night porter was on duty and to attend to the locking up, which out of season took place at eleven o'clock. In the summer it was always after midnight.

The morning was successful – all he had to do he accomplished with ease, and at twelve o'clock when he had a few minutes to spare he felt confident and free. So he drove to the call box in the village and telephoned Rosemarie.

The telephone at the May of Teck was fixed to the wall outside the staff room, and there was an extension in Rosemarie's sitting room. It was answered by any member of staff who happened to hear it and sometimes it rang for a long time. It did so on this occasion because the girls and accompanying teachers were never back from church until after twelve-fifteen. Other teachers were mostly reading Sunday papers in the staff room. Rosemarie, who attended church on alternate Sunday mornings, had preceded the girls on the homeward walk, making a brisk escape while they took their time forming up into their two-by-two crocodile and arguing about who was to walk with who. She noted that Miss Denny and Miss Whitehouse were in charge, organising the girls, quelling loud voices and pacifying grumblers. A choice existed between the longer way back by way of the front, and the shorter route down the main street. A vote was taken and the longer way got the most, then Hilary Lambert shocked everyone by saying quite loudly, "But I want to be excused." Rosemarie, already at the church gate, left the situation in the capable hands of the senior mistress – what was a senior mistress for, after all? – and returned to the school by the shorter route, for no particular reason, but she was in time to hear the telephone ringing as she went in by the main entrance.

She had been looking forward to twenty minutes relaxation before going down to the dining room so when she picked up the instrument she said "Hello" in the voice of a rather bad-tempered headmistress, which put Clive off for a moment. Had it been a friend or relative of a teacher they would have received very short shrift, though a parent would almost certainly have been graciously answered. Somewhat nervously Clive suggested they should depart from their routine and meet that evening at Warne Bay station. He missed her, he said, could not wait another week. He said exactly what he had planned to say but his voice lacked conviction because her manner had put him off. Without altering her tone she said, "Very well, the usual arrangements. Goodbye," and hung up the earpiece. There was an extension in her sitting room but to use it on this occasion she would have been forced to go upstairs, take the instrument off its hook, then return to replace the receiver in the passage downstairs, during which time some passing busybody might have replaced it, or even asked if anyone was holding. But Clive, not knowing this, was hurt and surprised. Of course, he told himself, she was afraid someone might overhear, or there might have been someone in the room with her, someone whom she could not dismiss. But her cool, impersonal response stayed with him, considerably reducing his anticipatory ardour.

When the midday dinner was safely over Rosemarie informed Miss Whitehouse that she had been called away, implying some sort of emergency in the fragile life of the invalid aunt. But she would be catching the six-twelve as usual, so the normal Sunday afternoon routine would not be changed. From three until four the sixth-formers would gather in the sitting room with their knitting or embroidery, in order to listen to their headmistress reading aloud from some classic but entertaining work. Sometimes they found the plots rather mystifying as Rosemarie was often forced to make considerable cuts in the text. *Jane Eyre* had been successful owing to its heroine's impregnable virtue; only Adele's origins had to be glossed over. But *Tess of the D'Urbervilles* was so filleted that no one really understood why poor Tess was so ashamed and desperate.

Daygirls were luckier, with their Sundays to themselves. Bronwen and Jo could put into action the plan conceived on the previous evening. The plan was to investigate Mrs Osterreicher, whom they suspected of being a spy. There were, as it happened, a few small circumstances which seemed to justify their suspicions.

That morning they had hung about in the foyer with their coats on, an innocent explanation ready for Beatrice if she saw them, until Mrs Osterreicher appeared from the lift – a prosaic figure, dumpy, dressed in quiet but 'good' black clothes – and handed in her key to reception. At a distance they followed her up the side road, across the shopping street and into an area of substantial Edwardian houses. At The Laurels Nursing Home she pushed open a wrought-iron gate, walked up the path and rang the bell, to be admitted by a nurse. This was not particularly exciting, but they remained at the top of the road for a few minutes, Bronwen taking off her shoe and sitting down on a low wall and rubbing her foot to allay suspicion if they were observed. After a time Mrs Osterreicher emerged accompanied, most satisfactorily, by an Army officer in uniform. They conferred briefly on the path, and then Mrs Osterreicher went back inside and the man strode off down the road.

Bronwen, officially invited to tea, returned to the St Andrews early in the afternoon. They hoped to combine detective work with roller skating along the promenade, permitted during the winter. But this time Beatrice, irritable because of Clive's continued absence after a hurried explanatory telephone call, saw them in the foyer and told Jo to go back upstairs and put on her best coat, that roller skating was an unsuitable activity for Sunday, they were to go for a walk only and Jo was to be back by four o'clock. All this was quite unlike Beatrice's normal attitude. Jo queried the roller skating, was sharply reprimanded and told that in their position they had to be concerned about what other people thought.

Crossly Jo went upstairs and changed her old brown tweed for her new camel-hair and rejoined Bron who said that Mrs Osterreicher had just come down in her outdoor clothes and was in the lounge. Jo was peering round the door when Beatrice reappeared and irritably packed them off. They crossed the green and watched the hotel from the distance of fifty yards. It was cold, dull, and very windy, and time passed slowly. After ten minutes they grew tired of waiting, decided that Mrs Osterreicher had settled in the lounge, and walked along to where a flagpole and some iron seats furnished a curved projection of the promenade. Here their view of the St Andrews was blocked by another hotel that had been built at right angles to the sea instead of facing it. They looked out over the railings at they grey, hostile-looking water, watching the great waves roll in and the tops crash over into foam. They counted them hoping for proof that the seventh waves were always the biggest. The tide was about halfway in, soon the water would be slapping against the lower promenade. They considered going down the steps, but Jo was not eager. She thought that Bron might want her to engage in some activity that would endanger her best coat. She was afraid this would bring on a fit of sulking at which Bron had plenty of practice and was relieved when she was able to draw her attention to Mrs Osterreicher, perkily crossing the green, her fur collar held up round her face, her sensible shoes enabling her to make speedy progress. Reaching the promenade she turned away from the girls and walked briskly towards the nearest 'shelter', a largish wood and glass structure, fitted with seats on three sides, where visitors could supposedly sit protected from the weather whilst they admired the view.

It was winter. The view was miserable, and it was far too cold to sit about, but as they sauntered past, keeping close to the railings and calling out to one another with elaborate casualness, they saw that Mrs Osterreicher was sitting in the shelter talking to a man. They really did appear deep in urgent conversation. Pausing before she was out of their line of vision Jo, turning uninterestedly away, heard Bron, leaning with her back to the railings, murmur, "She's given him something. A piece of paper. Now he's going."

And he was. The man, elderly, and wearing a shabby black

coat rose and walked away westwards. Then, horror of horrors, Mrs Osterreicher was up too, and not walking away but coming towards them.

"And what are you doing out here, my two little friends? It is such a cold, windy day. A real Culvergate day, I think. So bright here in summer, but now . . ." She was opening her bag. "Let me see if I have something for you." She drew two small, brightly coloured tubes of sweets out of her black leather handbag. "Refreshers! You know Refreshers? They are so good when you go on a journey, they quench your thirst. I always have some."

"Oh, we couldn't, really . . ." began Jo, "but—"

"You will not hurt my feelings by refusing a few sweets. No, take them. Such dear girls, so kind, such nice English girls."

Then, embarrassingly, she put her arms round them both, hugging them fiercely to her bosom and knocking off the beret which Jo had persuaded Beatrice to let her wear instead of the up-and-down brown velour. Then they were forced to walk all the way back across the lawn to the St Andrews with her, feeling silly and self-conscious as she took Jo's arm and talked to Bronwen about how lucky she was to have such a nice friend.

Up in Jo's room they discussed what they had seen. Obviously Mrs Osterreicher was passing messages to the Germans, represented by the man in the shelter. Was the Army officer at The Laurels a traitor? Or an innocent victim? Would it be dangerous to actually eat the Refreshers?

They made notes, and giggled a lot and conjectured wildly, but when Patty served their tea, with a message from Beatrice that they need not wait for her, they both became rather silent. Bron said, "We could do something else after tea, until Dad comes."

"We could do our scrapbooks. Yours is still in my cupboard."

So this was agreed and they spent a pleasant hour cutting pictures of Deanna Durbin, Robert Taylor, and other favourite film stars out of *Film Weekly* and *Picturegoer*, and hardly mentioned Mrs Osterreicher at all.

Beatrice invited her mother to dinner that evening. Just because Clive had gone crazy over this Territorial rubbish she didn't see why she should eat alone half the time. Well, alone except for Jo. She wanted someone to talk to. Clive wasn't actually a lot of use, but she did like to have him there. She wondered what he was doing that evening. He'd told her he often had to stay behind doing administrative work, or spend extra time at meetings with senior officers, and if there were to be a war he would at once have a well-paid senior position, probably in the Catering Corps, which sounded quite safe, though really he didn't know a great deal about catering. She felt that she herself could do any such job far more efficiently. Pity they didn't have women in the Army, except as nurses. She certainly didn't want to be a nurse.

It was dark, and windy, though clear, when Clive stopped outside Warne Bay station. He did not sit and watch the exit but glanced through a Sunday paper by the inadequate light of a street lamp. When she opened the car door he threw it onto the back seat. She took off her hat and he kissed her.

"I really shouldn't have come," she said. "I can't keep leaving the school. I'll have to stay there next weekend."

"The school will be OK and so will my place. They can both run themselves."

Rosemarie wondered what Beatrice would say to that but naturally did not say so. They were both rather tired and did not talk much on the way to the Hunter's Moon. As they drew up outside the tearoom the place looked very closed, and no lights showed from the front of the 'cottage' which deserved the name because of its thatched roof and diamond-paned windows, though there was a fair amount of room inside. The door was locked.

"I suppose you let them know?" said Rosemarie.

"Well, no, I couldn't, but I'm sure it will be alright."

"You should have phoned."

Clive did not say he had run out of change and also of time, and had been forced to take a chance. It was the sort of thing that would have made Beatrice really down on him. Luckily she wouldn't know about this. They had to ring again before a light showed in the tearoom window to the left of where they stood, and the olde worlde door with its small diamond-shaped pane of glass was opened by Miss Caxton. Recognising them, she looked horrified.

"Oh! It's not ... I didn't expect ... I thought it was next week."

She stood in the doorway, not asking them in, with hair that needed combing, and Rosemarie noticed at once, red-rimmed eyes.

"We don't want to inconvenience you; we just hoped ... as my husband had some unexpected leave ... but we can easily go somewhere else."

There wasn't anywhere else, of course, they both knew that. Not for miles, anyway, and no hotel would be as safe and private as the Hunter's Moon. Clive thought that if Miss Caxton refused to accommodate them they would have to part and go home, not only disappointed but ignominious. But the door was being somewhat grudgingly opened.

"Oh no, I couldn't let you do that, not now you've come all this way. Come in." Rosemarie went in and Clive got the suitcases out of the car. The tearoom was bright and tidy, as usual, if not very warm, for the Hunter's Moon was open till six o'clock all the year round, closing only on Mondays and at Christmas. Miss Caxton knelt down to light the gas fire, and with Clive's help pulled a table closer to it. If they would like to sit down, she said, she would make them a pot of tea which would warm them up while she prepared their room and found something for their dinner. As she was about to leave them Clive, trying to be friendly, inquired after the health of Miss Simms which caused Miss Caxton to rush precipitately out to the kitchen without replying.

"We really should not have come; we are putting her out." Rosemarie could not help sounding headmistressy when in a state of disapproval.

Clive, with a show of confidence, took off his greatcoat and hung it on the coatstand with his cap.

"She'll be glad of the money, I expect, once she's got used to the idea. After all, they must be very quiet here in the winter."

"I hope the bed's aired," went on Rosemarie, "and Heaven knows what she'll give us to eat. I don't think she cooks, as a rule."

"I'm sure Miss Caxton can cook," said Clive, without the slightest basis for this belief. "I wonder what's become of the little one?"

"I expect they've had a row. That kind are always having rows, and parting for ever and making it up. I know, I've come across them before."

Clive wondered where, but did not ask. He hoped Miss Simms would be back soon, perhaps even in time to cook for them. If it was only a quarrel . . . and she wouldn't be able to get far tonight without a car.

"I suppose she could be back any minute," he said vaguely, but Rosemarie had picked up a scrap of paper that was lying, screwed up, on the table. She smoothed it out, read what was written upon it and showed it to Clive.

The pencilled words were 'If I never speak to you again, it will be too soon for me'.

"It doesn't look like it," she said.

Clive read the crude message, so untypical of quiet, girlish Miss Simms, and then said, "Yes, but that's not the kind of thing you say when you're serious, is it?"

"We wouldn't. But she might."

"Oh, Lord." Clive sighed and stretched his khaki legs gloomily towards the hissing heat of the gas fire. "I shouldn't have done this. I'm sorry."

They felt better, slightly, after they had drunk their tea, their recovery aided by the fact that Miss Caxton's fringe now lay smoothly upon her forehead and she seemed reasonably in command of herself. She could give them soup, she said, but after that all she had to offer was bacon and egg, followed by a coffee gateau, and cheese and biscuits. Both by now hungry, they welcomed her suggestions and she said that she would put hot-water bottles in their bed, but she was sorry, she had let the boiler out and there would be no hot water for baths. This was a blow. She would put an electric fire in their room as of course the radiators would be cold. Their spirits sank again under these blows. The leisurely baths, with bath salts, Rosemarie's L'Aimant-scented talcum powder, the extra large soft white towels, the thrown-back bedclothes in the warm bedroom, were all part of their idyll.

"I'll bring up some hot water, when you go up," said Miss Caxton when she served their coffee.

But in the event she forgot to do so, because Miss Simms returned by taxi soon after nine. When they slid between the icy linen sheets they found she had forgotten the hot-water bottles as well.

Rosemarie was wishing she had not come. The egg and bacon supper had been greasy and gave her indigestion; the succession of interviews on the previous day followed by the usual busy Sunday routine of the school had left her tired. Cold in her chiffon nightdress she climbed into bed and pulled the covers up to her chin. She did not feel like making love. On the contrary, she thought with longing of a cup of Ovaltine and a nice book. Clive, chilly, unfresh and beginning to need a shave, pulled back the bedclothes to get in beside her. She exclaimed irritably as the cool air preceded him. He remained sitting up, his dark blue pyjama jacket with the smart braided fastening looking out of place in the cottagey room. He was tired, too, and thought he had a cold coming.

What on earth was he doing here when he could have been at home at the St Andrews, where he could have had a hot bath and a whisky and pretended to be asleep when Beatrice came up? He was too tired to be the great lover and anyway the thought of Miss Caxton and Miss Simms, now presumably passionately reunited, put him off. He sighed.

Rosemarie sat up and put her arms round him. However she felt at that moment, she did not want to lose her lover.

"It can't always be perfect," she said. "Let's just go to sleep. At least now Miss Simms is back we'll get a decent cup of tea in the morning."

Chapter Eight

BEATRICE had completed the first part of her morning routine before Clive returned, and decided to take an hour off to do some shopping. Mme Adelaide, the proprietress of Culvergate's most exclusive dress shop, was having a sale, and Beatrice hoped to buy a fur-trimmed winter coat at a greatly reduced price. Then she would give the one she was wearing, a black one with a Persian lamb collar, to her mother. It was quite suitable for an older person.

After trying on a number of coats, helped into and out of them by the almost frighteningly elegant Mme Adelaide in person, she bought one she really liked, made of dark green facecloth with shaggy red fox cuffs. It wasn't really very drastically reduced, and neither was the neat little hat she chose to go with it, but the personal attention of the proprietress made quibbling about the price an impossibility. When the coat and hat were taken away to be delivered that evening, the two women fell into an interesting chat about women's place in the world, during which, or perhaps after which Beatrice was easily persuaded to buy a smart knitted suit in black bouclé, softer than a tailor-made but equally suitable for a businesswoman, such as herself, constantly in the public eye. Pleased and flattered, she spent longer in the shop than she had intended, and almost decided not to call in at The Japanese Tearoom but the smell of coffee as she approached it was so appetising that she succumbed to temptation.

In the soft lighting of the cafe the black laquered furniture shone, the murals depicting Japanese scenes were cheerfully bright, and the young waitresses in their orange and black kimonos were attentive. Mrs Hewitt soon appeared. Her normal somewhat oriental appearance, which was due to her deepset eyes and her dyed black fringe was enhanced this morning by a high-necked ruby-coloured blouse, vaguely Chinese in style. Though busy, she found time to sit down at one of the too-small tables with her daughter.

"You're out early."

"I just bought a coat in Madame Adelaide's sale. A bargain."

"There's still plenty of wear in that one, I should have thought."

"I'm tired of it."

"Tired of it! You must have money to burn."

"Shut up, Mum. You can have it if you like. It'd suit you. You can have it shortened."

"Well, thanks, if you think Clive won't mind."

"It's nothing to do with Clive. Only don't go giving it to Doris. You're to wear it yourself."

Doris was Beatrice's second sister, who had married into the professional classes, but was always hard up. She and Beatrice had never got on.

"Of course I shan't give it to Doris," but Mrs Hewitt sounded unconvincing. Beatrice sighed.

"It will look nice on you."

She was anxious to stop her mother wearing the ancient twenties style musquash with its roll collar and one big fur-covered button, that she felt sure was a by-word in the town. But Mrs Hewitt had known hard times, and though now quite prosperous, never discarded clothes until they were worn out.

"Jo alright?"

"Oh yes, she's alright." Beatrice spoke without interest, adding, "Clive's out a lot, with this Territorial rubbish."

"You're sure that's what he's doing? Not up to anything, is he?" Mrs Hewitt was a mind-reader where her daughters were

108

concerned, no doubt about that. But Beatrice had hoped for reassurance.

"Course not, Mum. Clive? How could he be? Who is there, anyway?"

"He's a good-looking man."

"Used to be." Beatrice who had refused cakes in the interests of her figure, found herself biting messily into a small cube of sponge, to the four sides of which wafers of chocolate had been stuck, with apricot jam generously used as an adhesive.

"Mum, what is this ghastly object?. I've got jam all over my chin."

"People like them. I didn't ask you to eat it."

The cafe was filling up with women out shopping, and businessmen from nearby offices. Beatrice lowered her voice.

"He doesn't know anyone." She pushed away her plate.

"If you're going to waste that . . ." Mrs Hewitt appropriated the cake. Removing a slice of chocolate from one side, she ate it separately.

"There's that Miss Wells. Jo's headteacher, or whatever she is."

"Rosemarie Wells? Oh, Mum, don't be so ridiculous!"

Beatrice was so relieved that she decided, after all, to take a small delicious-looking macaroon from the cakestand in the centre of the table. The Japanese tearoom was a hotbed of gossip. If Clive had been seen with another woman, her mother would have heard about it. No, it couldn't be Rosemarie, so it couldn't be anyone. Having made this clear Beatrice enjoyed her coffee, finished her macaroon and left the cafe in quite a peaceful frame of mind.

When Clive returned to the St Andrews Beatrice was still out. After a bath, he dressed in one of his well-cut lounge suits and went down to the office, where he drank a cup of coffee and read the *Daily Mail*. This broadsheet with its many pages occupied him for some time, though unlike his wife he did not even glance at the financial section. The paper was running a

109

humorous series about married life called 'Behind the Scenes', which he read with amusement. The political news, when he came to it, was not encouraging. The shadows of conflict were looming nearer, and secretly he wondered how he would actually get on in the Catering Corps. He resolved to learn all he could from the chef, about how much of different things to order, and so on. Though the chef was temperamental and would probably think he was out to steal his job. Then he supposed that when the St Andrew's closed Beatrice would become simply an army wife. They would be allotted a house somewhere according to his status, already furnished with stuff that Bea would hate, and she would have to get on with the other wives as best she could. This train of thought proving negative, he left the office in order to tour the public rooms. After all he was still nominally the Manager. It was really only natural that a woman should take charge of the catering and housekeeping side. And of course she had such a good head for figures too. But the Company still held him responsible.

In the foyer he was waylaid by an elderly resident, Mrs Broughton. Mrs Broughton was not pleased. Her silver-knobbed ebony cane tapped the floor, her Queen Mary coiffure wobbled dangerously. The ropes of pearls and cornelian which rested on her corseted bosom were in constant motion because of her agitated breathing.

"Mr Livingstone! Ah, dear Mr Livingstone, I'm sure you can spare a moment for an old lady in distress. I really do not know what to do."

Clive recklessly offered his services in any capacity she cared to name. It seemed that some ill-mannered, inconsiderate visitor had usurped the easy chair nearest to the fire in the lounge, a position that she had made her own by dint of getting there before everyone else until the other residents tacitly accepted it as 'her' chair. She usually left her workbag, containing her embroidery, on the seat to signify her prior claim. Now some newcomer had simply placed the workbag on a side table, sat down, and refused to move. Perhaps dear Mr Livingstone could remedy the situation. No other chair, unfortunately, was possible for her, owing to her dreadful susceptibility to draughts. When Clive, assuming a managerial manner to hide his nervousness, entered the big room, the atmosphere was tense. He was not surprised to see that it was Mrs Osterreicher who, having arrived on the previous Saturday, was occupying the accommodation in question, apparently absorbed in reading a newspaper, while the residents, five ladies and two gentlemen, sat about with an air of suppressed excitement, pretending to knit or write letters. Such visitors as there were during this slack period had nearly all left the hotel to go for health-giving walks along the windy promenade. A good fire was burning in the mock-Tudor fireplace, and the room was additionally heated by huge ugly radiators, one below each of the five windows that overlooked the green. Mrs Broughton could not have been feeling cold. There were some people he could have asked to move, but the German lady was not one of them. He steered Mrs Broughton out of the room again and into the bar, although it was not yet open. Then he sent for coffee, offering her a brandy 'to warm her up' at the same time. This was graciously accepted. They chatted about the difficulties of dealing with foreigners while Clive wondered privately whether he could have Mrs Osterreicher called away by a non-existent trunk call. After ten minutes of sympathetic chat he was able, having seated himself so that he had a view of the foyer, to see the lady in question approaching the lift. No one looked up as Mrs Broughton majestically re-entered the lounge and took her place. Clive shook up her cushions, found her workbag, asked unnecessarily if everyone was warm enough, commented on the international situation to old Colonel Brindley, on the weather to old Mrs Porter, and the programme at the local cinema to old Miss Trigg. At the top of his voice he addressed a few cheering words to old Miss Kember. After which, with a comfortable feeling that he had done a good morning's work, he returned to the office. Beatrice was back, and he retailed the incident as amusingly as he could.

"You're so good at that kind of thing," she said. "I wouldn't have the patience. Now, I've been thinking. How about a regular tea dance? On Thursdays. We could get a trio or something, not a full band. We'll have to do something to increase turnover. You could MC it; I think it might be popular."

Clive agreed and they discussed details companionably. Leaving her at twelve-thirty to go down to the Knight's Bar he kissed her lightly on the cheek and for once she didn't tell him to mind her hair.

Returning to school Rosemarie took a taxi from the station and arrived soon after ten. She went up the steps to the front door and let herself in. The main hall, unlike the rest of the ground floor, or any other floor, for that matter, was well carpeted. Fresh flowers graced a side table. Brass door handles were well polished. The visitors room on the left was chilly but gleaming, and the fire was laid in the grate. She was aware of the low hum of work going on. The sound of a piano, uncertainly played, came from the basement where Miss Baker, the music teacher, had her room. On the first floor she passed the doors of forms IIA and IVB. These were back rooms, once secondary bedrooms in the house that was one of the three originally private homes occupied by the school. The front bedrooms in this part, beautiful rooms overlooking the square, with a view of the sea to the left, were now dormitories. Savouring the feeling of disciplined activity going on around her she reached her sitting room. There was a bright fire burning and the morning's mail lay on the large leather-topped desk, bequeathed by her father. She rang the bell, ordered her morning coffee a little earlier than usual, and sat down to read her mail. It was good to be back. Once or twice recently she had conjured up a picture of herself and Clive leading a quiet domestic life somewhere, free from worry and responsibility. At times it seemed an attractive idea, but today she knew she would find it indescribably dull.

Having sorted out the letters she drew the detention register towards her. A shabby exercise book with stiff red covers, it was filled in by the staff and left on her desk each evening. Detentions had been on the increase of late, particularly in the middle school, and she soon found that things had not improved, despite the apparent peace of the Monday morning. Analysing the punishments and the reasons behind them more carefully than usual, she came to the conclusion that something would have to be done. Running and talking in the corridors, whispering in class, drawing and passing notes were almost commonplace, while among the boarders, talking after lights out, a sin she usually looked on with some tolerance, had reached a new level. A high proportion of these detentions, she noted, had been handed out by Miss Card. Miss Craig and Miss Whitehouse were responsible for roughly equal, larger than usual amounts, while Miss Denny and Miss Curnock seemed to have been lenient. Miss Perkins had not even doled out ten minutes detention for talking in class. Rising, she studied the timetable pinned to the wall in what she considered the 'Office' area of the room, concealed by a screen from the rest. It also sheltered a filing cabinet and a table for the secretary who came on three afternoons a week, Rosemarie's own desk was in full view. The timetable informed her that Miss Perkins should currently be taking a French lesson with form IIIA. This classroom was at the back of the building, next to the dining room. Having been designed as a drawing room it was high-pitched, sunny, and had French windows opening onto what was now the playground. Close by this room, stairs led downward to the basement, where most of the daygirls hung their hats and coats on numbered pegs, and stowed their outdoor shoes tidily in compartments under the long low bench beneath. Rosemarie went down and stood for a few minutes in the corridor, keeping well back so that her shadow should not obscure the frosted glass panes in the upper part of the door. At first there was silence, then a young voice said something – a remark or question which was followed by far too loud a burst of laughter. A desk lid banged which seemed to be followed by a mild reprimand and then a long rather aggressive justification. Something wrong here. Rosemarie did not consider entering. That would only humiliate the teacher. She went thoughtfully upstairs, and by the time she reached the top she had decided to put the whole thing in the hands of the prefects.

The 'Pre's Pi' was a time-honoured tradition instituted when the Princess May of Teck School for Girls had been The Prince Rupert School for the Sons of Gentlemen. When discipline became slack as it periodically did, the prefects were encouraged to deal with the situation by inviting all pupils in the forms concerned one by one to the sixth-form room, where they would singly face the five prefects and the head girl, and be verbally bullied until almost in tears, when they would be allowed to leave having made promises of improved behaviour. In no circumstances could these invitations be refused. The school was divided into two Houses, Grange and Foreland, for the purpose of competition generally, and much was made of "letting down your House."

Rosemarie distanced herself, as her father had done, from what actually went on during these meetings, but she believed they were not only useful but democratic and somehow modern. Girls know how to deal with girls, she thought, stifling any misgivings.

Bron and Jo, sitting side by side in their double desk, with innocent expressions facing Miss Perkins while they shared a packet of fruit gums, were bored. The French text book was a masterpiece of dullness, and their teacher had not the personality and inventiveness required to make the lesson interesting. Under cover of her Rough Book, Jo was designing a new handbill in the hope of stimulating flagging interest in the JoBron Detective Agency. Other members of the class were also engaged on illicit enterprises. Maura Wolfe was drawing a cartoon showing Rosemarie very large and Miss Colwell, very small, dressed as Laurel and Hardy, for the amusement of her fellows. Joy Warner was doing her Botany homework, and Ailsa Sparks was practically asleep having, in her parents absence, stayed up late the previous night listening to a thriller on the wireless. None would be able to find the place when it became their turn to translate the simple sentences, but they knew Miss Perkins would patiently give them the page number and the line so what did it matter. She'd never tell anyone off; her colourless garments, her dreary hairstyle, her round-lensed glasses and her red nose made such a thing impossible.

Thelma lifted the lid of her desk unnecessarily high and let it crash down. She said, "Sorry, Miss Perkins" in a tone that indicated a total absence of regret. One or two people stifled giggles.

Miss Perkins said, "It wasn't necessary to make all that noise, Thelma," She didn't ask why Thelma was opening her desk in the middle of the lesson, but Thelma evidently chose not to waste her prepared answer.

"But I had to get my Rough Book out, Miss Perkins. I couldn't get on without my Rough Book."

Uncertainly the teacher said, "I thought I could see your Rough Book on your desk."

"That was my old Rough Book; it's full up now. I had to get my new Rough Book out so that I could take down the vocabulary. I must take down the vocabulary or I won't be able to learn it for the next lesson." She paused then, inspired to greater insolence for the benefit of her contemporaries, added, "I won't get it out if you don't want me to, only then I can't learn the words."

Miss Perkins, painfully flushed said, "That's quite alright, Thelma. You may get out your new Rough Book."

Thelma said "Thank you, Miss Perkins", managing to make the words sound like an insult.

"Can I go on now, please Miss Perkins?" Dora Morris, who had been translating, sounded bored and aggrieved at the interruption. Altogether the whole incident had been rather successful.

*   *   *

115

Valerie Maskell

At break-time Rosemarie sent for the head girl, Barbara Goodwin and drew her attention to the sagging standards of discipline and suggested she did something about it.

Chapter Nine

THE PRE'S PI was, after some consultation, arranged for 17 March, the following Friday.

Although rumours encircled the school the victims would not be officially informed until the notice went up on the board outside the staff room. The juniors hoped it would concern only the seniors. Hadn't Peggy Bates been seen waving out of a front window to an errand boy? Hadn't Betty Faulkes had five conduct marks this term? The seniors believed it would concern the juniors. The wretched kids were definitely getting cheeky, and needed taking down a peg or two. But the sense of dread hung miasma-like over them all. The seniors claimed to be totally unworried by what the prefects thought or said but the juniors were frankly terrified. Though many boasted of the snappy answers they had ready they knew they would never be uttered.

On the Wednesday of that week, war stepped one pace nearer, Hitler's army marched into Czechoslovakia. Rosemarie took the senior Current Affairs lesson herself that morning. Discussing what the innocent Czechs were enduring and would endure, she found that the girls in their inexperience seemed untouched, even excited, by what was happening. In an effort to bring the reality home to them, for after all they were sixteen and seventeen years old, young women really, she enlarged on the plight of the Kramer girls, on the Gestapo habit of banging on doors in the middle of the night and removing Jewish husbands and fathers to concentration camps, she spoke of interrogations and torture and told them that if war came as it almost certainly would, Hitler would try to bring these evils to England. Afterwards she wondered if she had gone too far, but decided she had only done what was necessary to break through their complacency and bring them into the real world. At the same time she wondered whether she should cancel the Pre's Pi. The subdued tone of the school for the last day or two told her it was something to be dreaded. Wasn't there enough anxiety in the air without that? She thought about it, but did nothing, not liking to be seen as indecisive.

That Wednesday was a half-holiday as usual, allowed because the girls worked until twelve-thirty on Saturdays. Jo and Bron, fortunately not on the games list for the day, were able to join other roller-skaters on the promenade. From October till April each year the council allowed this pastime. Not for the youth of Culvergate was the slow skating along pavements or the circling of empty car parks, the only spaces available to inland children. Five miles of unbroken asphalt, with the sea on one side invited them to speed along. It was a bright, cold afternoon, just right for skating, and detecting activities were temporarily in abeyance. The Jobron Agency had lost some of its appeal, since nothing really exciting had come to light. But they hadn't given it up, still in their wilder moments hoping to unmask a spy or set the police on the track of a jewel thief or a murderer. Patty, who was in their confidence, had told them severely that the game could get them into trouble, almost convincing Jo that it should be abandoned, and then spoilt it by relating the story of how her aunt had discovered that the man next door, father of a family and a good husband, earned his living by burgling. The aunt had been congratulated by the police on her powers of observation.

But this afternoon they were not detectives, they were skaters on a frozen river, prisoners escaping across the wilds of Russia. Jo had on her best coat because even Beatrice admitted that the old pink tweed was now too small, and stuffed her beret in her pocket because her newly-permed hair was a source of pride. Bron was wearing a camel coat as well. It was rather too big and had to be gathered round her with the belt, as Mrs Harries had bought it second hand. Mr Harries, having retired early because he was tired of living in foreign parts, could not afford expensive clothes for his daughter. Bronwen told Jo that the coat had been purchased at a special place in London where all the things had once belonged to film stars. She had, she said, definitely seen Nova Pilbeam wearing it in a film. Jo did not dispute this, although she knew it was false. She was sorry for Bron, wearing a second-hand coat.

Other girls from Form IIIA, as well as one or two boys joined them, nearly all of them skilful, their skates fixed to their shoes with clamps which were cleverly designed to separate soles from uppers, and reinforced with leather straps. They sped along in the pale spring sunshine, the grey-green sea on their left below the chalk cliffs, on their right the lawns, the clock-golf course, the closed kiosk where you ordered photographs, and the white-domed Koh-i-Noor Cafe, until they left the town behind and came to the last gap, leading down to a deserted bay. They returned at a more leisurely pace, some of them slowing down to demonstrate turns and stops. A small man wearing a black beret crossed the green towards them, and Bron dared Jo to ask him the time in French. This was an easy one. Jo skated to within earshot and called, "Excusez moi! Quelle heure est-t-il, s'il vous plait?" Disconcertingly the man came quickly towards her, answering her with a flood of totally unintelligible French, and trying to grab her hand as she skated away, calling out, in her execrable accent, "Merci beaucoup!"

They skated on to a safe distance leaving the others behind, this time in the direction of the cheaper boarding houses, the Lido, and finally the harbour.

"Its my turn to give you a dare."

"Think of a good one then. I'm in a daring mood." Bron indicated a Men's lavatory which occupied half of a little grey building ahead of them.

"I'll go in there if you like."

"Of course not; don't be silly. I'll think of something if you wait a minute."

"If you haven't thought of something in one minute I'm going in there." Bron had somehow managed to twist the whole situation. It was a way she had.

With Bron counting loudly to sixty Jo was unable to produce a good dare.

"I'll think of something on the way back."

"You needn't bother. I'm going in there. Say you dare me."

Jo did not answer. Bron was removing her skates. When she stood up she said peremptorily,

"Say you dare me."

Jo said nothing. She crossed the promenade and gazed out to sea

"I dare you, then" shouted Bron, but Jo did not turn round.

"I'm going then. It's the same as if you had dared me."

That was the rule. If the other person failed a dare you had to do it yourself. Jo would have liked to skate off at speed, towards the St Andrew's, but she waited. Supposing Bron fainted and she, Jo, had to go in and drag her out? Suppose she locked herself in and couldn't be released? How could she go to anyone and say that her friend was locked in the Men's lavatory? Then Bron appeared, sauntering towards her.

"It's different from ours, but of course they do it standing up, don't they?"

"You're horrible," said Jo.

"What's horrible about it? I like to know things." Bron had to sit down to put on her skates so it was a few minutes before she caught Jo up. The sun had disappeared; they would have to go in. Jo decided not to ask Bron to tea. But then, as they crossed St Andrew's Lawn Bron said, "I can have tea with you, can't I? I told my mother I'd be staying," so they went up the steps of the St Andrew's together.

They had to have their tea in the kitchenette because the

managing director of the Company was in the sitting room of the apartment with Clive and Beatrice. He had arrived unexpectedly, earlier that afternoon, in order to discuss Air Raid Precautions, and the probable effect on the hotel of the outbreak of war. It might, he said, become necessary to close down.

"We will try to fit you in somewhere else if we can," he added, but Clive was in the happy position of being able to say that this would not be necessary. The Territorial Army was to be expanded, he fully expected promotion, and if the worst happened he would be posted, possibly to some far flung outpost, as a Major in the Catering Corps.

Bea caught the managing director's glance and knew what he was thinking. How would Clive cope without his wife.

"I'd be glad of a job myself," she said. "I can't sit and do nothing."

"You won't be allowed to do that. When all the men are called up, ladies like you will be greatly in demand." He smiled. He was a big man with a lot of prematurely white hair.

"I hope you are right."

"You may depend upon it."

Clive realised she was seeing herself as manageress of a luxury hotel somewhere. He thought that Colin Weir was seeing her as something quite different.

"Perhaps you'd like to look round while you're here," he said, and a few minutes later he rose to take his superior on a tour of the hotel, saying to Beatrice, "Don't you bother, darling. You have another cup of tea."

She did so, but made a point of being busy and important in the office when the tour was concluded there, as she had expected it would be. She suggested sherry, but Clive and Mr Weir had already partaken in the bar. So she had little further opportunity to drive home the fact that it was she and not Clive who ran the place, which was a pity. She imagined herself in charge of some glamorous and sophisticated riverside hotel, with Clive away, and the managing director visiting at frequent intervals to see how she was getting on. He was quite a handsome man. Clive looked narrow shouldered beside him.

Clive, who was beginning to be worried by the complications of his life, thought the outbreak of war – awful thing to say really – might just save his bacon.

The approach of change excited both of them. At dinner they chatted in quite a lively fashion, and Jo, who did not like anything that was on the menu was allowed to have a poached egg on toast.

She thought about Bron who had been grumpy and bored while they had their tea. Afterwards they looked through Jo's old film magazines in case there were any pictures of their favourites that they had missed, but of course there weren't, and Bron had gone home earlier than she need have done, leaving Jo with a sense of foreboding. Though Bron worried her at times, seeming to be without any sense of what was ordinary fun and what was going too far, they liked so many of the same things. Their film-star games, their dress-designing, their exploration of the caves which they combined with re-enacting dramatic and highly romantic stories of smugglers, and then there was the detective agency which Jo thought would improve if they went on with it – no one else would be as adept as Bron at all these. She must think of something that she would really like, some daring and different escapade that would win her friend's respect, though not like that afternoon. Thinking idly of school she remembered how Miss Perkins didn't even tell you off when you were late and then she had the idea.

They arranged it during break the next day, Miss Perkins's French lesson being immediately afterwards. Classes were expected to be seated quietly in their places when the teacher approached, rising as the monitor opened the door to admit her. Girls were hardly ever late after break, and then only with good reason. Just outside this classroom the staircase led down to the daygirls' cloakroom. All the members of Form IIIA changed back into their indoor shoes after break as usual but then, instead of going up, they hid, giggling among the coats, waiting for Miss Perkins to enter the empty classroom. Dora Hayes, nearest the foot of the stairs, whispered loudly, "Here she is. She's gone in."

"What's she doing?"

Dora crept up a few stairs. "I think she's just sitting at the desk."

"Count ten and then go."

One by one they entered the room. It was long and narrow with double desks ranged one behind the other, four on each side of a central aisle. Jo, at the top of the stairs, heard Dora say, "I'm sorry, Miss Perkins, I had to get a handkerchief."

Miss Perkins apparently made no reply, Jo followed Dora. "I'm sorry, Miss Perkins. I couldn't find my shoes." She took her seat halfway down the room in the desk she shared with Bron.

"I'm sorry, Miss Perkins, I had to hand in some lines."

"I'm sorry, Miss Perkins, I had to be excused."

"I'm sorry, Miss Perkins, I felt funny, I had to sit down." This was Bron.

One by one the girls entered, spoke, and took their places. Some of the excuses were repeated because the bell had rung for the end of break before they could think up thirteen different ones. Miss Perkins did not turn her head as they paused in passing her desk, which had its back to the door. Her face flushed, she stared fixedly down at the pile of exercise books in front of her. At last they were all seated. The silence lengthened. Jo was worried. Somehow the whole thing had turned out to be not very funny after all. Would they all get conduct marks, be taken to Miss Wells?

Miss Perkins moved the pile of books which she usually returned to their owners at the start of the lesson, to one side. She opened her text book. Something that must have been a tear slid down from behind her heavy spectacles and splashed onto the page. They sat still, waiting in silence. Usually when she gave them back their homework they complained vociferously about their marks. Someone always whined, "Miss Perkins, you've only given me six out of ten and it took me the whole evening." Jo thought the books were being withheld for this reason, but knew that today they would have been received in silence. It seemed like hours before the teacher said unsteadily, "Open your books at page fifteen. Start translating, Josephine."

They worked quietly for the rest of the forty minutes. When the bell went Miss Perkins interrupted the reader, saying, "That will do." She gathered up her books quickly and rose.

Thelma Purvis leapt to open the door, and they all stood up as she left the room, saying "Thank you, Miss Perkins" in the polite way that was de rigeur at the May of Teck. She had forgotten to set their prep.

"She was crying."

"Well, she didn't give us any detention."

"She's stupid."

"We shouldn't have done it."

"Do you think she'll do anything?"

"She might tell Miss Wells."

"She might commit suicide."

"Don't be daft."

"She looked ever so upset, though, didn't she?"

"Shut up, here comes Miss Card."

Thelma flung open the door as the others hastily got out their Geography books. Miss Card, small, thin, bitter, took her seat at the desk.

"What are these?" She indicated the pile of excercise books.

"Our French prep, Miss Card. Miss Perkins didn't give them back."

"Well, Thelma give them out please. Be quick about it."

She spread out her books and papers, moved to the blackboard and wrote 'Exports'. Below it to one side she wrote 'Sheffield'. Then she turned to the class with the expected question to which, thank goodness, someone knew the answer. The lesson proceeded briskly. When Miss Card made a small dry joke, they all laughed sycophantically.

Jo felt guilty and miserable that evening. She had seen Miss Perkins's tears, the look of despair, the effort she had made to go on with the lesson. At the same time she was angry with her wretched victim. Why was her nose red, and her chest flat? Why did she wear horrible thick glasses and horrible cardigans and have dandruff on her shoulders and why did she do her horrible hair in a horrible old-fashioned bun? You couldn't like a person like that. But it was no good, she still felt awful. In the end she told Patty about it and Patty actually laughed and said it was up to the teachers to keep order, and she wouldn't be one for anything. She told Jo how her brother had got the cane for putting a dead frog on the teacher's chair and Jo felt quite a lot better.

That night Miss Perkins did not appear at the supper table. Miss Denny reported that her colleague had a headache and was going to bed early. Rosemarie told Miss Denny she could arrange for supper to be taken up for her. She did not approve of headaches and missed meals among the staff. Later she sent Matron up to take her temperature, and reporting back to her, Matron had said she thought Miss Perkins was upset about something.

"Perhaps she's had bad news from home", said Rosemarie. "It can't be anything here." Had she not glanced in at IIIB again that morning during their French lesson, and seen them all listening attentively to Dora Hayes who appeared to be translating? It looked as though the teacher had conquered her discipline problems, at least.

The Pre's Pi started at three-fifteen on the Friday and Bron was called at four-thirty. The two top junior classes were named on the list outside the staffroom, and IVB, the first of the seniors. Bron was the nineteenth girl out of thirty-seven who were forced to attend, or who thought they were forced to attend. It simply did not occur to any daygirl to go straight home instead, or to any boarder to refuse to present herself at the dun-walled closet that was the sixth-form room. They had been called, and they would go, climbing the narrow stairs that led to the second floor in the main building with weakening legs and churning stomachs, for such was the power of prefects at the May of Teck. Less than five minutes after Bron went in, she came out. Scowling and silent she brushed past Jo on the landing and hurried downstairs. Then the door opened. One of the prefects said, "Josephine Livingstone," and Jo entered.

A chair had been placed in the centre of the room, facing the long table which, replacing desks, was a mark of the prefects' seniority. The head girl Barbara Goodwin sat at the centre with two prefects either side of her – Joan Forster, Peggy Jardine, Mary White, and Mavis Welsh, all the magnificent, powerful righteous beings, more awe-inspiring than the teachers, more severe than the headmistress, who were at the top of the May of Teck, neat in their bottle-green gym slips, and striped shirts with ties neatly tied and cuffs that never lacked the right number of buttons, their bobbed hair, brown, black, fair or sandy all tidily combed and held back with slides. Under the table their black cotton stockings, totally free from holes, were tightly held up by proper suspenders attached to elastic suspender belts, not by unreliable rubber buttons on liberty bodices, like Jo's.

She sat down as directed, holding tightly to the seat of the chair as though she was liable to fall off at any moment.

In a not too unkind voice Barbara said, "Well, how do you think you've been behaving?"

Jo did not answer. The incident involving Miss Perkins, which she had been trying not to think about for the last two days, now came back to overwhelm her. Could they know about it?

Another prefect said, "She's had lot of detention. Mostly for talking in class." Rosemarie had made the detention register available to them.

"Why do you talk in class, Jo?"

Jo said she didn't know, so they told her. They told her she was rude to teachers, ungrateful to her parents, was letting down

126

her form and her House, not to mention the Junior branch of the League of Nations, of which Jo was a proud member. That is to say she was proud of the little blue enamelled badge to which membership entitled her. She hadn't listened when Miss Wells talked about it because that sort of thing was boring.

They went on to mention her repeated absence from games and her lack of prowess on the playing field. They pointed out that she was often bottom of the class without remembering that she was also the youngest, they thought her hair was untidy, that it was not acceptable for people in IIIB to have perms, asked her whether or not she had a clean handkerchief, which she had not, and generally made her feel that she was a stupid, grubby and valueless person. When she was asked if she intended to do better in the future she nodded, wordlessly. Seeing her tears, Peggy Jardine, whom she had worshipped for two terms last year, before transferring to Joan Forster, to whom she had breathlessly presented posies of violets and packets of Rowntrees fruit gums, told her not to be such a disgusting cry-baby, so of course the tears came faster still and a sob rose in her throat.

Then they let her go. Thelma was waiting her turn on the landing.

"Was it awful?"

"I hate them," said Jo.

The sub-prefect was at the door. At that moment Jo thought she heard a suppressed giggle and a quick "Shh" from inside the room. Thelma went in and the door closed. Had she imagined it? Could the prefects be enjoying themselves? Could anyone be as wicked as that? Had she been just as wicked, making Miss Perkins cry? But she was grown-up, a teacher, it was different. Wasn't it? Pondering these questions Jo went down to the cloakroom and put on her outdoor things. She surveyed her permed hair in the mirror before dragging on her green felt hat. It had been Beatrice's idea – she thought it might make Jo's soft blonde hair more manageable, but Jo could hardly expect to visit the hairdresser regularly, and the crimped effect of an unset perm was after all perhaps not much of an improvement. But still, it was nothing to do with the beastly prefects.

Bron hadn't waited, so she walked home alone.

Arriving there she was still visibly upset, and Clive elicited from her the statement that school had been horrible and eventually the whole story of the Pre's Pi had come out. Beatrice, once it became clear that no specially bad behaviour on Jo's part had brought about the unpleasant interview, and that thirty-six other girls had been called, had dismissed the whole thing. Though her father seemed more concerned, her mother's trivialising of the incident had helped Jo to see it as something that did not really matter. Clive wondered if Rosemarie knew what went on. The five girls at the long table, the isolated chair facing them, the closed door, guarded by the sub-prefect, all smacked of bullying and tyranny. Rosemarie's prefects seemed to be turning themselves into some sort of Gestapo. He wondered if he should speak to her about it. Perhaps not just yet. He was due, on the following Sunday, to meet her at the Hunter's Moon, the first time since their unsuccessful visit when they had been unexpected. He wanted everything to go well, and to complain about her method of running the school would hardly be conducive to romance, let alone passion.

The Pre's Pi undoubtedly achieved its object. During the following week only three detentions, for very minor offences, were entered in the register, all in the name of Miss Card, whom Rosemarie had begun to think simply did not like girls. Nobody passed a note in class, no one ran or talked in a corridor, or was noisy between lessons, and yet . . .

The next Monday Miss Curnock's history lesson with IIIA proceeded with unaccustomed quiet. The girls knew about her forthcoming marriage and had often by means of subtle questions and a spectacular show of interest deflected her from her intended path and led her into the byways of more personal revelations. The style of her wedding dress, her going-away outfit were often frankly discussed with enjoyment on all sides until the teacher said, "Now, we must get back to our lesson", and the loud groans which greeted this return to work did not even earn a reprimand.

On this occasion the voices of the girls, reading in turn, droned uninterrupted through the designated chapter of Dalton's *History of Europe*, Part III: The Nineteenth Century.

Jo, in the third row, was usefully screened by the back of the girl in front. This, plus the acuteness of her boredom gave her sufficient courage to slide a sheet of drawing paper out from under her Rough Book. She was designing a new wardrobe for her alter ego, Pearl Black, the film star, whose career had been at a standstill since the inception of the Jobron Agency.

Jo's dress designs were remarkably competent and very glamorous. Sketched in pencil and coloured with crayons or watercolours, she had made dozens of drawings of impossibly elongated women, their sculptured blonde curls drawn in detail, wearing evening gowns, low backed and clinging, coats with bands of fur round hem and sleeves, accompanied by Cossack hats, peasant-style summer dresses, and exotic nightwear. Many of her ideas came from the film magazines, *Picturegoer* and *Film Weekly* on which she spent her pocket money; some were her own. Sometimes she would draw and cut out paper dolls clothed only in brief underwear, then the dresses were cut out too and fixed to the dolls by means of tabs and slots. This was unsatisfactory as they often fell off.

The text book they were using was dull in format and devoid of illustration except for the frontispiece which took the form of an engraving of Disraeli, whose colourful personality and life played no part in Dalton's *History*, for this stultifying work concerned itself only with politics, ignoring the personalities of those involved. Jo became absorbed in her sketch of a wedding dress. She wrote underneath it; 'How would she look in this?' and slid it across to Bron in the adjoining desk. Unfortunately Miss Curnock saw the

129

movement and commanded Jo to bring what she took to be a note up to her.

Jo's low-necked, tiny-waisted, full-skirted design, surmounted by floral halo and bunchy lace veil were not the kind of thing that would have become the tall flat-chested teacher, who had described more than once the folds of creamy satin that were to give her a statuesque look on the great day, and Jo had not intended this question as anything other than a sarcastic comment on Miss Curnock's face and figure. It was the sort of thing she said to Bron because she wanted Bron to see her as clever and superior.

Jo walked up to the desk, handed over the drawing and waited, despairing, for retribution. To her surprise Miss Curnock smiled a little.

"You ought to have detention for this, Josephine, but as it's such a pretty drawing I will let you off this time. I don't think it would suit me quite as well as the one I have chosen."

She placed the drawing in her folder as she told Jo to go and sit down, afterwards saying seriously, "It is quite natural that you should all be interested in my wedding. After all, you will, most of you, be married yourselves some day. But we mustn't let weddings come between us and our work, must we? I'm letting Jo off this time, but the next person who misbehaves will get detention. Now, go on reading, please."

When she left the room she took the drawing with her. Everyone agreed she had been really nice and Jo tried to convince herself that she had actually meant to be nice herself. She couldn't think why she'd wanted to be nasty about Miss Curnock, anyway. She was grateful that the teacher hadn't given her detention; a punishment so soon after the Pre's Pi would certainly have earnt her another painful interview with the head girl.

Chapter Ten

THAT evening Jo's childhood came to an end. She started her first period.

At six o'clock, Bea, on her way up to change into one of her black dinner gowns was waylaid by Mrs Osterreicher. The German lady had begun to make a habit of this, apparently noting the times when Bea was in the habit of passing through the foyer.

"Ah, Mrs Livingstone, dear Mrs Livingstone, I know you will spare me a minute from your busy day. I must tell you about my friend Trudi Myers, she is coming to join me for a few days. She is so wonderful! You have not seen someone so elegant; you will be so proud she is in your hotel. I tell her that the St Andrew's is the best in England, and that Mr and Mrs Livingstone are so charming, and so careful for our comfort. Poor Trudi, it is all so dreadful."

And the story of Trudi Myers' suffering, her loss of her husband and oldest son and escape from Germany was told in some detail. After which Mrs Osterreicher continued, "So you will find her a specially nice room, I know, dear Mrs Livingstone, very close to mine, because poor Trudi, at night she is so nervous."

So Beatrice had to accompany her to the reception desk and deal personally with something that the receptionist could have handled with complete efficiency, tearing herself away afterwards, too late for the bath she'd intended to take and yet feeling guilty. Did these things really happen? She read the papers, knew that Jews were being persecuted, their assets

131

confiscated, their shop windows smashed, yet it was hard for her to believe that these things took place in the real world, the world she lived in herself. Mrs Osterreicher was tedious, and her wonderful friend would no doubt be tedious as well, but the guilt remained. In Berlin Mrs Osterreicher had lived in a sumptuous flat in an expensive building, in a magnificent tree-lined street called Unter den Linden. She had kept a cook and two maids and given dinner parties for twenty people at a time. Beatrice, seeing the quietly expensive clothes, the jewellery, the handbags and luggage which, though unostentatious, were all of the very best, could accept all this. It was harder for her to believe that the Myers family, in the flat above, had received a night visit from the Gestapo, and that Herr Freidrich Myers and his son Kurt had been taken away, never to be seen or heard of again. She wanted to think that the incident had been exaggerated, or that the Myers men had, unknown to Mrs Osterreicher, been criminals of some sort. But she could not convince herself of this and as at last she ascended in the lift she wondered what changes were in store for her own family. Supposing the threat of war that had rumbled around for so long became a reality? Colin Weir seemed to think it would and even if he found her a nice hotel to manage she did not want to leave her home just when she had finally arranged it to her satisfaction. In any case the whole of the St Andrews was her home. Then where would Clive be sent? Might he have to go abroad? Would his life be endangered? He was just the idiotic sort who would get killed trying to be a hero. And of course there was Jo. And Mum to consider. She longed for her relaxing warm bath, with her Coty bath crystals. She wanted to lie in the steamy silence with cream on her face, afterwards sprinkling herself with her Chypre talcum powder, slipping into her dressing gown while she did her face and hair, sitting at her triple-mirrored dressing table with a gin and tonic to hand. Well, it was nearly seven already, she would have to settle for a quick wash and tidy up, but she would have the gin and tonic first – it might buck her up a bit.

132

As she entered the private apartment she heard Jo calling from her bedroom. She called back but went on into the sitting room and opened the cocktail cabinet. Jo's cry came again, sounding distressed.

"Mummy! Come here!!"

Who did the wretched child think she was, ordering her about? She sat down on the white tweed settee. If anyone deserved five minutes peace she did, after listening to that woman's depressing stories for half an hour. She sipped her drink gratefully. After a moment, however, she rose and went to the door.

"You can come here if you want me."

She sat down again as Jo appeared in the doorway.

"What's the matter now?"

"I've got . . . blood . . . and stuff . . . coming from my inside. And I've got a pain. There's something horrible wrong with me. Oh, Mum."

Oh, Lord. She would start her periods at the wrong moment. Bea had never mentioned the subject to her and it seemed that no one else had either. That was the trouble with an only child, no one to tell her anything. Living with her two older sisters, Bea had never been in Jo's unfortunate position. Perhaps she ought to have given Jo a book about it, if such a thing existed. But what time had she to go looking for books?

Jo advanced a little into the room.

"Don't sit down," said Bea, thinking of her pale upholstery. "You're not ill or anything. It happens to everyone. Well, every woman, I mean. Go and wait in the bathroom, I'll come and fix you up in a minute."

Jo did as she was told, amd Bea finished her drink a little more quickly than she had intended and went to her room to fetch the necessary items. Of course, she hadn't got any. She'd run out at the end of her last period and hadn't been to the shops since. Damn! Crossly she rang the bell for Patty, who fortunately had a nearly full packet of sanitary towels in her eyrie. Waiting for her to return Bea went into the black and white tiled bathroom, where Jo was sitting carefully on the edge of the bath.

"You have to wear something," said Bea. "It will last about five days, then you'll be alright for three weeks or so."

"Five days? What about school?"

"You can go to school as usual."

Beatrice went back to the sitting room. She needed another gin though normally one was her limit at this time of day.

Jo waited. And as she sat there, cold with shock, with a dragging miserable pain low down inside, many areas of mystery became clear. The advertisements with their vague allusions to monthly pain, and women's ailments, and pictures of nurses in flowing white caps which made them all the more frightening. Only Camelia can banish this worry. What worry? Jo had puzzled over these, not once considering the possibility of consulting Beatrice. Sometimes she thought she might ask Patty, but it was so difficult to put into words. She didn't think Bron knew, because she would have talked about it.

Later Jo asked if she could have her dinner upstairs that night and reluctantly Bea agreed.

"But only this once, mind. It's no good letting these things get you down." Then leaving Jo sitting on her bed she paused in the doorway. "The only time you don't have this is when you're going to have a baby."

"Is it?" said Jo, for want of any other response.

Her mother hesitated. "That's when you're married, of course."

Giving her daughter no time to ask questions she went to her own room, changed hurriedly into a dinner gown and descended in the lift. It had been embarrassing, but she had, she thought, handled it all quite well. There was no need for Jo to know any more at present.

*   *   *

134

Later that evening Bron telephoned with a query about homework. Miss Braine at Reception put her through to Jo on the extension. There was another extension in the office.

"I'm in bed," said Jo casually, though she was actually standing in the little square lobby. "I might not come to school tomorrow."

"Aren't you well?"

"I'm OK. I just might not come to school."

There was a pause during which Jo enjoyed the rare pleasure of being one up on her friend. She was more grown up now than Bronwen who was nearly thirteen, and to whom this had not happened. She must join the conspiracy that protected girls from this terrible knowledge until nature thrust it upon them.

"So long," she said, in the familiar idiom of American films. Then she took down her latest Valerie Drew book and tried to read, but she could not concentrate on the story, the intermittent twists of pain and the burden of experience, not to mention a whole new set of mysteries kept coming between her, and the heroine's efforts to identify the sinister intruders at Clarewood School.

Later that evening Bea told Clive that his daughter had made this major advance towards adulthood.

"Don't say anything."

"Of course not. What do you take me for?" Clive answered in an offended tone as, sitting on the side of his twin bed with his back to his wife, he pulled on his silk pyjama trousers. Of course he would not dream of saying anything, but he thought he might give her the money to take her friend to the pictures on Saturday afternoon, if there was anything suitable for children. Then he realised that she was not, strictly speaking, a child any longer. He remembered taking her on the sands when she was younger, and digging great holes which other children had envied, or building castles with sand pie battlements and dams to keep out the tide. He remembered the excitement of helping her to reinforce the dams as the water rose, the sadness of eventually abandoning the castles to the sea; he recalled the racing car he had modelled for her in damp sand, and how she had been a racing driver for a whole afternoon, with the handle of a spade for a steering wheel. Sometimes they had clambered out over the slippery seaweed-covered rocks, looking for crabs and sea anemones. The rock pools were often pretty, filled with warm, clear water and fringed with green. Finding one of these, a lake in miniature, she had said how lovely if it had been a real lake, then they could build a house on one side – she indicated a flat space a few inches across – and live there together, just the two of them. That was long ago, of course, almost as long ago as the time when she had climbed into bed with him in the mornings, while Bea was dressing and demanded her favourite song, "One Fine Day" from *Madame Butterfly*, heaven knew where she had first heard it. Then he had made the mistake of telling her the story and after that she hadn't wanted the song any more because it was too sad. She had been such an appealing little girl, he had loved walking along with her holding his hand and now she had grown up and he hadn't noticed. But she was only twelve, wasn't she rather young for this to happen? He suggested this to Bea. Should she perhaps be taken to a doctor? But Bea said no, it was alright; though most girls were thirteen or fourteen she had only been twelve herself.

"There isn't any cure for growing up," she added.

Grown-up or not, when the Easter holidays came round, Jo and Bron revived the Jobron Agency. Roller skating on the promenade was now forbidden, and you weren't allowed to go to the pictures more than twice a week. Even so, it was really Clive who was responsible. Jo had become absorbed in her dress-designing, with some encouragement from Bea who thought her remarkably talented and wondered if it might be a possible career, but Bron was less good at drawing and soon tired of being a customer or vendeuse in Jo's imaginary salon. Finding them quarrelsome Clive said they had been indoors too long and that it was a nice day for a walk. Quite accidentally they saw Mrs Osterreicher and her friend in the distance as they dawdled gloomily along the promenade, and quite naturally they wondered where she was going and so it began again.

"I don't think your mother ought to let German people stay in her hotel." Bron used the virtuous voice that was one of her specialities. "My father says they do awful things."

"I don't think she's a real German," said Jo vaguely. "She's Jewish. Lots of the people who stay at our hotel are Jews."

"Well, her friend can't be Jewish, she's got blonde hair."

"P'raps it's dyed."

Despite this disagreement they continued along the promenade together, keeping the suspects in sight, simply for want of anything better to do. Mrs Myers's visit had been delayed for several weeks, Mrs Osterreicher on her regular appearances having made elaborate excuses for her. Bea thought that perhaps the much expected Trudi found Mrs Osterreicher as wearing as she did herself. She had eventually arrived that morning, a haggard woman with straight blonde hair in the new page boy style, looking much younger than her friend, but just as expensively dressed with noticeable diamond rings. Mrs Osterreicher had introduced her.

"Mrs Livingstone, dear Mrs Livingstone, I know you can spare a moment to meet my friend, Mrs Myers. I have told you about her. She is wonderful. And Trudi this is my friend Mrs Livingstone, who is so kind and looks after me so well when I am here. So I will need a table for two now, Mrs Livingstone, a nice one, not too near the kitchen and out of the draught."

Bea was no kinder to Mrs Osterreicher than to any other guest, but it was evidently essential to the lady's well-being that she believe herself to be a special person in receipt of special treatment from a specially charming – to her, that was – hotelier, who appreciated her own specialness and that of her elegant and heroic friend.

137

"I expect they've come out here to tell each other secrets," said Bron. "They wouldn't talk indoors in case anyone heard."

"P'raps they'll meet that man again."

"What man?"

"The poor-looking one she gave a message to."

"I don't suppose he was really poor. I expect it was a disguise."

The afternoon was disappointing, the German ladies met no one, spoke to no one and called nowhere, simply walking along as far as the Koh-i-Noor and turning back. Jo and Bron sat down on a seat near the flagpole and pretended to be looking out to sea. Mrs Osterreicher glanced at them as she passed but did not pause in her walk or in the flow of unintelligible speech to her companion. She seemed impassioned and angry, and Mrs Myers could have been crying.

"Why didn't she say anything? She's supposed to like you so much."

"Well, I don't like her. She makes me feel embarrassed, always hugging me and saying how pretty I am—"

"She doesn't mean it. She just wants your mother to think she's nice."

"Well, I don't think Mum does. She tries to keep out of her way. Sometimes I have to go down and make sure she's not in the foyer, if Mum wants to get to the office without seeing her."

From the far side of the green they watched the two women enter the hotel. When they went in themselves Mrs Osterreicher was in the glass-doored telephone booth in the corner and Mrs Myers was waiting outside. She gave them no sign of recognition as they passed, but as they slowly, very slowly climbed the first flight of stairs they saw Mrs Osterreicher leave the telephone. Looking pale and very upset, she spoke to her friend for a moment and then they both went to Mrs Braine at Reception and began asking anxious questions. In the apartment Jo and Bron decided that the phone call had been a warning of some sort and the two spies were going

138

to make a quick getaway. She had obviously been asking about trains.

Patty, serving their tea at the table in the kitchenette because Bron was there – Bea didn't like crumbs on her pale grey carpet – said they ought to drop the spy game, they would get into trouble following people about.

"It's just nosey-parkering. Curiosity killed the cat."

"But what about your aunt, Patty, the one that caught the burglar?"

"She was lucky the burglar didn't catch her if you ask me."

Mrs Osterreicher and her friend left in a taxi the following morning, which did not surprise Jo, who excitedly passed the news on to Bron. It seemed to them to confirm their suspicions.

On the Saturday they went to the Astoria in the afternoon, but it turned out to be an A film, and they were refused admission. Bron boldly approached a stranger, a respectable-looking, middle-aged man and asked him to buy their tickets. Jo hung back. Bea had told her many times that she must never speak to strange men, even in the hotel. Jo believed that the danger was of being kidnapped and held to ransom. The man appeared helpful, however, and Bron handed him the money for two ninepennies. When he turned away from the box office he had bought them shilling seats. Jo, worried by the whole situation, protested, but Bron was quite pleased. They took the tickets and went through the swing doors into the stalls. It was very dark, the black and white feature film *Love from A Stranger* had been showing for nearly ten minutes. The uniformed usherette flashed her torch around, looking for empty seats and indicated two in the centre block. They'd got rid of the man, thought Jo, thankfully. They settled down happily and were soon engrossed in the film.

When it came to an end the woman on Bron's left went away, almost before it was over. Then during the News a disturbance made them look up. The man who had bought their seats was pushing his way along the row of irritated spectators to the vacated seat. Jo, in horror, pushed her way out and sat down across the aisle, leaving the seat at the end of the row for Bron, believing she would follow immediately, but Jo remained isolated and vulnerable, with an empty seat on either side, for several minutes. She could not concentrate on the story on her own and was relieved when Bron at last slipped into the seat beside her. She leaned eagerly towards Jo, and whispered, "He touched my leg; I wasn't going to move but he started touching my leg."

Jo did not know why a strange man should want to touch Bron's leg. It wasn't as though Bron was at all glamorous, in fact she was a very ordinary schoolgirl. But the incident was disturbing and nasty and she didn't enjoy the rest of the three-hour programme at all. When the lights came up she looked round for the man and was on tenterhooks until an innocent-looking couple took the seats on her other side. She sat through it all then – the supporting film which had a complicated plot to do with oil wells in Texas, the cartoon film about Donald Duck, the advertisements and the organ interlude. She usually enjoyed the music and the way the coloured lights played on the draped curtains which temporarily concealed the screen behind the white organ when it rose from its subterranean hiding place with the man playing as it ascended, but this time the entertainment gave her no pleasure. She was so glad to leave that she forgot to look at her favourite picture of Robert Taylor on the way out. But Bron was unworried, seeming almost to have enjoyed the incident.

"It was better in the shilling seats," she pointed out.

Jo remembered her own deliberately vague answer when Clive had asked her what film they proposed to see. She couldn't tell him what had happened, but she wouldn't do it again. She thought Bron would, though. It almost seemed as though she had liked having the strange man touch her leg. How worrying it was. Very worrying and very baffling. Part of her wanted to know all the secrets, like why you didn't have a baby unless you were married, though Patty's sister had one and wasn't married. Part of her wanted to understand, while another part of her

140

wanted to stay as she was, never to be told. That night she dreamt that Patty's Ken had touched her leg in the cinema and the next minute she was holding a baby but of course there must be more to it than that. She knew where babies actually came from. Many well-to-do expectant mothers stayed at the St Andrew's. They wore flowing dresses with plenty of 'neck-interest' and complained about their backs, and Beatrice was always sympathetic. But what started them off? According to her mother it was simply the state of marriage. But Patty's sister Ada wasn't married. So it went round in Jo's head as she tried to sleep that night. Who would tell her the secret, frightening, horrible thing you had to do before you had a baby? What with that and the menace in *Love from a Stranger*, in which the beautiful Ann Harding unwittingly married a murderer, she decided it might be better to become a nun, which was a pity when she had always hoped to be the mother of four or five children, in a big house with a sunny garden.

The last weekend of the Easter holidays was spent by Rosemarie and Clive at the Hunter's Moon. By now the rapidly expanding Territorial Army was much more demanding of Clive's time. A second drill hall had been hastily erected, and Clive thought he might soon be promoted to Major. The mere thought of the crown on his shoulders instead of the three pips gave him enormous satisfaction. And the pay, if he became a full-time soldier, would be quite good. If the hotel closed he would still be able to support his wife and child in comfort. The advent of war would, he thought, certainly bring his affair to an end and he wasn't altogether sorry. He would miss their times together of course, but it was all a bit of a strain, and with Rosemarie evacuating the school to north Wales it would be impossible to continue. He'd probably be sent abroad, anyway.

He had instructed Rosemarie to take a taxi to the Hunter's Moon from Warne Bay station because he could not guarantee getting away in time to meet the train. She arrived as dusk was falling, and the golden light gleamed from the diamond-paned windows, and the floodlit hanging sign with its full moon glowed invitingly. Having paid the taxi she walked straight into the tearoom, where one or two tables were still occupied. The Hunter's Moon was on the main road to Ashford, so there was a good deal of passing trade. She was glad to see that fluffy-haired Miss Simms was there, seeming as efficient as ever.

"You know your room," she said to Rosemarie, resting her loaded tray on the corner of an an empty table. "It's so nice to see you, Mrs Livingstone. How is the Captain?"

"He's very well, but desperately overworked. The international situation . . ."

"I know."

They both considered the international situation and Clive's weighty responsibilities for a moment before Miss Simms said brightly, "Well, I expect you want to get settled in," and Rosemarie carried her own small suitcase up to the pretty flowery bedroom where she had spent really not very many nights with her lover. Not nearly enough, and it looked as though there might only a very few more. The news was bad. German troops had marched into Czechoslovakia, Dutch troops were massing on the German border, Mussolini had occupied Albania . . . while at home conscription was almost a certainty. For her, personally, Rosemarie thought that the outbreak of war might have certain advantages. A scandal in Culvergate, with Clive's wife divorcing him would almost certainly bring about her own bankruptcy. No parents would leave their daughter with a headmistress who had been involved in a divorce. But if she and the school were buried in north Wales they probably wouldn't even hear about it and eventually she and Clive could marry quietly and live happily ever after. Well, as happily as most people. She wanted him to be permanently and publicly her own. Of course at forty-four she was not as desperately in love as she had been with her cousin, although it had been quite exciting to begin with. But she was very fond of him, he was kind and reliable and didn't lay the law down like so many men did; being in bed with him was amazingly enjoyable and it was nice having a man to admire the chiffon nightgowns and expensive scent she would soon be too old to wear. Beatrice would be perfectly happy managing a hotel somewhere, and the child, a bright little thing, could not really be attached to such a cold woman. Rosemarie would be a second mother to her, and see she passed all her exams and fulfilled her potential. While these thoughts passed through her mind Rosemarie laid a new peach satin negligée across the bed, and set out her talcum powder and bath salts in the bathroom. When she washed her hands she was pleased to find the water extremely hot.

Downstairs the cafe had emptied. Miss Simms was clearing tables as Rosemarie took her accustomed seat near the fire. It was almost six o'clock but Miss Simms was quite willing to supply tea and cakes. When a pot of tea for one, with assorted fancies, had been unloaded from her tray she did not leave the room, finding a number of little jobs that needed doing. The flowered curtains had to be carefully drawn, shutting out the blue dusk that Rosemarie was rather enjoying, and more coal to be put on the fire, extinguishing the cheerful orange glow. Crumbs were brushed away, and ashtrays collected. Moving about making a series of small noises she irritated her only customer, who would have liked to sit peacefully waiting for her lover, finally saying rather breathlessly, "I expect you noticed I wasn't here when you came last?"

"Yes, we missed you."

"Well, I wouldn't have gone, not if I'd known, but you hadn't booked in, you see."

"No, we just came on the spur of the moment. It was an unexpected opportunity for my husband to get away."

"Yes, well, I'm ever so sorry. Was it alright?"

Rosemarie chose her words carefully. "Well, I expect it's a lot of work for one person." That, she thought, would please Miss Simms without actually criticising Miss Caxton.

143

Miss Simms came to where Rosemarie was sitting, and brushed an imaginary crumb off the pink tablecloth.

"She's a wonderful cakemaker, I will say that."

Rosemarie agreed, permitting herself to choose a second delicious example of Miss Caxton's art.

"But it's very hard sometimes. She doesn't think I can do anything, you see."

"Oh, I'm sure she does."

"Well, some things. Some things she thinks I can do. Like cleaning the baths, and laying the tables. But I can make cakes too, you know, everyone used to love my scones, and she gets so tired, but still she won't let me help. Half the time I'm not even allowed in the kitchen."

"I'm sure you have plenty to do . . ." murmured Rosemarie.

"But I'm not appreciated, you see. That's what upsets me. She thinks its nothing, all the work I do, and she's always telling me not to forget things. When I went into town this morning to get the shopping, she said 'And make sure its caster sugar, not gran. I can't use gran.' As if I didn't know that. I've been with her for nearly five years, of course I know about her never using gran, always caster, but she doesn't give me any credit."

"I'm sure you're mistaken."

The cake, a macaroon, was delicious, but really this woman was spoiling Rosemarie's enjoyment of it. "She just doesn't say, I expect."

"Its very hurtful, day after day, being reminded of things you haven't forgotten, as though you've got no brains. I don't know if I can stand much more of it," and Miss Simms took out a small handkerchief and wiped her eyes.

Rosemarie said, "Yes, I can see it must be," and asked Miss Simms if she might take her second cup of tea up to the bedroom, to drink while she ran the bath.

Miss Simms said, certainly she could, and apologised for telling her troubles to a guest, but Mrs Livingstone had such an understanding way . . . Rosemarie escaped, and was sitting upstairs drinking the tea when there was a knock at the door. It was Miss Caxton, her neat, girlish bob and her toothy smile both restored. Rosemarie feared that she was now about to hear the other side of the story, but Miss Caxton merely asked in a businesslike way what time she expected the Captain, and was everything alright and went briskly down the ancient awkward staircase to her inviolate kitchen. Clive did not arrive till after nine, but the beef casserole was delicious, none the worse for being kept hot.

Clive was a happy man. He liked the Army, you knew just where you were and what you were supposed to do, and there was always a right way to do everything that was written down, so you didn't make mistakes. Major Upcott had been really pleased with the way he was training the new recruits, and Clive couldn't refuse to have a drink wth him in the village pub before coming on to the Hunter's Moon.

"See you in the Knight's later, perhaps," said Upcott, as they parted, but Clive explained that when he got back there would be much to do. Catching up on the weekend. Upcott said it must keep him pretty busy, running the hotel on top of his commitment to the 'Terriers'. Clive said it did. He had to hang about a bit, polishing the windscreen of the Hillman Minx, until it was safe to turn the car and set off in the direction of Warne Bay.

Chapter Eleven

"WHAT will you do if there's a war?"

Everyone was asking this question of everyone else during that summer of 1939. On this occasion Beatrice was asking her mother. She was a little afraid that Mrs Hewitt might wish to accompany her to whatever hotel she might be sent by Colin Weir. She need not have worried, the old lady had no intention of giving up her independence.

"I shall stay on here as long as it's worth keeping open, then I shall see. I might find a little place in a reception area, just something to keep me interested. You needn't worry about me."

"I thought p'raps you'd go to Doris . . ."

"Lord, no. I'm too old to change my ways to fit in with Doris, or Joan, or you."

They were not in the cafe – Beatrice was paying a rare Sunday visit to the flat above. The summer term having started Jo was at home doing her prep, under protest. She seemed to have a sniffly cold starting and was hoping that it might develop into a justification for staying at home on the Monday. She had been out with Bron in the morning, but her symptoms had worsened rapidly. Clive had, as usual, departed in his uniform on the previous afternoon. Beatrice no longer referred to his military activities as 'playing soldiers'. His evident competence and the possibility of war had increased his stature in her eyes. He looked smart in the uniform, too, with his cap at a rakish angle.

Beatrice and her mother were sitting in the living room over the cafe. It was arranged for comfort. The big plush-covered settee had a checked travelling rug draped over its back, and many extra cushions. Dozens of china ornaments and framed photographs covered every surface. The copper fender incorporated a box at each side, the lids of which, being upholstered in brown rexine, formed seats on which you could sit almost literally on top of the fire. These seats were dented with many years of use, and their inner sides scorched by the searing heat given out by the coke that Mrs Hewitt favoured. She even favoured it on this Sunday in May.

Beatrice's mother, whose business premises were so pleasing to the eye, had not had time or money to consider the decor of her home when she and her daughters had moved in over twenty years earlier. Now she was on her own it didn't seem worth the bother. It was cosy, it was home, and anyway she was hardly ever there. Beatrice thought it was awful and frequently said so. For her, there was too much softness, too much heat from the fire, too much shutting out of the street and shutting in of the room behind the thick velvet curtains. Even the seldom-used dining table in front of the window was covered with a brown chenille cloth, and in front of the hearth on top of the worn brown and orange carpet lay a grubby black sheepskin rug that to Beatrice's own knowledge had been there for eighteen years. As girls she and her sisters had sprawled on it, close to the fire on winter afternoons; now she would not have sat on it at any price. She tried to keep her feet clear of it too, it being the favourite resting place of the two elderly cats, which almost certainly had fleas.

Mrs Hewitt had been enjoying her Sunday off. She was tired, too tired to dress up and go out, and had refused Beatrice's invitation to dinner. But she had been quite pleased to see her daughter. Before going down to open the door she had hidden her glass of whisky and water behind a photograph of Doris, aged nine, dressed as a ballerina, and on the way up she told Bea she could make a cup of tea if she liked, but Bea did not like. So they smoked and gossiped enjoyably, and Bea talked about

Colin Weir, and assured her mother that there was nothing like that, and Mrs Hewitt said there always was, with men. Then she asked what about Clive? Bea said well; she still felt sure it couldn't be another woman, he simply didn't have the time. She supposed he'd simply gone off it, being over forty, as she had herself, and as they certainly didn't want any more children . . . Mrs Hewitt looked sceptical.

Beatrice re-entered her own home with relief. She was fond of Mum, who had really done her best by her three daughters, and she had a useful store of common sense, as well as a satisfying relish for local scandal, but the buried-alive feeling that sooner or later always overcame her in the room above the cafe was almost more than she could stand. The space and light in the St Andrew's welcomed her, and her own rooms, with their smooth shiny surfaces, clean pale walls and upholstery, with bright reflections in the chromium fittings pleased her even more than usual. Here you could breathe, here you could walk about, there was no feeling of being shut in. Outside the windows there was the endless space of the sea. She would not draw the curtains until it was quite dark. She sat down with the Sunday paper and a gin and vermouth – no need to go down just yet.

Then of course, Jo appeared.

"I've got an awful cold," she snuffled, miserably. She did look rotten.

Beatrice said, "You'd better go to bed. I'll send up some supper for you."

"I've used all my hankies."

"Oh, dear. Take one or two of Daddy's. Don't come too near me. I can't afford to have colds."

"I've got a headache too."

"I'll give you an aspirin later. Go to bed now, and don't forget to clean your teeth when you've had your supper."

"When's Dad coming?"

"Tomorrow sometime. Now go to bed."

"I wish he didn't go away so much."

149

"You'll have to get used to that. He'll be away all the time if there's a war."

Bea turned back to her newspaper. Strange of the child to want her father. You'd think she'd want her mother more if she didn't feel well. All the same, she could understand because she shared her feelings. Clive should be at home, sympathising with his daughter, who didn't look at all well, and being a companion to his wife, who needed someone to talk to when she came upstairs. And she hated eating alone in the restaurant, which she would have to do, with Jo in bed. She would have no protection from the elderly residents as they passed her table on the way out. No doubt someone would find it convenient to draw her attention to an oversight, to voice some petty complaint, while she ate her cheese and biscuits or drank her coffee. Thank heavens Mrs Osterreicher's friend in the nursing home was not demanding her company this weekend.

By the time Clive returned on Monday, the doctor had diagnosed Jo as having measles. A conference was held. Jo had a high temperature and seemed ill, Clive thought she should not be left. Bea demonstrated that it was impossible for her to stay in the apartment, she was no good with illness, she said, with some pride, seeming to imply that Jo's infection was due to sheer wilfulness.

"You can stay up here," she added to Clive, reminding him tacitly of the lightness of his responsibilities in the hotel.

Eventually it was decided that Patty should be released from downstairs duties to look after Jo. Patty, who had been an experienced nurse by the time she was twelve, was not ill-pleased, and Jo through the miseries of the illness was glad. Clive visited her every hour or so, bringing grapes and magazines and a cuddly toy which embarrassed her because she was not quite old enough to be sure it was a joke. Patty helped her out of bed to sit on a chamber pot, tucked her back in again, washed her gently and supported her when, with a tongue frighteningly like a piece of black cardboard, she tried to drink.

There was a bad time, a whole afternoon, when the doctor thought she had fallen victim to unnamed complications. She rambled in her speech, talking of cheese which seemed to be somewhere near the ceiling, her fair hair was darkened with sweat and with her oddly puffy face she was almost unrecognisable. Patty sponged her, as directed, with lukewarm water, to bring down her temperature, Bea caused oranges to be squeezed in the kitchen and herself carried the jug of juice upstairs, afterwards waiting in the apartment for the doctor's third visit of the day. Clive's anxious pacing about irritated her.

"For God's sake sit down. You're driving me mad."

He did not sit down but stayed at the window, looking out, not answering.

"He's late isn't he? What time did he say he'd come back?"

"I don't know! You saw him last time."

"You should have come up too. He asked where you were."

"There was no need for both of us. Somebody's got to keep this place going."

"Jo's more important than anything else."

"Of course she is. But its only measles. Not diphtheria or scarlet fever, not one of those. Only measles. What did he say last time?"

"He said he was . . . a little worried."

"What did he mean by that?"

Clive turned to face her. "Complications, I suppose."

"What sort of complications can you get with measles? All kids have it. I had it when I was nine."

"I don't know!" Clive almost shouted at her. "Shut up, will you?"

Bea was staggered by the strength of his reaction to what she considered her innocent words. Clive almost never lost his temper. But she was too anxious to be really aggrieved. Going into her bedroom she remembered how companionable Jo was

151

to be when she reached the mature age of eighteen, how people would take them for sisters and to her own surprise she was overcome by tears. Clive called from the lobby.

"The doctor's here, I've just seen his car."

Hearing Clive leave the apartment to meet the doctor, she blew her nose and applied her powder puff, then she picked up her comb and tried to tidy her hair, but she seemed to a have forgotten how to do it. She could not achieve the neat centre parting and symmetrical waves that encouraged people to remark on her resemblance to Wallis Simpson, now the Duchess of Windsor. Well, it didn't matter, anyway. I've been a rotten mother, she thought. I've been a lousy bloody mother, Jo. Give me another chance.

When the doctor had left, still looking serious, she sat beside Clive on the settee. He took her hand.

"She's been such a good kid," he said. "Never any trouble. It hasn't been the right life for her, living in a hotel."

"We had to earn a living. Or I had to."

Clive ignored this, knowing his wife's bitterness sprang from her anxiety. After a moment she said, "Sorry. I didn't mean that."

"She's grown up so quickly. It doesn't seem any time since I used to read her those Rupert Bear stories. She always liked them."

"D'you remember her in that pink sunbonnet, sitting up in her pram?"

"Yes, we put her in for the bonny baby competition."

"I was amazed when she didn't win."

"She was easily the prettiest."

Patty's voice came from the door. "Could you come a minute, please. She's . . . different."

They followed her to Jo's bedside. Jo breathed slowly with endless pauses between each intake of breath.

"Can we get the doctor back?" said Patty.

Clive hurried away to ring down to Reception, but he was too

152

late. At once he telephoned the surgery to be told, maddeningly, that Dr Tree was out on his rounds. They stayed by the sleeping Jo until he eventually returned an hour and a half later. He felt her pulse. They waited for him to say "I'm so very sorry," or something like that. What he actually said was, "I think she's turned the corner."

Jo, after measles complicated by pneumonia, missed over four weeks' school, and when she got back she was informed by Bron, who had been suspiciously cool on the telephone, that they were no longer best friends. Bron was now best friends with Thelma. Well, you couldn't stick to one person all your life and there were plenty of other people Jo could be best friends with. She suggested Elsa Parrish, who, as well as having poor parents, had blackheads and BO and had never had a best friend at all. All this was said in the playground in break-time with Bron trivialising the whole thing by talking through a mouthful of toffee. Afterwards she went back to Thelma, leaving Jo, taller, thinner and paler than before, with the top of her hair flat because the perm was growing out, standing alone. Bron and Thelma walked away, arms round each other. Jo went and sat by herself on one of the benches, giving a look of contempt and dislike in the direction of Elsa Parrish as she passed her.

That was a miserable term for Jo. She missed Bron, she felt tired most of the time and was excused from tennis and cricket, which, though she was not good at the first and thoroughly bored by the second, was not altogether a relief. She felt more and more excluded as tennis tournaments and cricket matches approached, and then Miss Card had somehow got her knife into her. It started when Jo, on an errand for a teacher during class time, met another girl as she passed the top of the basement stairs in the main entrance hall, in the middle house. Jo, understanding that the rule of silence in the corridors was necessary to avoid pandemonium when everyone was moving about, nevertheless

153

believed it hardly applied to her situation at that moment. All she said was "Hello, Audrey" to Audrey Stanton and Miss Card popped up from the stairwell rather like the demon king in a pantomime, immediately sentencing Jo to ten minutes detention for talking in the corridor. Jo had the temerity to argue.

"But I only said—"

"Don't answer me back."

"But Miss Card—"

"Right, make it twenty minutes, Josephine, and come to the staffroom in breaktime."

This was far the worst part of the sentence. Miss Card was fond of giving private venomous tickings off outside the staffroom door, during break. Jo was bitter and angry and decided not to go to the staffroom, but at the last minute, of course, she went, only to receive a message from the teacher that she was too busy to see her. Perhaps Miss Card regretted her own harshness, but perhaps not. From that time onward she took Jo to task on every possible occasion. One of her favourite ploys was to hold a page of her writing up in front of the class, inviting the other girls to comment on the activities of the spider that must have walked across the page. Jo, despite her drawing skills, wrote a small crabbed hand, though she made honest efforts to improve. Miss Ward also constantly suggested that Jo had an unduly high opinion of herself. This was totally unjustified, but it became fashionable to belittle Jo and her work, and no new Best Friend materialised. Almost everyone in the class adopted a sneering, sometimes bullying attitude towards her. All except Elsa Parrish, to whom Jo, in a misguided effort to regain her self-respect, meted out exactly the treatment the rest of the girls afforded her.

So when one Sunday afternoon towards the end-of-term holidays Bron telephoned to say that she had noticed Mrs Osterreicher walking along the front, and suggested a final effort to unmask her as a spy, Jo agreed gratefully, eager to resurrect their old companionship. She was waiting on the steps of the hotel for Bron at half past two, wearing her grey pleated shorts and navy and white striped knitted jumper. She looked trim and smart, and Bea had let her have another perm. She'd had a set too, the previous afternoon, so that her hair after she had combed it fiercely on her return home, waved in a soft, natural way. Bron was wearing rather shapeless beige shorts made by her mother, and a white sweater. She'd slept in curlers the previous night and her hair stuck out rather strangely. Not that this mattered to Jo. What did matter was that Bron was not alone. She was accompanied by Thelma. Thelma was to become a member of the Jobron Agency and join in the afternoon's activities. Jo was forced to accept the situation.

Mrs Osterriecher soon appeared and set off towards the nursing home. They kept her in view, waited outside at a distance and followed her back to the hotel. It was all quite boring. Jo had planned to ask Bron to tea, but she didn't want Thelma as well, and in any case it soon transpired that Bron was going to Thelma's house for tea and to spend the evening. Dispirited, Jo watched them go off together, and went into the hotel alone. When the phone rang in the lobby she was consoling herself with *Film Weekly* and a Crunchie bar while she waited for Patty to bring tea. Beatrice wanted her in the office. This was not particularly unusual, Jo ran errands for extra pocket money, sometimes even helped with teas in the kitchen when they were short of staff. She was quick and neat, cutting sandwiches and setting trays quite professionally.

She was surprised to see Mrs Osterriecher in the office. Bea was sitting behind her desk, wearing her spectacles

"Jo, Mrs Osterreicher has a complaint. A complaint about you. I've told her that she must be mistaken."

Even then Jo wondered if she had been unduly noisy, or lacking in politeness. Bea continued. "Mrs Osterreicher thinks you have been following her about. You and that friend of yours, Bronwen is it? I thought you weren't friendly with her any more."

"I went out with her today. And . . . another girl . . ."

"Did you follow Mrs Osterreicher?" The direct question was too much for Jo.

"Yes."

"But why, in heaven's name?"

Jo, her face already scarlet, looked desperately at Mrs Osterreicher. Short, fat, dowdy and harmless, how could she ever have imagined . . . ? The whole thing had been a stupid, babyish game of pretend. She said, "I don't know," and stared at the floor.

Mrs Osterreicher said, "Don't question her further, dear Mrs Livingstone. You see, I do understand. I am so fond of Jo, and she is so fond of me, and of Mrs Myers, but you see, I have been too busy lately to pay her attention, and she and her little friends, I am sure that is all they wanted, just a little of my time. I should perhaps not have spoken but I have been through so much, and poor Trudi even more, she began to worry, when the children followed us before, and then it started again and she does not feel safe anywhere, you see, so you will not do it again, my Josephine will you? And as soon as my friend is better and can spare me, you and I will go for a long walk together and have a nice talk."

That said she rose and hugged Jo, disarranging her careful hair and displacing the red celluloid Alice band, a recent purchase from Woolworths.

She left the room, with several more expressions of appreciation and admiration, and renewed promises of time to be spent with Jo.

When she had closed the door behind her Bea said, "What in heaven's name have you been up to? Were you following her?"

"Well, in a way we were."

"Why? What was the point?"

"We thought she was a spy." Jo muttered the words, their silliness overwhelming her.

"A spy? Mrs Osterreicher? Well, thank God you didn't tell

156

her that. Was this that Bronwen's idea? It's time you gave up these infantile games, you'll get us all into trouble, me most of all. Haven't you got any brains at all, you stupid, stupid little idiot?" Bea's temper rose as she wondered what Colin Weir's reaction would be in the unlikely event of his hearing about the incident. "Go up to your room. I don't want to see you again today."

So Jo went. She knew she had been foolish, only it was so difficult to say 'No' to Bron. And it was all that stupid Thelma's fault, playing about and making noises so that Mrs Osterreicher had noticed them. Not like a real detective at all.

She sat miserably on her bed until Patty brought her tea, when she told her an edited version of the story. Patty's reply was an elaboration of I-told-you-so. But somehow this didn't matter. Later on, when Bea sent a message that she was to come down to dinner after all, she had almost recovered from the incident. All that worried her was that Bron did not, after all, seem to want to be best friends again.

This disappointment preoccupied her for days. Even when Beatrice went with her to an empty shop in Southdown Road where they queued for nearly an hour in order to be fitted with gas masks, which they were instructed to take with them wherever they went, she was hardly disturbed by the possibility of actually having to wear the thing, but Beatrice was thoughtful as they walked back to the hotel.

The current events lecture that week was given by Rosemarie herself, and she decreed that third, fourth and fifth forms were to attend. When they assembled in the gym hall they found a large map of Europe suspended over a black board.

Rosemarie explained about the Polish corridor, and about Danzig, and how England was committed to defending Poland if necessary.

"We would declare war on Germany," she said proudly, "if Hitler, metaphorically speaking, took one step over the border."

Bron put up her hand.

"Yes, Bronwen?"

"Why?"

"Why what?"

"Why would we fight for Poland? It isn't ours is it?"

"No, it is not ours, but we have signed a treaty. We have made a promise and we must keep it."

"But Miss Wells, if we do that, a lot of people will be killed, won't they, like before. And they didn't sign the treaty, did they? It wasn't them. Perhaps they don't want to fight for Poland."

"I told you, Bronwen, we have signed a treaty."

"Well, my father hasn't signed a treaty, but he says he'll have to go abroad again if there's a war, because all the young men will be in the Army."

"Well, that's very upsetting for you and your mother of course, but promises must be kept, otherwise chaos would ensue."

Rosemarie was rather proud of that phrase, and hoped that Bronwen would be silenced by it. But she was not.

"But I don't see why people should have to keep promises that other people have made, without asking them."

There was a slight stir among the girls, who were seated in rows on the floor. Rosemarie looked a little uncomfortable and Bron seemed to be winning the argument. But she was going too far. They were disturbed by this reversal of the natural order of things. Grown-ups, especially teachers, knew best.

Jo was not sitting next to Bron. If she had been she would have nudged her with her elbow, as she had done on previous occasions when Bron had not known when to stop but now Thelma failed to see where her duty lay and, best friend or not, Jo blushed for Bron as she refused to bow to the headmistress's patriotic platitudes. Jo blushed for her, then told herself she didn't care now they were no longer best friends. It was just one more example of Bron's refusal, sometimes worrying, sometimes exciting, to observe the accepted boundaries of behaviour. Afterwards in the classroom Bron was reprimanded by the Form Captain, but seemed not to understand what she had done that was wrong.

Chapter Twelve

AS THE END of term drew near Jo remained thin and pale, The effort of catching up on the work she had missed, combined with intermittent verbal bullying and the lack of a best friend made her feel depressed and tired almost all the time. Clive, when he saw her, which was by no means every day, was anxious about her, and communicated his anxiety to Bea. Bea decided that Jo was 'outgrowing her strength' and made her drink Horlicks Malted Milk, which was advertised as being a cure for this condition. Jo loathed it, and usually managed to drink less than half of what she was given. Mrs Hewitt voiced doubts as to whether the child was happy at school. Both parents vetoed the idea that she could possibly be miserable at the Princess May. But she was. Somehow the girls in her class had by this time convinced one another that Jo, living at the St Andrews, with, they believed, huge rooms and innumerable servants at her disposal, considered herself superior, considered herself, in fact, because of the palace which was her home, to be a princess. They nicknamed her 'the princess'. And even Elsa Parrish, so frequently snubbed by Jo, was now allowed to take her place among the tormentors. Jo was proud and silent, kept her dignity, and made no friendly overtures, making it easy for them to call her stuck-up and conceited.

Rosemarie, who made a habit of noticing whether or not her girls looked well and cheerful, was worried by Jo's appearance, and invited her to the sitting room during break on a Thursday morning. In Jo's nervous state, this always ominous invitation struck terror into her soul. She entered the sunny, comfortable room trembling.

"Don't worry Jo. I didn't send for you to scold you. On the contrary. I think perhaps you are working too hard."

Rosemary was at her desk, but she left it and seated herself on the chintz settee, hoping to put Jo at her ease. She looked carefully at Jo's pale face. There was a decided resemblance to Clive which endeared his child to her.

"Bring that chair a bit nearer, Jo, and sit down. You look as though you could do with a rest."

She indicated a light, upright chair, which Jo, as instructed, moved closer to the settee, placing it in front of the easy chair on the opposite side of the fireplace. She perched uncomfortably on its edge. The kindness in her headmistress's voice did nothing to lessen her unease. Could she have heard what a horrible time she was having? Could she be going to sympathise with her lack of a best friend? These were wild ideas but Jo had never heard of anybody's being called to the sitting room for reasons other than disciplinary ones. Rosemarie's friendly, personal approach was to her profoundly disturbing. Perhaps – the thought struck her suddenly – her mother and father had, since she left that morning, been killed in an accident! It couldn't be that, could it?

"I know you've had a great deal to catch up on, after your illness."

Jo agreed, feeling embarrassed. The headmistress seemed to be on her side, but she didn't want her on her side. She was a girl, and she wanted to be on the same side as all the other girls.

"Your teachers tell me you have done very well, considering. And then you've had your elocution lessons, too."

This was an extra. A visiting teacher gave private lessons in elocution on Thursday and Friday afternoons.

"I'm going to tell your parents that I think you should drop elocution for a time."

The half-hour each week given to reciting poetry and acting scenes from Shakespeare with Miss Summers was greatly enjoyed

162

by Jo. Apart from these Friday sessions, only English and singing gave her any pleasure. All the maths lessons were difficult, geography might have been alright if taught by someone other than Miss Card and the rest were boring most of the time, but she said nothing.

'Extras' were a source of income to Rosemarie and normally she encouraged pupils to take them. She congratulated herself on putting a child's welfare first, but she knew she had not got to the heart of the matter. Suddenly she said, "You're happy here, are you? Plenty of friends?"

Jo said oh, yes, plenty, thank you, and stared at the carpet. Rosemarie, after a very few more questions, minimally though politely answered, let her go. She would have to talk to Clive, though so far they had tacitly agreed not to discuss his family.

Thankful to be free, Jo went down the stairs and out to the playground. Fourth-form girls did not tear about playing Rescue or Wolves at breaktime. They strolled up and down or sat in groups talking. Jo's classmates would be Form IVB next term and had already abandoned childish games. Bron was sitting on a bench, learning the Shelley sonnet about Ozymandios, which she should have done the night before. The rest of the class were hurriedly going over their own pieces. Jo, who had learned hers, Harold Monro's 'Milk for the Cat', with ease the previous evening, sat down beside her and said, "D'you want me to hear your words?"

Bron agreed grudgingly and Jo took the book, prompting helpfully as Bron stumbled through the poem. Then she made the mistake of offering advice on how to say it, out of the knowledge gained in her discontinued elocution lessons. Bron was offended and said Jo thought she knew everything better than anyone else, so the situation was not, after all, improved.

When Jo had gone Rosemarie returned to her desk. In the event of war all children would sooner or later be evacuated from danger areas, which included Culvergate in its exposed

163

position at the south-eastern corner of England. Those at state schools would go to strangers; anyone who had room to spare in a safe area would be forced to take in one or more young evacuees. The private schools would move independently. From the Princess May building overlooking the tennis courts pupils, furnishings and equipment of all kinds would travel to north Wales, where Rosemarie had provisionally arranged to rent a somewhat dilapidated country mansion, currently in use as a charity home for unemployed – mostly unemployable – men. This was the best the agency could offer, having assured her that the men would be absorbed into the Army long before the staff and pupils of the Princess May arrived. They would arrange for the place to be cleaned as well. The journey, in hired coaches, would take over fifteen hours. Rosemarie hoped it would not happen, but believed that it would. Meanwhile every parent had to be written to, explaining that girls could, if war were declared during the summer holidays, return to school immediately, from there being transported to their insalubrious haven; or there would be stopping points on the way where boarders from distant parts could join the travellers. It all meant a lot of correspondence, and carbon copies would not do. Rosemarie and her part-time secretary had one hundred and twenty letters to send. There was also a list of instructions for each member of staff, and all the complexities of closing the school building to be considered.

Beatrice's task was lighter. In the event of war, her guests would depart soon enough without any help from her. Colin had said that the hotel should be only partly closed down, at least to begin with. The cellar would be turned into an air-raid shelter, made as comfortable as possible, and most of the staff dismissed. They could join the Army or go into munitions.

Culvergate faced north. The threat from Europe was not on the other side of the stretch of the North Sea visible from the St Andrews windows, it was around the corner, on the opposite side of the channel. Nevertheless being right on the front seemed to make the hotel vulnerable, and perhaps it did, but still Beatrice was not eager to leave. Jo would be in Wales with the school, Clive heaven knows where. She supposed, if the worst came to the worst and Colin Weir let her down she could join the new women's branch of the Royal Air Force. She would certainly be given a commission straight away, especially when they knew her husband was an army officer. She thought she could be a success with her eye for detail and her administrative and organising abilities. How high up would women be able to get in the Air Force? Perhaps it would be more interesting than running a small hotel in some out-of-the-way place.

But when she and Clive entered the restaurant at lunchtime with Jo, who returned to the hotel for the midday meal, the attractions of the WAAF faded. There were very few vacant places, the waiting staff looked smart and fresh, the tables were perfectly appointed with starched white cloths and little vases of summer flowers, and subtly appetising odours emanated through the swing doors from the kitchen. The guests in their holiday clothes, some of them quite tanned, as Clive was, with Culvergate's much advertised sunshine, looked healthy and rich. This was her achievement, this perfectly run hotel, this successful business. And upstairs was the home she had created, in stark contrast to the traditional old oak style of the public rooms. It hadn't been easy, getting it right, with Colin Weir protesting about the new fireplace she'd wanted, and Clive anxious to keep some of the awful old furniture from his parents' home. But there it was, black, silver and white, with touches of deep fuchsia and lilac. And there seemed little doubt that she would have to leave it, after only eighteen months. For over nine years she'd had to put up with the hideous wallpaper provided by the owners, which even Colin Weir seemed to think was quite alright, and having transformed the place into the elegant home of her dreams, she was to lose it because politicians couldn't somehow get on together. It seemed so desperately unfair.

* * *

Rosemarie held similar views of her own situation. She had suggested to Clive that the removal of all parties from Culvergate might make his divorce from Beatrice easier, saying this in a joking sort of way in the context of its being an ill wind that blew no good, but he had not taken her seriously, quickly changing the subject. Well, she would not insist – that way she might lose him altogether, and really she had a very pleasant life. She had him as a lover, she had the pleasure and excitement of their stays at the Hunter's Moon and her daily life was interesting and successful. The school seemed to have come through a rather thin patch, and there were now 127 girls, 65 of them boarders. It was true that the father of seven-year-old Mollie Jackson, who lived and presumably worked in Singapore, seemed to have lost all interest in her, having paid no school fees for over a year, and the Rosenberg girls had no idea what had happened to their parents and younger brother, nevertheless the financial situation was reasonably good and she had hoped to have major redecoration and refurbishing done during the summer holidays. If it weren't for the threat of war! If Hitler invaded Poland and England went to her defence the place might be standing empty for months, or even destroyed by enemy action. She had worked hard to get where she was; now who could say if the Princess May of Teck would survive moving to Wales?

She went down to the dining room in good time, put on the pristine white coat handed to her by the head dining-room maid, and set to work to carve the huge joints of beef. She always did the carving herself, and was an expert, taught by her father who had carved even thinner slices for his sixty-odd boys than she did for her similar number of girls. The meat was accompanied by boiled potatoes and cabbage and reasonably good gravy. Not an ambrosial meal, but adequate, especially if you were hungry. The pudding was jam tart. Mrs Hepworth's pastry, being a little over-cooked, was always rather hard, with a tendency to leap off the plate when attacked with a fork. The technique of coping with it involved smothering it in custard and stabbing it with the prongs. Most people were quite good at this. Rosemarie wondered why the smell of the cabbage was so pervasive and lingering when it was actually cooked down in the basement and brought to the 'pantry' leading out of the dining room in a service lift.

Barbara Goodwin seated next to her, raised the subject of Sports Day, fixed for the last Saturday of term. Would it definitely take place? she asked. Rosemarie said it would, unless they were all hiding in the basement, when they would be forced to substitute a tiddly-winks match. This joke naturally went down well and the conversation became quite lively, though with perhaps a slightly hysterical note. The tiddly-winks match might be a flight of fancy, but the hiding in basements could well come to pass. The young women of the sixth form, having listened attentively to the lectures on Current Events, knew this quite well.

The Sports Day was held as planned. The girls walked from the school to the playing field at half past one, and changed in the pavilion into the short white spongecloth dresses they always wore on this occasion. These were not their own but the property of the school, distributed and tried on a few days before the event. They were quite shapeless with elastic round the middle, and the correct length was usually obtained by pouching them over at the waist. The younger girls looked charming with their brown legs and ankle socks, the older ones, especially those with well developed busts like Barbara Goodwin were not flattered by the extremely simple cut. However, the march round the field, tallest first and smallest last, to 'Colonel Bogey' on the loudspeakers was nevertheless impressive. The sun shone, the flags fluttered, almost everone was excited and happy, for this was a special event. The mothers wore garden-party dresses in printed silk or diaphanous voile and ninon, most of them printed with flowers in soft pretty colours, pink and lavender, mauve and primrose and powder blue. The flared calf-length skirts were graceful and the shady hats became most faces. In this kaleidoscope, Beatrice was easily distinguishable in a black and white dress. Disliking floral patterns, she had chosen a design of black crescents and arcs on a white ground, geometric yet voluptuous, her wide-brimmed, black straw hat being trimmed only with a flat bow of white ribbon. Clive was proud to be seen with her, and Jo thought she looked like a film star. Mrs Hewitt, who was naturally present, looked eccentric but not unpleasing in a sapphire blue velvet jacket trimmed with fur, originally designed for evening wear, over the cream shantung dress she had owned for fifteen years. It was rather on the short side for the current fashion, and she told her daughter she would have let it down if she'd had the time. But she had not had the time and Beatrice spent much of the afternoon urging her mother to pull her skirt down over her knees as they sat side by side in deck chairs. Clive, like most of the males present, was prosperous-looking in a lounge suit. His own version was double-breasted, in light grey worsted, in which outfit he won the parents race and later when everyone gathered in front of the marquee for the presentation of awards, he received a silver-plated butter dish from the hand of Councillor Mrs Munns, who had been invited for the purpose of making a graceful speech in praise of the May of Teck, and presenting the prizes.

Rosemarie, standing beside the shorter and quite slender Mrs Munns, who wore a tailored suit in cream linen, looked opulent in her grey georgette, with a pink rose on the shoulder, and a pink hat. She said, "Well done, Captain Livingstone," and smiled charmingly and impersonally. Clive thanked her, feeling he could hardly match her performance. In about an hour the cups and certificates were all presented. The cups, apart from the coveted 'All-Round Cup' for the best sports woman of the year, were all awarded to teams and houses, individuals receiving mere certificates of success. One by one the winners and team leaders approached the dais which raised Rosemarie, Mrs Munns and one or two other local personages, above the surrounding crowd. Barbara Goodwin had won the hurdle race which had posed a severe threat to her bust, Bron came third in the fifty yards flat, and actually won the three-legged race with Jo, whom she had chosen as a partner, she said, because they were of equal height. Together they collected their precious pieces of paper, shaking hands with the right, accepting the certificate with the left, as they had been taught, and saying thank you.

Jo was almost happy. As they sat on the grass untying the handkerchief which bound her left leg to Bron's right, after winning the race, Bron had said abruptly, "I don't mind being friends again if you want to."

Jo had some pride. Not much, but some. She said carelessly, "What about Thelma?"

"She's boring."

This pleased Jo, but still she managed to hold back. She hesitated, and Bron, rising, said, "Oh, it doesn't matter, if you don't want to," and started to run off towards the others.

Jo had to catch her up and say, "Yes, alright then, I'd like to," breathlessly.

But later, after quite a convivial dinner with her parents she had some doubts. She and Bron could have good fun together much of the time, their film star scrap books, their home-made fashion dolls, their 'acting' games when they hid in caves and pretended to be escaping from kidnappers, all were pleasurable, and their newest game invented just before Jo's illness, when one was a sort of Judy Garland auditioning for a part, and the other a film director, had immense potential for enjoyment, yet friendship with Bron had its darker side. Jo knew that, with Bron, she did things she would never have chosen to do, left to herself. The Jobron Agency had turned sour, she had definitely gone off 'Calling for Peggy', and anyway they were getting too old for that sort of thing. Bron needed to be kept under control but Jo doubted her ability to do it.

The dinner had been convivial because Beatrice and Clive were

169

both pleased with themselves. Beatrice knew she had looked twice as elegant as any of the other women that afternoon, and Clive, having obtained special leave to attend his daughter's Sports Day, would be changing into his uniform soon after dinner and departing to the Territorial Camp. He thought of the many evenings he had spent hanging round the hotel with nothing much to do, so bored that a complaint from one of the elderly residents provided a welcome respite, drinking too much in the Knight's, with Beatrice gradually assuming more and more of the minor responsibilites he had tried to make his own. In the Officer's Mess he was liked, and he thought, respected. He could perform his allotted tasks competently and the men looked up to him. So he wasn't a nonentity facing an evening at a loose end, but a busy man, fitting in a meal with his wife and daughter before returning to the real business of life.

Beatrice had suggested inviting Rosemarie to dinner, but Clive had told her it wouldn't be fair to Jo. He believed this and made it sound like an adequate reason. That afternoon Rosemarie's blend of massive dignity with sensual allure had been as much as he could stand. He had smelt her scent – *Je Reviens* – as he accepted his butter dish and nearly dropped the thing, he had been aware of her delicious lips and the curves of her full – very full – bosom beneath the draped folds of silvery stuff. He had admired her air of easy authority, her calm acceptance of being the central figure among the four or five hundred people present, all of whom must be totally convinced of her rectitude and chastity. Thinking of all those well-groomed fathers – doctors, solicitors, and businessmen – with daughters being educated at the Princess May, who, seeing Clive go up to receive the prize for winning the parents race, would be totally amazed, disbelieving, thunderstruck, not to say deeply envious, if they knew what he and Rosemarie would soon be getting up to in bed at the Hunter's Moon, was the most potent aphrodisiac he could imagine.

In the school dining room Rosemarie presided as usual, unaware that she might have been eating fresh salmon poached in white wine at the St Andrew's instead of sliced luncheon meat and beetroot where she was. Yet the atmosphere was lively and festive, despite the fact that more than half of the boarders were out with their visiting parents for the evening. The remaining girls needed to let off steam, she thought, and decided to authorise an impromtu social evening, with some dancing to the gramophone and a few games in the gym. She would put Miss Colman in charge, just dropping in for twenty minutes herself to see that things weren't getting out of hand.

She had spoken to as many of the parents as possible that afternoon, and exchanged a friendly word with Beatrice whom she really rather admired. At one point it had seemed likely that she might be invited to dinner but this had come to nothing. It would have been rather bad taste to accept, if she had been asked, she supposed, but still, sitting alone in her sitting room for most of the evening was an anti-climax after such a successful afternoon. It was the best Sports Day they'd ever had, she thought – the weather had been perfect, the girls nearly all looked healthy and brimming with vitality, there had been no accidents, no sprained ankles or dislocated shoulders, and no other untoward incidents. She recalled the previous year when someone's very elderly grandmother had choked on a burnt current in a scone and very nearly died. The scones on this occasion had been plain.

Mrs Munns had made a very good speech, saying what an asset the Princess May was to the town, and how fortunate the girls were to have Miss Wells as headmistress, and then they had sung the school song, one hundred and twenty-seven girls in white dresses standing grouped in the early evening sunshine, and Jo the middle girl of thirteen in the middle line of seven, singing and looking as though she was enjoying herself.

Which she was. She had forgotten about about Miss Card, and how beastly everyone had been lately, and about Miss

171

Wells saying she had to give up elocution. The Princess May was the most wondeful school in the world and she was singing as loudly as she could.

But Rosemarie, with every reason to be happy and satisfied, was missing her lover. As she ascended the staircase outside the dining room, the shortest route to her bedroom on the second floor, it occured to her that it would really be quite easy for anyone to come and go unobserved through the door which had once been the front entrance to number seven when it was a private house. It was now used only by those daygirls whose outer clothing was accommodated in that particular section of the basement, and in the school holidays it was kept locked, since excepting at mealtimes, this part of the building was deserted. The rooms above could be reached from the landing which had been 'knocked through' during her father's time. But the staircase was there, leading straight up to Rosemarie's sitting room on the first floor at the front of the house, with two staff bedrooms at the back, and her bedroom and the bathroom she used on the floor above. The only part of this house where girls might be seen was in the ground-floor dining room. Surely, when the normal population of the school was reduced to such a small number at the end of the summer term, she might give Clive a key, and entertain him sometimes in her own quarters? Of course there were the maids, and Matron, and the four or five girl holiday-boarders, but there would be hours and hours when it would be perfectly safe. In fact the empty silence had sometimes got on her nerves. With the future so uncertain . . . Rosemarie decided to have a spare key made for the entrance concerned.

Chapter Thirteen

JO was incensed at being forced to give up her elocution lessons, especially when Bron suggested that she could hardly expect much of a part in the school play, the best ones always going to Miss Summer's private pupils. Clive, when she complained to him, said, "You'll be lucky if there is a school play next term. I shouldn't worry about it," and in answer to further questions, said, "Well if there's a war the school will have to be closed."

This sounded delightful to Jo; she imagined never having to go back to school. Perhaps no one went to school when there was a war, perhaps it would be too dangerous. Like most other Culvergate children, she had no idea of the proposed evacuation, adults conspiring to protect them from this worrying plan, hoping still that it would never have to be put into action.

It was Mrs Hewitt who suggested a new elocution teacher for Jo. Mrs Marion Matthews had the necessary qualification and took private pupils at her home. If school work left Jo with no time to spare, then she could have lessons during the holidays. Jo, though this plan would not get her into the school play, was quite pleased, and Beatrice thought it a good idea to keep her daughter occupied, perhaps to get her away from that friend, Bron, whom she seemed to have taken up with again.

So at half past three on the first Wednesday of the holidays Jo presented herself at the Matthews family home. Towards the back of the town, it was not one of the new residences on the tree-lined estate near the sea, but it overlooked the park and had a substantial, established look. The house and its front garden were six feet above the pavement behind a brick wall. Jo climbed the steps, rang the bell and was admitted by a dark-haired boy a year or so older than herself who shouted up the stairs,

"Mum, here's your latest victim!"

He then showed Jo into a big rectangular sitting room, where nothing was spectacularly modern or particularly old, there were a lot of books, a piano, the top of which was heaped with music, and the furniture was arranged to give plenty of floor space. He said cheerfully, "Welcome to the torture chamber," and left her.

Jo had barely time to go to the window and look out at the square, enclosed garden, not very well kept or flowery, the main features of which were a dolls pram and a miniature wigwam, before Mrs Matthews arrived and said, "Well, Josephine, let's see what you can do."

Jo, eager to please, recited a poem by Walter de la Mare, and then gave a speech of Viola's from *Twelfth Night*. As soon as she began "I left no ring with her," she knew that Mrs Matthews was impressed.

Miss Summers had always been sparing with praise, but this new teacher, a thin, bespectacled woman, yet with a pleasant, maternal air, believed in appreciation and encouragement. She made some careful comments, saying, "I'm criticising you on a very high level, of course," and repeating the speech, Jo was even better. When the lesson was over she was invited to stay to tea. She had to telephone the St Andrew's and ask, but she was allowed to stay.

Tea was in the dining room, with the whole family present. Mr Matthews, who had come home, briefly, from his shop – he was a chemist – sat at the head of the table, with Mrs Matthews at the other end behind the tea tray. John, the boy who had greeted her, sat next to Jo, facing his two younger sisters, Eileen who was a year or so younger than Jo, and Beth, a captivating three-year-old. Grace was said and Jo enjoyed a splendid meal. There were plates of bread and butter, two kinds of jam in little glass dishes, Marmite and fish paste, their pots standing on saucers with little knives to help yourself, with currant bread and butter, and delicious rock cakes. Conversation was general and there was much cause for laughter. Seeing Jo temporarily without food Marian Matthews instructed her son to "Watch Jo's plate" and his subsequent refusal to avert his eyes from it for one moment caused considerable mirth. Afterwards all the children including Jo helped to clear the table, even Beth carrying an almost empty fish paste pot. The kitchen was inhabited by the daily maid, Elsie, in black, with white cap and apron only slightly less dressy than Patty's afternoon uniform. She was finishing her tea at a corner of the kitchen table, and thanked them for their help.

"We do this to save Elsie's feet," said Eileen.

Jo thought. But she's only a maid" and was mystified. Later the idea seemed to typify the Matthews' way of life.

Although Jo had long ago abandoned her dream of a home in which the central figure was a plump, aproned mother, eternally making apple pies in a cosy kitchen, the Matthews home reminded her of it. After Mr Matthews had returned to his shop, two more girls and another boy arrived. They also were pupils of Mrs Matthews and had come to rehearse a play that was to be presented at an old people's home nearby. They would rehearse in the garden, they decided, because it was a pity to be indoors on such a sunny evening. Jo helped them to carry out kitchen chairs and so on to set the stage and then watched the rehearsal, enjoying John's clowning as an absurd vicar while the girls played two very old-maidish spinsters whose robot servant ran amok. Eileen was splendid as the robot. When Jo left, Mrs Matthews promised her a part in their next production, and Beth hugged her and begged her to come again tomorrow, and Eileen went with her to the front door and waved to her from the porch, calling "Thank you for coming," as Jo reached the bottom of the steps that led down to the pavement.

Walking back to the St Andrews Jo wished that she and Eileen were the same age and went to the same school. She had been told that Eileen took the train to the Grammar School in the next town, having won a scholarship. She was not only clever, but beautiful, with golden brown curly hair and a glowing out-of-doors complexion. Good at so many things too, it appeared, not only school work and acting but playing the flute, and gymnastics. The idea of Eileen joining in anything like 'Calling for Peggy' or following Mrs Osterreicher was ludicrous. She would always have something better to do. And although Jo and Bronwen had given up both of those games, Jo knew that Eileen and Bron would not like each other, and Bron could never fit in to that family as she had done herself that afternoon. She decided not to say much about the Matthews to Bron, and at the same time not to be tempted by her into any activity of which they would disapprove. Bron would probably think they were boring anyway, but they weren't. They were nice. The nicest people she had ever known.

The sun shone on Culvergate that August. Down by the pier the day trippers from London wore Kiss-me-Quick hats, ate fish and chips out of newspapers and had their photographs taken astride long-suffering donkeys. Eastwards in the more salubrious district of Eastonville a concert party gave twice daily performanceces in the Arena bandstand, the sands were crowded; children built sandcastles, boys played cricket or clambered over the slippery rocks to collect crabs, mothers read novels or got on with their knitting or both at once. The ordinary families made little camps, spreading out towels and hiring deckchairs, while the residents of Palmers Bay took tables and chairs out of their canvas huts, set them up on the lower promenade, and put on kettles for tea. They too bought ice cream cornets from passing vendors, posed for itinerant photographers and went swimming in the calm, cold sea at intervals.

People who had decided not to take holidays in view of the uncertainty of the political situation telephoned the St Andrew's to make hasty bookings. Why not enjoy themselves while they could? Beatrice was happy and busy, pleased when Colin Weir made a surprise visit and saw the place full to overflowing, yet running smoothly in the absence of Clive who was away more and more. Early in the season Clive had erected their own hut on its rented site eastwards of the hotel at Palmers Bay. It would seldom be visited by Beatrice, who was busy, and disliked the sands in any case, but Jo would use it often, with Bron, and sometimes Patty would be freed from her duties to take the girls a picnic lunch or tea. Clive himself still managed to spend an hour or so two or three times a week stretched out on an inflated mattress in front of the hut, aquiring the tan of which he was absurdly proud. Between Clive and Patty, the girls, Beatrice convinced herself, were adequately supervised but in fact they were there for hours by themselves, swimming, climbing, visiting the caves at the far end of the bay, walking the breakwaters and generally risking life and limb. Late in the afternoons, when the crowds thinned out they would join a group of their contemporaries to play hide and seek. Some of those that played were in their teens, handsome boys and lively girls who did a lot more hiding than seeking, which rather spoiled the games. But still, it was fun.

Naturally Jo and Bron did not spend all of every day on the sands, they liked to look round the shops, to visit Woolworths in the old town, and to pay sixpence to go on board the lifeboat. One or two afternoons a week Jo helped Patty to prepare teas at the hotel, and they still went to the pictures regularly, even on sunny afternoons sitting in the cool darkness, munching liquorice allsorts or Sharps Kreemy Toffee whilst they were entertained by the monochrome shadows of the stars – Judy Garland and Deanna Durbin, Robert Taylor and Loretta Young and all the others. Best of all, perhaps, was Dorothy Lamour with her short sarong and her black hair falling to her waist, forever on her tropical island, forever the object of a handsome hero's desire. Jo was happier than she had been for weeks, wishing the holidays need never end. She had Bron, she had Patty, she was one of a crowd on the sands, and she had her weekly visits to the Matthews. She never went to the house at any time other than three-thirty on Wednesdays, but she was always invited to tea, and always accepted. When the play was ready for performance at St Mary's Home for the Elderly, Mrs Matthews decided that a humorous poem or two would enhance the programme, so Jo learned Hilaire Belloc's 'Matilda' which was very well received. The old ladies who formed the audience were most appreciative, applauding enthusiastically and begging them to come again. Jo told Bron all about it, and Bron said she supposed it was alright if you liked old people, but she didn't like them herself; she thought they smelt.

"None of these smelt," Jo was offended on behalf of the St Mary's Home ladies.

"You probably didn't notice it," said Bron, adding, "It'll soon be term-time again; we've had half the holidays already. We ought to think of something exciting to do."

Jo said she supposed they ought. She would have to think of something herself, something that would satisfy Bron and yet would not be disapproved of by the Matthews family. They were hardly likely to find out what games she played with Bron, but Jo wanted very much to be the kind of person they liked.

Matilda having served her purpose, Jo was given another poem to learn by Mrs Matthews, and enthusiastic as she was she started work on it as soon as she reached home on the Wednesday following the performance. The sun had left her back bedroom so she curled up on the white tweed settee, carefully removing her sandals first. The room faced north-west, so a glancing shaft of sunlight played on the end wall, It was very light, though after seven o'clock, with the brilliance of clear air and reflections from the sea. The room was perfectly tidy, highlights glinting from polished chromium and sparkling glass, the grey and white striped curtains framing the clean, open view of green and sea. Jo thought of shabby armchairs with flowered covers, a faded carpet littered with toys belonging to a younger sister, and French windows that opened onto a garden with a tennis court and a summerhouse which, in the fantasy world which she sometimes inhabited, was her own secret retreat, her own and Juliet's. She would have, she thought, an older sister too, who knew lots of boys and played the gramophone, and an older brother who would bring his friends home. And the house would be called Willow Lodge, after the one she had read about in *The Girls of Willow Green*. Forgetting her poem, Jo began to think of names for this imaginary family and had just decided on Marguerite for the older sister and Shirley for the younger when she heard her mother entering the apartment and hastily concealed her sandals under the settee.

Beatrice had come up to change for dinner, allowing herself, as usual, time for a drink and a bath. It was an interval when she liked to be joined by Clive, so that she could sink down and kick off her shoes while he poured her a Martini, and she could chat about her day, the problems she had solved, the new ideas she hoped to put into practice, and the tiresomeness of the staff and the elderly residents, who really ought to find somewhere else during the season. But as Clive had already gone off in his uniform and would return late at night or possibly on the following day and she did not feel like being alone she sought what companionship she could from her daughter. After all, she was growing up now, no longer really a child.

"Want a drink? Keep me company?"

Jo, surprised, asked what was available. Beatrice poured sherry into a liqueur glass, not quite filling it and feeling a very modern mother as she did so. She passed this to Jo and poured a larger sherry for herself – it seemed too much bother to mix a Martini.

She sank into an easy chair, although she preferred the settee, already occupied by Jo.

"Did you have a nice time at the Matthews?"

"Oh. Yes, lovely."

"It's been hectic here. I think we'll be full up again this weekend."

179

Jo said, "Good," absently, and went on with her learning.

Persevering, Beatrice asked her, "D'you think you'd like to run a hotel when you're older?"

Jo was amazed at this question. "Oh, NO! I want a proper home."

"But we have a proper home, a beautiful home," and Bea looked round at her favourite room, her triumph. Cool, elegant, luxurious, in perfect taste.

"This isn't a proper home." said Jo. "I mean, well, it isn't homely, its not the kind of place you want to get back to."

For Jo, the big shabby house of her imagination, with the little round summerhouse beyond the tennis court, was the kind of place you wanted to get back to. A place that didn't change, where you would return long after you were grown up, and would go to your old room and it would be just the same as it had always been. Beatrice was hurt.

"Well, I don't know what you want," she said. "Most girls would love to live in a nice modern place like this."

Jo, realising she had said the wrong thing, seized on an aspect of the situation for which her mother could not be blamed.

"But it's a flat, isn't it? Flats aren't the same."

But Beatrice had not lived in a house for years, having spent her girlhood in the flat above the Japanese Tearoom, and, on her marriage to Clive, moved into another. She rose crossly, finding her daughter's company thoroughly tiresome.

"Don't spill that sherry on the settee."

She took her own drink into her bedroom where she undressed for her bath. As she slipped on her fuchsia-coloured dressing gown that matched the furnishings she dwelt on Jo's ingratitude. She had that lovely little bedroom, grey and white to blend with the rest of the decor, but with touches of dusky pink, the divan bed with its luxurious eiderdown, the lamp with its frilled pink shade; she had chosen everything so carefully and Jo had straight away ruined it with her pictures of film stars stuck up on the wall, and now complained that it wasn't a proper home. What on earth did the kid expect? It was a pity they hadn't sent her to boarding school then she might have been more appreciative. Sometimes you really wondered what it was all for, with a husband off out more and more of the time, and only a wretched, ungrateful brat for company.

Later, when, in her black moss crêpe dinner gown and double row of pearls, she decided to inspect the restaurant, she found a number of instances of neglect or carelessness which made it necessary to speak severely to the head waiter. After that she felt better, but there was still coolness and silence between her and Jo as they ate their minestrone soup, sole meunière, and their noisettes of lamb. Jo thought of the Matthews family, seated round their dining room table and then immersed herself in her Willow Lodge fantasy, with Juliet, Marguerite and John – her brother would certainly be called John – and herself and the mother and father, and little Shirley. Dad could be the father of course, she didn't want to change him, but she needed a more motherly figure than Beatrice. Suddenly she thought of Miss Wells, big and fat and yet quite pretty; it was not too difficult to imagine her as the mother of a family. But then she felt ashamed and disloyal, as her own mother having snapped at the waitress, turned to her and said she could have icecream for pudding if she liked.

Later on in bed Jo tried and tried to think of a game that would satisfy Bron, but without success. And on the following Saturday, as they lounged on the sands Bron told her about the secret game she had invented, and which Jo must play, or once more be bereft of her best friend.

Bron had based this new enterprise on a situation in a recently-seen film. The two protagonists, a young handsome man, and a blonde girl, not major stars because this was only a supporting film that happened to be shown with *Mr Deeds Comes to Town*, starring Gary Cooper, were for satisfactory reasons forced to break into a huge country mansion in order to search for evidence of some kind. The plot was convoluted,

181

had something to do with oil wells and neither Jo nor Bron fully understood it. This search formed the climax of the film, building up a series of near discoveries with footsteps that approached and faded, hasty concealments and risky dashes for the stairs. Bron's idea was that they should enter the nearly deserted Princess May, visit some forbidden place such as the sixth-form room, and leave, naturally without being seen. It would, she said, be part of a training scheme she was devising for members of the JoBron Agency, or a sort of test they could set for aspiring detectives.

"But we're not doing that any more."

"We're not following people any more, but you never know when we might get a chance. And we might need more people. If we have a test we shan't get silly ones like Thelma. Only we must do the test ourselves first."

Jo was appalled. The idea seemed to her sneaky, and somehow low-class, but she did not know how to explain this to Bron. She said, "We might get into trouble. Supposing we're caught?"

Bron was impatient. "Oh, that's you all over. Always afraid. If we were caught I'd just say I'd left my holiday reading book in my desk and had come back to get it."

Jo wondered how this excuse would work if they were discovered upstairs in the sixth-form room.

"It's different for you. I've never been a boarder."

"What difference does that make? Anyway, what if someone does see us? It's not like somewhere we have no right to be. It's our school."

Bron's arguments were so often unanswerable. Jo sat silent, then Bron said, "You're always afraid to do anything the least bit exciting."

This was so obviously untrue that Jo wondered which defence to choose first. Hadn't she climbed on the iron struts under the pier when the tide was high and the cold, deep water swishing about beneath? Hadn't she scrambled along the narrow chalk passage that led from the back of the biggest cave at Easton Bay to another cave that opened halfway up the cliff face?

Hadn't she . . . but Bron knew all this as well as she did
herself, yet she would be labelled a coward and a spoilsport
if she did not join in this game that was not really a game at
all. She sighed, but Bron was adamant. They laid their plans,
deciding on dark clothes, and rubber-soled shoes; they chose a
day, the next Tuesday which would be Patty's afternoon off –
Patty was often nosy about where they were going – and they
fixed a time: mid-afternoon when the holiday boarders would
be on the sands with nurse. Then they waited, Jo avoiding the
subject and hoping that something would happen to force Bron
to abandon the idea. If Bron's mother were to die suddenly, or
be taken to hospital, would that be enough? She felt guilty for
wishing such a thing. If Bron herself were to be run over – she
tried to feel guilty about that too but somehow did not, which
was worrying since Bron was her best friend.

Nothing happened, and on the Tuesday morning Bron arrived
early at the St Andrew's to complete the arrangements. In Jo's
bedroom she drew maps of the first and second floors, with which
Jo, always a daygirl, was less familiar. They should each take a
torch, she said, and since Jo did not possess one they spent the rest
of the morning walking to Woolworths and spending all of Jo's
pocket money on a small flashlight. They separated for lunch.
Jo was very silent, but Clive and Bea, absorbed in a discussion
of the day's news, which was very threatening, hardly noticed.
   A few days earlier France and Great Britain had reaffirmed
their pledge to defend Poland, and now Hitler was demanding
that the Polish corridor, Poland's pathway to the sea, and
Danzig, the port to which it led, be ceded to Germany. It was
the end of hope that war could be avoided. The preparations
already made at the hotel, the clearing of the cellars for use
as an air-raid shelter, the labelling of the square, cardboard,
gas-mask boxes, the blackout curtains ready to be hung up at
windows criss-crossed with sticky tape by Clive and the hall
porter, these preparations took on a more sinister quality. It

183

was just a matter of time. And Beatrice had received one of Rosemarie's letters and agreed that Jo should travel to Wales with the school within twenty-four hours of a declaration of war. Clive had agreed to this plan. He wasn't happy about it but there seemed to be no alternative. Culvergate had been bombed in the 1914 war and would certainly be bombed again. But he didn't want Jo to be told until it became necessary. It would only upset her, he said. So her probable departure was not mentioned at the dinner table, and the idea of sleeping in the cellar, and being careful never to show a light seemed to her quite exciting. Beatrice, who had been eleven years old at the start of the earlier war remembered the fear and deprivation of those years and remembered also her own father who had not returned from France.

"You wouldn't be sent abroad, would you?"

"Why not?"

"Well, in catering . . ."

"Troops have to eat abroad."

"Well, perhaps you'll be too old." But Clive was only thirty-eight.

"It seems so unfair, after all we've built up here." She said 'we' though they both knew that the building up had been almost entirely her own achievement.

"War's always unfair," said Clive.

Beatrice thought that he didn't seem particularly worried about the prospect. That, she supposed, was being a man. Staying at home worrying was worse than anything, really, and she loved Clive, in her own way. He suited her, she thought, quite affectionately. She didn't want to lose him, to become a woman on her own. She looked so downcast that he took her hand across the table.

"Cheer up. It may never happen."

This annoyed his wife. What was the point? It was going to happen and it was just like Clive to be an ostrich. She sighed irritably and took away her hand.

* * *

After lunch Rosemarie held a conference with Matron. It looked as though they might well be leaving soon. Unless war were averted at the last moment – and really that moment had already arrived: in a few days' time a coach would arrive at the Princess May to take those of the staff and boarders who had returned early to Wales, while others would be picked up en route by a second coach. Most of the boarders would be going, but it seemed that many of the daygirls might stay in Culvergate. The evacuation of state schoolchildren from the town had been delayed, giving all parents a sense of security that perhaps was not justified. Rosemarie was pleased that she would have the responsibility of Clive's daughter, also feeling that Jo's presence in the school would form a link that she might need, once Clive was absorbed in service life.

When Matron, with instructions to start packing for the holiday boarders, had left, Rosemarie made herself coffee on her gas ring and sat down, to relax for a few moments before going up to sort out her own clothes.

The room was light with the cool brightness of the seaside, though it was nearly eight o'clock. How nice, she thought, if Clive, whom she had not seen for several days, were sitting with her now, discussing plans, giving advice. Well, she didn't know about advice. He didn't seem to be a particularly perspicacious man, but he was considerate and charming, and once she had accepted the fact that he had neither her business acumen nor her wide-ranging imagination, she had found him very lovable. Brains, she thought, weren't everything. And her life of late had been very satisfying, combining professional success and a love affair with a very very attractive man. That Sports Day, at the end of last term, was that to be remembered always as the happiest day she had ever had, never to be repeated? The obvious success of the school, with so many rich-looking parents, the splendid way the girls had sung the school song, and Clive receiving his prize as though butter wouldn't melt in his mouth. The Sunday night, at

185

the Hunter's Moon, had been memorable. Now she might lose all of it, her school and her lover. How long did they have? Would war be declared tomorrow? Or next week? Would there be even one more Sunday night at the Hunter's Moon? Almost certainly there would not. But Clive had his key, any afternoon he might arrive unannounced. Their arrangement was that he would go straight up to her bedroom, on the top landing where the only other bedroom was occupied by staff not at present in residence, and knock on the floor so that in the sitting room below she would hear him. They would always be safe until five o'clock, unless the weather turned really bad and the girls came in early. Even then, was he not the father of a pupil? Once down the first staircase she could see him out through the front door quite legitimately. The main thing was never to look furtive. But how many more times could she expect to see him? The TA was now genuinely absorbing most of the time he had once claimed for it. Sighing she climbed the stairs to her bedroom, stepping heavily, feeling middle-aged and depressed. The bed was neatly made but she turned back the counterpane and picked up the pillow on which his head had lain a few days earlier. She pressed her face into it, imagining that she could still smell the brilliantine with which he smoothed his brown, wavy hair – the wave he disliked and tried so hard to flatten. She was, she knew, behaving like a love-sick girl, but who cared? There was no one there to see.

Chapter Fourteen

JO and Bron slipped into the school by the basement entrance, which admitted them to a corridor which led to the kitchens – strangely situated as far as possible from the dining room – the practice rooms and the boarders' cloakrooms. The odour of years of stewed meat and boiled cabbage, combined with the powerful effulgence of sweaty plimsolls and lacrosse boots would have been overwhelming if they had noticed it, but they did not. Had the basement smelled of fresh air instead, they would have wondered what was amiss.

Surprisingly, the sound of the A Minor scale, hesitantly played, drifted mournfully from one of the practice rooms. The kitchens were silent, and Bron and Jo crept up the linoleum-covered stairs to the back hall, passing the door to the playground by which they could perfectly well have entered. But creeping through the basement was more exciting. The three classrooms in this area were naturally empty.

In the oppressive silence the dusty air weighed upon them. The shabbiness of their surroundings was more obvious than when the stairs and corridors and classrooms were thronged with people. They peered through the glass panes in the brown doors, looking in at dead rooms, with rows of scarred desks, and grey blackboards, noticing shabby floor covering and chipped paintwork that had never previously been apparent. Bron, showing off, knocked lightly on the door of the staffroom, and hearing no sound, opened it.

"It's alright, There's no one here."

She went in. Jo remained outside, shuddering with fear.

"Bron, come out. You musn't. We'd get into awful trouble. Do come out. Bron. Supposing somebody comes."

"There's nobody here to come. They're not back yet."

"What about Matron?"

"She wouldn't care."

"And Miss Wells."

"She never comes here. Don't be so soppy. Come in and have a look. Its so small, you'd never believe . . ."

Jo put her head round the door and seeing nothing too alarming, crossed the threshold to stand just inside. The room was indeed small. There were half a dozen shabby armchairs of various sizes set against the walls, a scratched dining table taking up most of the central space, bookshelves, cupboards and a mirror over the fireplace. This room, having been intended for a servants' hall, was notably unpretentious, its main feature being a black grate set between ugly cracked tiles, with a brown-painted surround. On the mantelshelf a small clock sat silent, on one of the chairs was some forgotten fawn-coloured knitting, but nothing else lay about. The maid who had cleaned the room at the end of the previous term had arbitrarily stuffed away the few overlooked papers and scattered books. The curtains, porridge-coloured, framed a dismal view of the asphalted playground.

"It's so small," repeated Jo, in a whisper. Was this really the secret place where Miss Whitehouse, Miss Colman and the rest of those superior beings, lived and moved when they were not actually teaching?

Bron was wandering about, trying an easy chair, opening a cupboard.

"I can smell Miss Craig's BO," she said. "It must be awful in here with her."

Jo thought she was imagining this, but the room was undoubtedly stuffy.

"I'm going to let in some air." Bron pushed up the lower half of the sash window.

"This is the one they lean out of to yell at us," she said, leaning out herself. This was true, break-times were punctuated by the sound of the sash being raised and an irate voice calling for a reduction in noise.

"Do shut it, Bron, someone could get in."

"We'll shut it on the way out."

"Let's go now. We've done what we said. Come on."

"We haven't done anything yet. We've got to go upstairs."

"Why?"

"Because we have."

"We've seen the staffroom. Can't we go now?"

"Can't we go now?" Bron mimicked her plea cruelly. "You can if you like. If you want to let me down."

In their code, letting down a friend was unforgiveable but Jo was mystified. Would she be letting Bron down? Couldn't they both go? In any case they must not separate. To be discovered together would be appalling, to be discovered alone unspeakable. She had no faith that Bron's flexible code of honour would force her to admit her complicity. So she stayed. They left the room, turned to the right and crept along the wide passage that ran parallel to the front of the house to open out into the main entrance hall, with its carpet, display of flowers and the door to the sacred "visitors' room." Jo was relieved that she was not obliged to enter it, but Bron's objective was the broad central flight of stairs which led not to classrooms but to more interesting apartments. Jo followed her, trembling. They were doing something wrong. Not just in an against-the-rules sense, but something shifty, of which to be ashamed. In a whisper she urged Bron to turn back, but there was no stopping her now. She was excited, reckless.

"I'm going to see where Collie sleeps," she said.

The large front room on this floor was a dormitory, with six beds. Nurse slept in the smaller one next to it. At the back five teachers shared two quite spacious rooms. There was a bathroom with two baths in it, screened from the room by curtains and opening off this, two lavatories. Handwritten notices in metal frames were fixed to the bedroom doors, stating the names of the occupiers. None of those on this floor bore the name of Miss Colman. Jo gave a despairing sigh. If only they could find Collie's room and then go back. She would leave openly by the nearest door rather than transverse the corridor again.

"I'm going on up."

Bron was already mounting the narrower staircase to the second floor. Desperate with anxiety Jo set her foot reluctantly on the first stair. Then, just above them a door opened, voices were heard, the door closed and firm, somewhat heavy footsteps crossed the linoleum-covered landing above. Bron turned, almost knocking over Jo, who hestitated, unsure whether her friend would permit a retreat.

"Go ON," hissed Bron in a stage whisper. They ran down the stairs, and along to the back entrance. Closing the door behind them, they ran down the steps to the playground then round the corner of the building, past the garage where Miss Wells kept her new Morris Minor and out into the street. There they slowed down and walked sedately towards the sea. Only then did Jo remember the staffroom window. Bron said it didn't matter, but Jo thought that if no one closed it, the school might be burgled in the night, everyone could be murdered in their beds and it would be their fault.

It was a relief to Jo when Bron said that her mother had insisted that that she return home by teatime. She added that she would call for her the next morning but Jo said no, she was going to Mrs Matthews in the afternoon for her elocution lesson, she needed to practice and would not be able to to see Bron till Thursday. At that moment she would have preferred to avoid Bron's company indefinitely, but she knew from experience that this feeling would wear off.

The foyer was empty when she entered the St Andrews. She went up to the private apartment where her mother was already having tea.

"You're late, Jo." she said. "You've missed Daddy, and heaven knows when he'll be back. I suppose you realise there's going to be a war."

"Daddy hasn't gone away, has he?"

"How should I know? He's in the Army now. They could send him off anywhere, at a moment's notice."

Beatrice rose. "I must get back to the office. Don't go out again tonight."

"But Mum! Its not five o'clock yet!"

"You heard what I said." Beatrice put down her cup and left Jo alone. In her bedroom she smoothed her already immaculate hair, powdered her face, renewed her dark red lipstick and changed her high-heeled black court shoes for another pair. These were no more comfortable or less tiring to wear, but she had heard that frequent changing of shoes rested the feet. In her case this was necessary, years of high heels and pointed toes having given her corns and an incipient bunion.

In the restaurant every available member of staff was helping to put up blackout curtains. Two thirds of the hotel was to be shut up at once in the event of war being declared, so only twenty bedrooms, the bars, the restaurant and the foyer needed the heavy black drapes. Bea had a team of seamstresses working in the lounge. Colin Weir had applauded her preparations, and believed the hotel could be kept open for a time at least, and when Clive was called up she would become manageress officially. It was a relief to know this, and that he would not put in another manager over her head. The Knight's Bar, below ground level, should, they thought, prove even more popular than before, so it was an ill wind, and they had air-raid shelters ready-made in the wine-cellars which ran underneath the building. Beatrice and her secretary were making large notices headed IN THE CASE OF AN AIR RAID WARNING, giving directions to the cellar stairs. These were to be placed in all the bedrooms and in prominent positions downstairs.

Later that evening, to Beatrice's surprise, Patty appeared in

191

the office with a letter from her father. This carefully written note stated in no uncertain terms that his daughter was no longer to sleep in the glass dome, which would be unsafe if bombs were dropped and if she could not be moved to another room she would be forced to give notice. Rather proudly, Patty laid the envelope in front of her employer.

"I suppose he's right," said Beatrice, "what with the blackout and everything. You'd better take one of the single rooms on the second floor until there's a staff room available. That way you'll be near Jo if anything happens," she added vaguely.

"And another thing, Madam," said Patty nervously, "Ken and me want to get married . . . so . . ."

"Married?" Bea was startled into giving the girl her full attention." But you're only . . . what? Are you sixteen yet?"

"Oh yes, Madam, I was sixteen last week, and now Ken's joined the Army . . ." Ken had indeed joined the Territorials, enthusiastically encouraged by Clive, when he was filling up the car with petrol. Bea looked at Patty. Her straight greasy dark hair, her pale skin covered with Poudre Tokalon in a rather too peachy shade, her pretty mouth, sticky with bright red lipstick, her lace apron pristine over her well-worn black crêpe dress. Married! This child!

"Surely, Patty, you're far too young."

"Yes, well, that's what my Dad says, but Ken says I might as well have the allowance, and anyway, in a war you never know what's going to happen, you might as well be happy while you can."

"I see. Well, I think you should listen to your father." Bea wondered if Patty knew anything about birth control. It seemed unlikely that her mother, with her ten children, would be in a position to inform her. Poor kid!

"Well let me know when the wedding is. We'll get Chef to make you a cake. You can stay on here while we're open. I suppose Ken will be called up straight away."

"Oh, thank you ever so much, Madam, and Madam, we

192

was hoping that you and Miss Jo could come to the wedding."

"Well, I'll try to come certainly, Patty, but it looks as though
Jo will be going away with the school."

And I shall be too busy, thought Bea. How painfully out of
place she would feel. She said, "Well, go now and move your
things, and see that Jo does her practise."

"She was learning her piece for tomorrow when I came down,"
said Patty. 'She's ever so good at that elocution isn't she? How
she remembers all them words! And thanks ever so much about
the cake, Madam. I'll tell Mum and she'll be ever so pleased."

"Alright Patty, go along now."

Patty left the office and went back to clear away the tea things,
which she would wash up in the kitchenette. Jo was learning a
poem about daffodils that seemed to her to express exactly the
joy and purity that characterised the Matthews household. She
would stand up to Bron in the future, refuse to do things which
she knew would be disapproved of by Eileen Matthews, and
her brother, let alone Mrs Matthews. She could imagine Eileen
being baffled by this latest escapade, saying, "But why? Why did
you want to go into the school in holiday time? What was the
point?" and she pictured John looking at her with a kindly yet
puzzled expression, as though she were some animal with strange
unpleasant habits. She thought that the next time she and Bron
went out together she would persuade her to go to Woolworths
in search of American film magazines; she would buy her one
if necessary. She walked about her bedroom declaiming the
words of her poem, disliking her own thin fairness whenever
she passed the mirror, and comparing herself unfavourably with
rosy-cheeked Eileen's wholesome open-air appearance.

Rosemarie put away the Morris Minor, steering it in to the
narrow garage rather slowly and uncertainly. She had only
recently learned to drive and having completed her course of
lessons had been out for an hour's practice. She had bought

it partly because driving to the Hunter's Moon would be more convenient than going by train and waiting for Clive at Warne Bay station, but she had found herself a nervous driver and had never yet made the journey by road. She wanted to have the car with her if they were forced to evacuate the school to Wales, but doubted her own ability to drive it there safely. Besides, she really ought to be with the girls in one of the coaches, in case anything untoward happened. Matron and nurse would be there of course and they would be picking up most of the teaching staff en route, but it was all very worrying and she did not know when she would see Clive again.

And there was another little worry that nagged at her. She thought she had heard intruders in the school earlier that afternoon. Only a shuffling sound on the central staircase which she might have imagined, but she hadn't imagined noticing that the staff room window was wide open when she went to get the car out. No one had any occasion, or any right, to go in there during the holidays. Normally one of the maids would clean it before term started, but that was all. Had one of the six holiday boarders trespassed on this forbidden ground? If so who? Not the two seniors who were far too conscious of their position, certainly not the German girls and the younger ones would not be tall or strong enough to raise the heavy glass pane. And Elsa was far too lacking in initiative to enter a room without being directed to do so, let alone open a window. Returning inside to close the window, she noticed how shabby the room was, how meanly furnished. Well, it didn't matter now, it seemed very unlikely that it would ever function as a staffroom again. She heaved a sigh. Unless the crisis was averted the removal men would soon be packing desks, books, bedding, crockery, so that they could precede the coaches to Llanbedr Hall, the house which Rosemarie had never seen but which the agents had told her would suit her purpose admirably, and anyway there wasn't much choice. Places in "safe" areas were being snapped up and she was lucky to have secured it.

Had there been an intruder? Should she give orders that the back doors were to be kept locked? How inconvenient. Surely it wasn't necessary. Even the main door was not locked during the term, when there were people about. Sighing, she rang for Elsa to bring her tea. She had bought herself some rather nice cakes at the Japanese Tearoom, a chocolate-sided one, a macaroon with a large cherry on top, and a little sponge cake with lemon icing topped by a blob of cream. Perhaps she wouldn't eat all three. On the other hand, perhaps she would. You had to have something.

Jo spent the next afternoon at the Matthews, staying, as usual, to tea after her lesson and rehearsing a play called *The Grand Chams Diamond*, though hopes of actually presenting it at the St Mary's Home were fading. After that she was allowed to help Eileen put Beth to bed, and then to read the little girl a story about a toy golliwog who came to life. The golliwog's owner was said to fail in loving him because of his black face, but the said owner's mother solved the problem by recovering his face with a bit of an old white sheet, and embroidering his features anew. Beth was unaccountably upset by this story, cradling her own shabby golliwog in her arms and saying, "I'd have loved him whatever colour his face was."

John and Eileen were deputed to walk part of the way home with Jo, but before this, after Beth was asleep, they had half an hour to spare. John suggested drawing, and Eileen said painting would be better as far as she was concerned, and Jo was delighted with the idea. She hoped to impress Eileen with some original designs for a film-star wardrobe. They sat round the dining-room table, speaking very little, absorbed in artistic creation. John was working on a design for an ocean liner, which he was drawing in section, with a great deal of minute detail. Jo thought this was clever but boring. Eileen was copying a snow scene from a book of paintings lent by her father.

"You have to realise," she said, "that white isn't ever

195

really white." She carefully applied a pale mauve wash to the distant fields.

For once Jo had no wish to emulate her. When Mrs Matthews came in to say it was time they cleared up, Jo and Eileen had companionably changed paintings with the idea of appraising each other's work. Jo thought the snow scene wonderfully painted, but then it was only a copy and didn't really count. Eileen, with a slight frown, gazed at Jo's dashingly executed evening gown, backless to the waist, in the height of fashion and trimmed with white fur round the hem.

Eileen's mother looked disapprovingly over her shoulder.

"What's this? Eileen, why are you wasting your time on this sort of thing? I certainly hope you'll never wear it!"

Jo blushed. Eileen said quickly. "Of course not. Neither would Jo. It's just a design. For someone in a film. I think Jo's very clever."

Mrs Matthews said, "Oh, I see, yes of course, Jo. It's excellent of its kind."

That she did not approve of its kind was obvious.

The painting things were quickly tidied away and Jo, John and Eileen set off towards the St Andrew's, first through streets of Edwardian houses, then across Southdown Road and down an avenue of newer, brighter-looking homes to the seafront. Conversation was a little awkward. John talked of films he had seen, and though they all seemed to have had some educational content he was at pains to let her know he found nothing distasteful in going to the cinema or in designing costumes, and Eileen said Jo ought to try painting portraits, and mentioned portraits she had seen in the National Gallery. Jo, whose few visits to London had been for the purpose of seeing a pantomime and wandering round Selfridges was not comforted by this. Their too-obvious kindness made her feel inferior and she was glad when they reached the corner, when she could say, "It's not far now. Thank you for coming."

They assured her it was no trouble. Then they turned away

from her, walking, as she did, a few steps, and then all three began to run.

The next day Clive returned briefly at lunchtime, after a radio announcement that Army and RAF reserves were being called up. He was excited and happy, expecting soon to be posted to a new regiment, where he would be in charge of catering. Having by now run many weekend camps for part-time soldiers he felt reasonably confident of his ability to do the job. After all, if he was ever in any doubt about quantities to order, for instance, he could always get on the telephone to Bea. He would be Major Livingstone before he knew where he was. For the moment he was doing quite a lot of running around in his own Hillman Minx, commandeering premises and supplies of food, snatching a few minutes for a brief visit home to collect more underwear and other necessities. He kissed Beatrice and hugged Jo and they both went down to the foyer to see him off, Jo openly weeping and Bea feeling more bereft than she had ever expected as he drove away with a cheerful wave out of the car window.

"Well, now we'll just have to look after one another," said Bea. A remark which gave Jo considerable food for thought. She had never really noticed that her father looked after her, except that he took her to school in the car when it was raining. It was Patty who looked after her if anyone did, and Patty was still there. Had her father looked after her mother? She didn't think so, though once when Beatrice had caught a severe cold Clive had told her to go to bed, but she hadn't gone. She'd stayed in the office drinking hot lemonade with whisky in it, and got on with her work. It seemed to his daughter that Clive's absence would make very little practical difference to their lives, but she would certainly miss his company at meals, his kindness, his interest and his jokes. Mum never made jokes.

In fact the whole atmosphere of the St Andrews was different now that Clive had finally taken his leave. Patty was miserable, because Captain Livingstone was so nice and always made it up to you somehow if Mrs L was in a bad mood, and also because his leaving meant that Ken would soon be going too. The elderly residents, worried about their future, had lost their defender and advocate, their concerned receiver of complaints who had time to chat with them and didn't make them feel they were a nuisance, who would sometimes stand Colonel Webster a small brandy, or one of the ladies a dry sherry, who would even sit down and shout at poor old deaf Miss Kember when he had the time, which had been quite often before he joined the Territorials.

"What are you going to do now?" asked Bea. Jo said rather dispiritedly that she didn't know and Bea said kindly that she could have Bronwen to tea if she liked. She had to suggest something, the poor kid looked so wretched, and though she didn't care for the other child she couldn't really think of anything else. She fleetingly considered suggesting they went to the pictures but somehow she didn't like the idea of Jo in a cinema with everything so uncertain. People said the Germans would not attack without warning but Beatrice had no faith that this would not happen.

"Go and ring her up," she said, "and I'll see that you get an extra nice tea."

"Thanks, Mum," said Jo, and went away to do as she was told. Not very enthusiastically, Bea thought. Honestly what did you do with kids? She went to talk to the receptionist and forgot about the special tea.

Bron duly appeared, but they did not spend the afternoon indoors. It was bright and sunny and Bron wanted to go out. When they were out she suggested another illicit visit to the Princess May. Jo suggested one or two alternatives but these were scorned by Bron so they slipped in by the area door again, and toured the basement and the ground floor. Jo refused to go upstairs, which annoyed Bron who then insisted on using one of the lavatories, the one with the extra noisy flush, by the flower room. But they heard no one, the place seemed utterly deserted, a circumstance for which Bron quite unfairly held Jo to blame. They walked back without speaking, and Bron left as soon as they had finished their disappointing tea.

On the Saturday morning, after listening to the news on the radio, several more guests left the St Andrew's, and one of the residents was removed by a daughter-in-law in a chauffeur-driven Rolls Royce. Since Mrs Palmer-Brown had for three years been accommodated in a small back room with a view of the fire escape this was surprising. Beatrice reproached herself for not having taken advantage of the situation.

In the morning Jo did her piano practice and thought about going on with her dress designs, but somehow the joy had gone – her creativity was at a low ebb. Why had Mrs Matthews not liked it when she thought Eileen was drawing clothes instead of painting her snow scene? What was wrong with it? Was it because they went to church? Jo had heard them speak of attending the Sunday morning service and John was going to be confirmed. The last time Jo had been inside a church was six years earlier, when she had been a small bridesmaid at her cousin's wedding. Perhaps they thought drawing clothes made you vain, or that low-backed dresses were rude. If so, lots of rude ladies came to the St Andrew's Hotel. Jo asked Patty if she thought there was anything wrong with wanting to be a dress designer, and Patty said no, she thought it was a good idea, and Jo being so clever at it, would become rich. This was not altogether a satisfactory answer. Jo didn't think riches would endear her to the Matthews family.

Later on, just before lunch, she took some drawings down to Bea, for further reassurance and Bea, after a perfunctory glance, took hold of the paper, examined the sketch of a skating outfit – bright scarlet, with a minimal skirt – and said it was extraordinarily good, and perhaps Jo should go to art school one day. The shortness of the skirt did not seem to worry her as the low back had evidently worried Mrs Matthews. And yet

199

Mrs Matthews was nice, and Jo wanted to be like her, more than she wanted to be like Patty or her mother.

So the last thing she felt like doing that afternoon was to go back to the Princess May, but when Bron came round and said it would probably be their last afternoon together because her father was coming out of retirement to help with the War, and they were all going to London, where she was very likely to be killed by a bomb, Jo gave in.

Chapter Fifteen

SO THIS was Bron's afternoon, and because she wanted to go by way of the promenade that was what they did. They peered over the low fence at the edge of the cliff and saw the rolls of barbed wire that were meant to repel an invasion, and Jo thought with regret of a new bathing costume she had left in the beach hut and now would have to abandon. Other people had dismantled and removed their huts as soon as instructed to do so, but Clive had been too busy, or forgotten, or both.

"I wonder where we'll be next summer," Bron gazed thoughtfully down on the deserted sands.

"I expect I'll still be here." and Jo looked forward with relief to a summer without Bron, without 'dares' and without the continual mild sense of guilt she had felt recently.

"You won't be here, you'll be going away with the school."

" 'Course I won't, that's only the boarders."

"Well, my father says they'll have to evacuate the whole town soon; no one will be allowed to live here."

"Well, we'll have to, because of the hotel."

"Anyway, it's not only the boarders, its everybody. I'd be going if we weren't going to London. We'll be alright there. There are plenty of air-raid shelters. My father says we'll be as well off in London as anywhere."

The probability of death overtaking her seemed to have dwindled, now that Jo had acceded to her plans for the afternoon. They left the promenade where so sadly few people were enjoying the late summer afternoon, and turned up through the square towards the school.

Hopefully, Jo said, "I don't see any point in this, now we can't be detectives any more."

"What does that matter? It's fun anyway. You said you'd come. Let's be spies, looking for secret plans. If we're caught we'll be tortured to death."

Jo thought such a pretence was unnecessary, the game itself was disturbing enough. Bron modified it a little.

"I'm the chief spy and I'm testing you to see if you'll be any good. To see if you're brave enough."

They went in the side gates and round to the back, with excuses about visiting the holiday boarders ready in case anyone was in the playground. They passed beneath the staffroom window, and descended the steps to the basement door. Inside, the usual stuffy smell assailed them, though weaker now towards the end of the holidays. The kitchens were empty and no one was practising. In one of the cell-like practice rooms Bron dropped some sheet music down behind the piano, in the cloakroom she muddled up the lacrosse boots. Jo watched, not taking part.

"What are you doing all this for?"

"Because you are so boring."

"But what's the point? If there's no one here?"

"We don't know for sure yet. Hitler might change his mind. Come on, let's go up."

There were three staircases from the basement, which ran under all three of the houses. Bron chose the middle one that came up near the flower room in the passage off the main hall. It was the most conspicuous, the one where they were most likely to be caught, or so Jo believed. Her heart was thudding. Once this was over she need never see Bron again, never be made to do wrong things that she didn't want to do.

They stood in the hall, listening. The grandfather clock ticked, that was all. The doors that they could see, to the visitors' room on their right, to classrooms on their left, were closed.

"You go along to the dining room, go upstairs . . . and bring . . . bring some soap from the top bathroom. There's a staff bathroom on the top floor at that end. I'll go this way, meet you by the practice rooms in five minutes. And remember, we're spies, we don't give one another away. If I'm caught, I won't say anying about you, and you mustn't say anything about me. I'll count five, and then we'll go."

They stood silent for a moment, then, "One. Two. Three. Four. Five."

Jo tiptoed away along the passage towards the dining room. At the foot of the stairs she looked back. Bron was standing still, watching her. She had not moved. Jo started to retrace her steps, but Bron made a vehement gesture, telling her to go on up, and then disappeared in the direction of the flower-room door. Jo went slowly up the stairs.

It was dark because there was no window to give light, only fan-lights over the doors of the various rooms, and a skylight on the top landing. This part of the house contained only one classroom, the long narrow one on the ground floor at the back, where they had tormented Miss Perkins. Jo did not want to remember that. And it had been her own idea, she could not blame Bron for that shameful episode. The first-floor landing had parquet patterned linoleum, a slight improvement on the plain brown in the rest of the building. Jo thought this was because of its proximity to Miss Wells's sitting room, the door of which was the one facing her, now that she had changed direction on the half landing and mounted to the top of the second flight. She meditated briefly on the idea of knocking on that door and sort of giving herself up. She wanted to be anywhere – anywhere, at the dentist's, in hospital, lost on a desert island – anywhere other than where she was. One of the four doors was open and she glanced in. If it was a bathroom she could take the soap and go; the test would be over. But it was a staff bedroom. On the wall were travel posters, with pictures of Greece and sunny Spain, and a dramatic one depicting the prow of a Cunard liner. Jo was surprised, she had never seen the teachers as ordinary human beings who wanted to go to sunny Spain or even to brighten up their sleeping quarters.

A board creaked behind her. She turned, expecting some voice to say, "What are you doing here?" and all the reasons and excuses flew round in her head like birds, each one more inadequate than the last. But there was no one.

She set her foot on the next flight of stairs, holding the bannisters as though she was weak and unsteady. At the top she saw three doors, one of which stood open to reveal a bathroom. It was small and tidy and there was a smell of lavender from the lilac-coloured tablet of soap in the soap dish. This bathroom was not like their smart black and white one at the St Andrew's. The walls were green, covered with shiny paper that was supposed to look like tiles, the bath had a dark wood surround and the brass taps needed cleaning. Apart from the soap there was nothing personal in the room, but Miss Wells, if you got close to her, often smelled of lavender – the soap would be a hallmark of success. As Jo stretched out her hand to pick it up, she heard the groan. A dreadful, gasping, long drawn-out moan like somebody dying. Terrified and appalled Jo stood on the landing, listening. It seemed to her that somebody was calling. Someone who was lying ill and forgotten, and helpless, unattended in this far corner of the deserted building. Jo hesitated. Obviously whoever it was had no intention of chasing her down the stairs. She could almost certainly get out now, without being seen. Then when she was three steps down she heard the sound again. She could not ignore it. Excuses could come later, nothing mattered anyway if you saved someone's life. She would fetch water, telephone the doctor, find Matron. She retraced her steps. Softly, carefully, so as not to disturb the sufferer, she opened the heavy-panelled door of the front bedroom.

For a moment she tried to understand the tangle of nudity, of huge white, blue-veined thighs, that hung over brown shoulders, of bedclothes pushed to the floor, of massive naked breasts. Then a head was raised from the pillow, and the eyes stared at her, the

204

legs jerked and then there was another face peering over the fat white thigh.

Jo ran, not quietly, down all the stairs, back through the hall down to the basement because even now she could not let Bron down. She managed to get outside before she was sick and when they got to the front she sat down on a municipal seat – they were meant for old people, she had never sat on one before – and shivered. She wouldn't tell Bron. She wouldn't tell Bron she had seen her father and Miss Wells doing something. Something so unspeakable that she could never be able to forget it, however hard she tried.

As soon as she could, she rose and set off towards home. Bron kept pace with her, asking questions in reply to which Jo could only shake her head. That was her answer, too, when they reached the St Andrew's and Bron asked if she could come in.

"I might be going tomorrow," she called, but Jo was already halfway across the foyer.

Running along the front, she had been running to her mother, to unburden herself of the horror, to confess her guilty knowledge, but as soon as the hotel was in sight she abandoned this idea. She had never confided in Bea, and anyway there were no words, what could she say? Patty? Could she tell Patty? But she couldn't burden Patty with what she had seen. Patty did not know that people did things like this. Or were her father and Miss Wells the only ones?

She ran along the second-floor corridor to the private apartment. In her bedroom, breathless, she pulled off her shorts and her jumper, and got into bed, though it was only half past three and the sun was shining. She dived down into the middle of the bed, under the white, cool sheet, the blanket, the pink bedspread and the flowered eiderdown. She pressed her eyelids with her fingers, trying to keep out the picture that would not go away. She tried to think of something else. Eventually she started to whisper the daffodil poem and, some time later, fell asleep.

*   *   *

205

Patty roused her soon after seven. "Where were you at teatime? You didn't say you were going out?"

"I was here."

"Well, I've been looking for you everywhere. What are you doing in bed? Don't you feel well?"

"I'm alright."

"Your Mum says you're to go down to dinner."

"Is Daddy there?"

" 'Course not. He's gone, hasn't he? So's Ken. They're miles away by now."

But he hadn't gone. Or he had come back.

"Are you sure?"

" 'Course I'm sure. Why? Have you done something you shouldn't? If I was you it's your Mum I'd worry about, not your Dad. Come on, get up, Jo, and put a dress on. I've got to do the guest rooms. And don't forget to put clean socks on, or are you wearing stockings?"

Jo's attainment of puberty had been marked by a gift of two pairs of silk stockings and a lace-trimmed suspender belt, from her grandmother. She kept them for 'best'. When Jo had risen Patty went to attend to the turning down of beds and tidying that visitors expected to be done while they were at dinner. Jo dressed, washed her face at the wash basin in the corner of her room, combed her hair and supposed that somehow she would have to go on with life. Either that, or commit suicide, and she didn't really want to do that. She would have to go on, burdened and oppressed, doing ordinary things which wouldn't seem ordinary any more, hoping never to see her father, never never to return to the Princess May. She hoped there really would be a war, though even that was wicked of course, because people would be killed, but then the school would be taken away.

Although there were very few occupied tables in the restaurant, Bea had changed for dinner as usual.

"Bron's going to London tomorrow." For some reason Jo wanted to mention Bron's name.

"Is she? Well, you'll miss her I suppose, but I don't think she was a good influence on you. You're better off with her out of the way."

If only her mother knew just how bad Bron's influence had been; if only she could know without actually having to be told. She might say it was not Jo's fault, she might say none of it mattered. Jo ate silently, brooding on this faint ray of hope.

"I suppose you'd better get Patty to help you pack. You must have grown out of your winter uniform. I'll order a new one to be sent. You won't want it for a couple of weeks."

Jo, picking desultorily at her steak and kidney pie, looked up.

"Pack? What for? Where am I going?"

"To Wales, of course. With the school."

"But you didn't say. You didn't say I had to go. I thought I was staying here."

"Of course we said. You don't listen. You've known for ages. We've talked about it."

"I knew the school was going. I thought it was just the boarders. I can't go. I can't."

"Oh, don't be ridiculous, I've got enough to worry about without you being difficult. I don't suppose it will be for long."

"But I'm a daygirl. It's the boarders who are going. There won't be room for daygirls."

"Of course there will, it's all arranged. You've got to go somewhere safe, and you've got to go to school. What do you want after that?"

"Nothing. I can't eat any more."

Bea looked at the almost undiminished contents of Jo's plate. The child looked pale and anxious, but it was not surprising. Perhaps she understood more about war than they had realised. Those current events lessons. She'd always thought they were a mistake. Perhaps Jo thought there would be an invasion. Perhaps she had heard Mrs Osterreicher's terrible stories and was afraid. Of course she must be afraid. Bea herself was afraid, if not of an

207

invasion, then of air raids, of losing the hotel, of not knowing where Clive was, and what the future held.

"You can have a strawberry sundae," she said. "Just for once."

Jo said thank you, but when it came, a mixture of ice cream, strawberries, chopped nuts and whipped cream, with extra wafers because Chef knew she liked them, she ate it without enjoyment. She did not think she would ever enjoy anything again.

Rosemarie ate supper with the boarders as usual. Naturally the conversation was all about the move to Wales. She assured the younger children that their parents were perfectly safe in India and Singapore, and discussed the probable course of events rationally, if optimistically with the seniors. To the German girls, whose family had not been in touch, she offered what comforting words she could. They sat side by side, seldom speaking, the older girl trying, and failing, to speak cheerfully to her sister.

There was virtually no hope now; that was why Clive snatched half an hour during an official trip back to Culvergate, to say goodbye. The girls were out for a walk with Nurse, matron packing bedlinen, no one about when he entered by the south door. Having been in possession of a key for weeks, he had used it only three or four times. He would really have preferred to restrict their meetings to the Hunter's Moon. So when, writing in the sitting room, she had heard the pre-arranged signal – three muffled taps on the floor above, a pause, then two more – she had not really believed it could be him, but had mounted the stairs hopefully, though half expecting to find herself deceived, perhaps by the breeze from the open window knocking over a photograph frame or a vase.

He was standing in the middle of the room. This was his last chance to see her, he said. He wanted to say goodbye, and thank you for all the wonderful times, and perhaps one day they would meet again.

But Rosemarie could not let it go at that. No more Hunter's Moon, certainly, no more Sunday nights, but he'd get leave, they'd be able to meet, halfway between wherever he was stationed, and Llanbedr Hall. Every few months.

Well, he didn't know about that. He might be abroad, he'd have to see how things went. At the moment, with so much responsibility . . .

Rosemarie realised that he was trying to say a permanent goodbye, her love affair was over. As he stood before her, handsome in his well-cut khaki, she thought it wouldn't be long before he found another mistress if he wanted one. And she wasn't looking her best. She'd had a busy, tiring week, writing letters, making arrangements, organising the departure which even then might not actually happen. Her blue linen button-through dress was crumpled; her hair was a little untidy; she had taken no trouble to arrange it becomingly; she was wearing no make-up.

He held her quite tenderly, however, saying, "I've been really fond of you."

The past tense of this statement was not exactly reassuring. She was losing him, she knew, and wanted him to leave her with the reality of their physical love fresh in his mind and body. So that he would remember not a tired, overweight middle-aged woman, but his love, mistress of the exotic pleasure-prolonging caress.

He drew back a little, sensing her desire. "I've only got ten minutes, darling . . ."

Rosemarie, however, was used to having things her way. They moved to the divan with which she had replaced her parents' high double bed. It did not occur to her to lock the door. No one ever intruded on Miss Wells – her privacy had always been absolute.

Chapter Sixteen

THE NEXT morning, warned by early news bulletins, guests and staff at the St Andrews gathered to listen to the Prime Minister. At 11.15 the bars were deserted, the reception desk unattended, the games room silent. In the lounge the residents clung to their usual chairs, visiting couples seated themselves close together, some of them holding hands, parents hushed their children, and Jo and Bea stood with senior members of staff just inside the door. Patty was with the rest in the kitchen, where Chef and his assistants paused only briefly in their preparations for luncheon to hear Mr Chamberlain announce that, since Herr Hitler had not undertaken to withdraw his troops from Poland, England was now at war with Germany. No one wanted to hear any more. In the lounge someone turned the wireless down though not off, and Colonel Webster said he needed a drink and led a partial exodus.

Bea said that coffee would be served to those remaining in the lounge and sent Jo to the kitchen to order it. She then reminded them that, in the event of an air raid, they should repair at once to the cellar, reached through the lounge bar. She suggested that, after they had partaken of coffee, they should all fetch their gas masks and keep them handy in case of an attack, and added that luncheon would be served at the usual time. Mrs Broughton said she did wish Captain Livingstone had not left them; to have an army officer about was so reassuring. Beatrice remembered to point out that the verandahs were now out of bounds because of the danger of flying glass, then she went to make sure that Stanley, the bartender, had returned to duty.

It was all so novel and absorbing and dramatic that Jo hardly felt frightened at all, and for a while the scene she had witnessed on the previous day sank out of her thoughts, only to surface with renewed intensity the moment she was alone. She argued with herself, that it had been Bron's idea, that she had only opened the door of the room because she thought someone was ill, that it was they and not she who were dreadful people, beyond the pale of human decency. None of this helped at all. She should have stood up to Bron; she need not have looked in rooms; she had stood there staring for that unbelieving second before running away down the stairs. It seemed that she and the other two – she did not so much as think their names – were locked in a loathsome conspiracy from which she could never escape. She knew, of course, that it was somehow related to what they had learned in biology about Reproduction, but that had only been about rabbits and seemed to have little to do with humans. The teacher's explanation had been embarrassed and garbled, and Bron had put up her hand and said, "Please Miss Curnock, do the rabbits come apart afterwards, or do they stay like that for ever?" and one or two people had giggled and their informant, blushing painfully, perhaps with her own imminent nuptials in mind, had said of course they came apart and if anyone didn't understand they could come to her afterwards. Naturally no one did. There had been a lot of private discussion, to which Jo had not contributed, though she listened. Some of the girls had the impression that intercourse was followed immediately by birth, but this did not seem likely. Jo was inclined to think it was something you had to do, by law, about once a year, if you were married. Since no one could possibly like it, it would have to be a legal requirement. But what she had seen was much worse, and the participants were not husband and wife.

She exhausted herself with trying to understand, and was silent at lunch with her mother and grandmother, Naturally they put it down to the declaration of war and the prospect of her departure to Wales. Just as they reached the coffee stage, the air-raid siren sounded. They had heard it before when it was being tested, but now it really meant something. The loud wail rose and fell, seeming to gather menace with each succeeding peak. All the adults in the restaurant rose to their feet.

Bea called out, "The cellars, please everyone"

Charles, the head waiter began ushering people out, saying, "Children first please, let's get the children down first."

Conversation broke out as they crossed the foyer, some openly doubting whether the cellars were the best place. What if the hotel received a direct hit and collapsed on top of them? Rather die in the street than be buried alive. But they all descended the stairs, to find the kitchen staff already coming down the back way. Charles asked Chef if he had remembered to turn off the ovens, and received a rude answer. Beatrice directed the most elderly to chairs and said they would be bringing down more seating for next time.

"They must have gone over by now," said a white-faced young woman hopefully. She took her small child from the nanny's arms and held him close.

"It's the return journey we've got to worry about. If they haven't used up all their bombs they'll drop them here as they cross the coast."

"Shut up, you fool," the man's wife hissed at him, nudging him hard with her elbow at the same time.

"It's true," he protested sulkily.

"What does that matter?" She smiled encouragingly at the other woman, and asked the baby's name. The man looked injured.

Jo was glad that both her grandmother and Patty were with them in the safety of the cellar. She asked herself whom she would miss the most if somebody had to be killed by a bomb. It ought to be her mother, of course, but relentlessly honest with herself she decided that Bea was the one she would miss least. Without her, Jo decided, she would go and live with her Gran over the tea shop, and Patty could work there so that she could still see her every day. Her almost readiness to sacrifice Bea increased her already crushing load of guilt.

"Listen! I think its the All Clear."

Someone ran up the kitchen stairs and threw open the door at the top. The single steady note blared joyfully. Noisy with relief everyone returned to the ground floor. Most of them forgot their gas masks and had to return to collect them. The children had rather enjoyed the experience.

Later, while Patty was ironing Jo's dresses and handkerchieves in the kitchenette, Jo sat on the small table which had been pushed up against the kitchen cabinet to make room for the ironing board. Patty was so approachable that Jo almost thought she might be able to confess the events of the previous day, but apart from the difficulty and embarrassment of putting the main incident into words there was always the fear that Patty might be as appalled as she was herself, would not want to speak to her again, being as she was, the child of someone like that.

"I'm not going, you know, so I don't know why you're doing all this."

"That's up to you." Patty carefully spread out the full skirt of Jo's favourite blue and white striped cotton dress. "All I know is, I've got to get your stuff ready."

But Jo knew it was not up to her. Despite her brave words she would have to go. She would have to go miles and miles away to this place in Wales, where she would see Miss Wells every day, with this terrible secret lying between them. Would Miss Wells actually speak to her? Surely not.

The next morning Bea called Jo to the phone.

"Daddy wants to speak to you. He was hoping to be able to come and say goodbye, but now he can't."

Clive, from his tiny office in a hut on the edge of the greatly enlarged camp, hoped to detect from Jo's tone of voice whether the face peering round the door of the bedroom yesterday had indeed been that of his daughter. His lover had been quite sure,

214

or appeared to be quite sure, that it was not. It was one of the maids, a small fair-haired one called Molly, who had not remained there long enough to see anything and would not dare to say a word anyway, for fear of being sacked. But to Clive, in that split second, it had looked like Jo, though what she could have been doing in the school during the holidays, let alone apparently being about to enter the headmistress's bedroom, he could not imagine. And if it had been Jo . . . well, he simply couldn't think how to rectify the situation. Could he ever look her in the face? Would she understand what she had seen? She was sure to tell Beatrice. And then what? He'd always known it would be a mistake to let their affair spill over onto school premises, but Rosemarie had been so importunate, it would have been unkind, churlish even, to refuse. But they had been wrong. Well, of course the whole thing had been wrong. Most of the time he had managed to see himself as a bit of a lad, not doing anything most men wouldn't do, but yesterday had put a different complexion on things. He'd always led a decent life and he had let himself down. Guy Upcott, if his reputation was to be believed, did this sort of thing and got away with it, but he, Clive Livingstone, wasn't the sort. And if only Bea had been a bit more interested, it need never have happened. It wasn't all his fault. Some of the blame could be attributed to his wife and her coolness, not to mention her usurpation of his job, which made him feel inadequate in more ways than one. Well, he'd let it all happen, and now it was too late and had ended in the worst possible way.

As he dressed that afternoon, he had explained to Rosemarie that this must be goodbye. "I'll be posted any day, quite possibly to France."

Rosemarie buttoned her dress. She had not replaced her corset, concealing it under the bedclothes. It was lightweight, expensive, lace-trimmed, but a corset nevertheless.

"Only au revoir, surely, my darling. I'll wait. So long as we are together in the end."

Desperately he said, "It'll be difficult. I may not be able to keep in touch. You must be free."

Rosemarie made it quite clear that freedom was not what she wanted. "You'll get leave, my dearest. The War may not last long. Then we shall be able to discuss our future."

He said vaguely, "Well, we'll see. We'll see what happens." Then he left, kissing her goodbye without enthusiasm. Driving back to camp he wondered if he had ever really been in love with her. He made up his mind to phone the St Andrew's on the way. If he spoke to Jo he might be able to judge from her manner whether the intruder had been her, or the maid Mollie, whom he strongly suspected had never existed. Rosemarie had spoken of Elsa, and he'd seen one or two servants about, none of them slim, or fair, or likely to be mistaken for his daughter.

When he finally succeeded in speaking to Jo the next morning she was monosyllabic, even when he said he was being moved and might not see her for a long time. She did ask him whether she really had to go away with the school, and her reluctance confirmed his fear. He told her to let Mummy decide, whatever she thought best.

So Jo knew it was no good, and five days later she boarded the coach outside the Princess May of Teck and was transported, by nightfall, to Llanbedr Hall, a run-down Welsh mansion that had until the previous week been St Benedict's Home for the Alcoholic Unemployed, and still bore all the marks of its history.

It was already dark by the time the two coaches laboured up the steep, rutted drive of Llanbedr Hall, drawing up on what had once been a gravel sweep outside the front entrance. The eighteenth-century building was still beautiful, but only its outline was detectable on this cloudy, dark night. It was past eleven o'clock as drivers, girls and staff wearily trailed into the house. They found themselves in a long panelled room, with an oak staircase at one side. It should have been welcoming, but the stone-flagged floor was stained and the panelling scratched and dusty. They were given cocoa, in thick white mugs, after most of them had thankfully visited the lavatories. These seemed fairly clean, and smelled chokingly of disinfectant.

Two or three of the inmates, unfit for army service, lurked in the kitchen. One had made the cocoa. Silent, shabby, looking tidy if not well washed, they were to be accommodated in the gatehouse at the top of the drive, with the commandant, a retired army officer.

"A temporary arrangement, I hope," murmured Miss White-house to Rosemarie. "One must be aware of the realities of life." Rosemarie felt that she would be the last one to forget them.

The nadir of the whole experience was reached when the girls were alotted bedrooms. Things, Rosemarie told them all firmly, would look better in the morning. Certainly that night they could not have looked much worse. Jo and three other girls, boarders whom she hardly knew, were led to a room with four beds. The beds being those that had been slept in by the deprived and depressed beneficiaries of the St Benedict Trust. They were narrow iron beds similar to most of those in the dormitories at the Princess May, but these were covered with dark grey blankets and the sheets on the one that Jo was destined to occupy were stained with a pinkish stain, and when she unwisely examined the pillow inside the crumpled pillowcase it was dark with grease.

"I can't sleep here. I can't sleep in this bed."

"You'll have to. Its all there is." Janet Porter, a fifth-form boarder who had been collected on the way, with a number of others, avoided examining her bed. She put on her dressing gown as well as her pyjamas, the top of which she had tucked firmly into the trousers, and slid under the covers and Lois Neave did the same, taking the extra precaution of spreading her cardigan over the pillow before laying her head on it. Eunice Banks, a thin girl who wore glasses and at least was not frighteningly bossy like the others, plaited her long fairish hair, got into her night clothes and then sat unhappily on the side of her bed. Jo did not even sit down. She stood in the middle of the room, still wearing her

217

green and white striped blazer, with her school hat in her hand. Rosemarie had ordered that uniform be worn for the journey. Now Jo could not see how she was ever going to take it off. All the surfaces in the room appeared grimy, though smeared, as if someone had cursorily wiped them over with a grubby cloth. She could not even put down her hat.

The grudging light of the unshaded sixty-watt bulb that dangled from the centre of the ceiling evidently prevented sleep from overtaking Janet and Lois. Janet sat up crossly.

"When are you two going to bed?"

"I can't," said Jo. "It's dirty." She indicated the pink stain.

Janet rose from her bed, pushed her feet into her black lace-up shoes and left the room. Jo walked to the window and looked out between the faded cretonne curtains, but could see only blackness. She went back to the centre of the room, then paced again to the window, back and forth, back and forth; she could not keep still.

Janet returned with Matron.

"She says the sheets are dirty."

Matron looked very tired indeed. Though still wearing her hat – navy straw trimmed with white ribbon – she had taken off the jacket of her navy costume and assumed her badge of office, a starched white apron.

Jo said, "I'm sorry, Matron," in a forlorn voice, and perhaps because of this Matron assured her quite kindly that the sheets had been washed, but were rough-dried. Jo showed her the pink stain and Matron pulled open the bed revealing an even more sinister yellowish one further down.

"Well, yes. Perhaps yours missed the boat."

Having examined Eunice's bed and pronounced it fit for use she fetched clean sheets and pillowcase and made up the fourth bed afresh. Even then Jo was reluctant to undress, but she did so, putting on her dressing gown like the others, and leaving her socks on too. She lay, carefully still, not wishing to expose any part of her body to contamination, which she thought might easily penetrate the clean school sheets that Matron had supplied.

"I hope you're satisfied," said Janet Porter crossly.

Jo was very far from satisfied, but she was desperately tired. Just before she fell asleep she wondered whether an outcast from the human race such as she believed herself to be had any right to scorn a bed just because it had been slept in by a man without a job, who drank too much.

Rosemarie was exhausted and full of doubts at the end of the long day. Had she made the right decision, bringing all these girls to this grubby, run-down place? Should she have made an effort to come and see it for herself first? But the agency had seemed reliable, and safety the main consideration, though at that moment she would willingly have traded the remoteness of Llanbedr Hall for a hotel in the middle of London with considerably less certainty of being alive in the morning. She supposed they would get the place cleaned up in time. She was sharing with Miss Whitehouse a room previously occupied by two members of staff. It was Spartan indeed, but at least the mattresses were clean. She would have to arrange for bedding to be brought from the school, which would be costly. The agency had assured her this would not be necessary, but she ought to have known.

There was so much to worry about that more personal considerations did not enter her mind until Miss Whitehouse, in smart silk pyjamas, had switched out the light. Then she began to wonder if she would ever again see Clive. How bleak the future was without him. Of course many women would be saying goodbye to their men, wives, fiancées . . . and mistresses. And for the last group it would be worse than for the others. Without rights, without any claim to information, without sympathy. And in her case perhaps even without love. Leaving her had hardly seemed to matter to Clive after that wretched child had stuck her nose round the door. That had spoilt everything. She hoped she'd convinced him that it was one of the maids, but the young fair-haired servant called Molly had been a fabrication, because she herself knew perfectly well it had been her lover's daughter, and the incident, shameful and embarrassing if it had merely been a servant, was in truth utterly appalling. But not her fault. In the afternoons there was absolutely no reason for any of the maids to enter her bedroom, which in any case none of them would ever do without previously knocking. Locking the door, although there was a key, simply hadn't occurred to her. And what was the child doing in the school? Let alone on that particular landing? Had it been some sort of escapade? But it wasn't the kind of thing Josephine Livingstone, the pupil, or Clive's daughter Jo seemed likely to do. It was the kind of thing one might have expected from . . . Bronwen Harries, say, who always had something mad and oddly furtive about her. And they had been friends, even when Bronwen had boarded. She wouldn't have been surprised if the Harries child was at the bottom of the whole ghastly episode, and she remembered her suspicion that there had been intruders in the school earlier in the holidays. She should have followed her instinct and got rid of Bronwen Harries somehow. The price for not doing so had been high. And what had it all done to Josephine? By common consent, they had avoided one another successfully during the journey, but in school that could not continue. Did the child know the facts of life? Probably not, or not in detail. Rosemarie had always thought that sort of thing was best left to the parents, though it did come into biology lessons, to a certain extent.

A new biology teacher would be coming at the beginning of term. At the interview she had seemed a sensible, down-to-earth sort of person. Could more knowledge lessen the shock and horror she had seen on the child's face? If they had just been in bed it would have been bad enough, but . . . Oh Lord, what on earth could be done? She didn't want the wretched child's life to be blighted, as it would be if the episode left her with a horror of men and sex, though what in hell she'd been up to, creeping round the school and peering into bedrooms, God alone knew. Well, it was the child's own fault and she would have to put up with any psychological consequences.

She would never again hear from Clive. She was sure of that. And she was stuck in this awful dump with only teachers for company, until the war ended. Which could be months. And might be years.

A light snore came from Miss Whitehouse in the other bed. How many years since she'd shared a room with another woman? She must try and change things round in the morning, so as to have a room to herself. But this might not be possible, in which case she'd just have to get used to it. At least it was Laura Whitehouse, whom actually she rather liked. How awful if it had been Miss Craig!

During the first night without Jo, Beatrice found she disliked sleeping alone in the apartment. During the next afternoon she walked up to the Japanese Tearoom which seemed to be surprisingly full of customers, and suggested to her mother that she moved into the St Andrews.

"Whatever for? I'm alright here."

"Well, we have got the cellar, if there's an air raid."

"I've got a cellar here, haven't I? But I certainly shan't go down there. If I'm going to be killed by a bomb I'd rather be in my own bed. No, don't worry about me, dear. I got through the last war and I expect I'll get through this one. Now, I'd better give the girls a hand."

"I was surprised to find you so busy."

"Well, I think people like to be in a crowd, you know. Have another cup before you go."

Mrs Hewitt, in her oriental blouse, black skirt and blacker fringe went out to the kitchen. Beatrice returned to the hotel to find that Clive had telephoned in her absence, and would try to ring again, if possible. Colin Weir had also phoned, but had said nothing about trying again. Although she was perfectly entitled to go out whenever she liked, she wished he had found her in the office. And missing Clive's call was even worse. She didn't need him to help run the hotel, she didn't need him in bed, but there were periods of time when his absence was really very trying. Why had he been so stupidly keen to join the Army? He should have considered her more.

When she had finished her dinner, lonely although there were over twenty other people in the room, she found Patty and told her to sleep in Jo's room. She felt responsible, she said, and feared that Patty might not hear the siren. She could continue to use a guest bathroom and leave her things where they were. Just the nights were to be spent in the apartment.

Although the air-raid warning remained silent, Patty continued to sleep in Jo's room for many weeks, and sometimes she and her employer shared a pot of tea before retiring. Only when Jo returned for Christmas did she occupy her single guest room.

But Christmas was a long way off. In north Wales as on the south-east coast the weather continued mild and sunny. Rosemarie ordered picnic lunches and led the girls on country rambles while the two maids who had come with them and some helpers from the village spring-cleaned the great house. When the van load of bedding arrived and the unappetising mattresses had all been stacked in an outhouse everyone felt more cheerful. Curtains were washed and ancient bits of carpet thrown out. Beatrice had caused the baby grand piano to be expensively transported from Culvergate, and this proved to have been a good idea. Sing-songs in the evenings were a success, and Miss Whitehouse went by bus to the nearest town and bought a lot of sheet music, popular songs and dance music and somehow the dancing and singing in the big entrance hall bound them, teachers and girls, together, and keeping cheerful became a duty that, for most of them, was not too difficult to fulfil.

Even Jo was almost happy at times. The countryside was wild and beautiful, quite unlike any she had seen before; there were crags and lakes and waterfalls and the dramatic scenery enthralled her; and often, walking with a dozen or more other girls, keeping her distance from Rosemarie, she was able to forget. But at night, or when they had their afternoon rest on their beds, during which twenty-minute period reading was forbidden she would once more be overwhelmed by the misery of guilt, shame and anxiety. What if the war ended and Clive came home and expected things to go on as before? She could not ever, ever speak to him, or let him touch her. When they started school work, at the end of September as usual, she was grateful for the occupation it gave her. Each week she received a letter from her mother, and another from Mrs Hewitt. Beatrice urged her to write to Clive, saying, 'Do write a note to Daddy, just a few lines. I will enclose it with mine. He will be glad to know you are thinking about him'.

Beatrice was in no danger of forgetting her husband. She missed him at mealtimes, taking her meals alone at the corner table, and pouring her own tea in her elegant sitting room. She missed the Martinis he had mixed for her before she changed for dinner, and in the late evening she disliked being forced to make the final round of the premises, and wondered why she had voluntarily taken it on before he left. She had wanted, presumably, to prove that there was no area of managership in which she was less capable than a man. And until the absence of expected air raids led to a belief that they would never actually happen, she missed the security of his presence in the other bed. He would, she thought, have made sure all the old people got down safely, have knocked on doors in case anyone had slept through the warning, which old Miss Kember was only too likely to do. Now she would have to carry out this duty herself, risking death until all were safely below ground. And where, in any case was he? After his embarkation leave, most of which he had spent in the Knight's Bar, she was given no idea of his whereabouts, his address simply being On Active Service.

*   *   *

223

Gradually Culvergate became used to the idea of being at war, and the Mayor made an announcement to the effect that there was no reason why the hotels and boading houses should not do well in the following year, adding that air-raid shelters for the express use of visitors to the town would be provided. Bea suggested to Colin on one of his rare visits that it might be a good idea to put 'Cellars available in case of enemy action', or something like that, in any advertisements, but he thought it would be best not to mention that eventuality.

Christmas came and went, with subdued gaiety, and Jo, home for the holiday, begged to stay on. Keswick Lodge, a small second-rate private day school for girls, was still functioning in an Edwardian house not far from the home of the Matthews. Why couldn't she go there?

Mrs Hewitt approved of this idea. "Well, that place in Wales doesn't seem to have done her much good. I'm sure she's lost weight, and her hands are covered with chilblains.

"And I've had this cold since half-term," put in Jo. "Everyone has a cold, all the time. The whole place is freezing."

"It will be better in the summer." Bea was doubtful. A child, even one of thirteen, was a responsibility. She had no time to spare. Although half the St Andrews was under dust sheets, there had been a corresponding reduction in staff, and there was plenty to do.

"You said the garden was beautiful."

This was true. Major Summersby had kept the inmates occupied and often exhausted by making them work long hours in the gardens of Llanbedr Hall. He was justly proud of the rose garden and the parterre, but the kitchen garden actually added to his income. It was a nice little sideline.

"We're not allowed in the garden," said Jo triumphantly, "because of the men." She explained about the remaining beneficiaries of the Trust, failing to mention that there were now only two left.

Mrs Hewitt was indignant, having been kept in the dark about this aspect of the situation at Llanbedr Hall, and Jo was not sent back.

Keswick House was not bad, though their record in the School Certificate was unimpressive. Jo turned out to be something of a star turn, which raised her self-esteem a little. A very little. She still, most of the time, felt separate from these other, ordinary girls, who had not seen what she had seen, did not know what she knew. One or two of the girls had newly married sisters and because she avoided all the furtive, giggly discussions about honeymoons and wedding nights she was thought prudish, and excluded from the long-established cliques, but this did not matter to her because once again she was regularly visiting the Matthews. John and Eileen still attended the Grammar School in the next town, journeying there by train daily. In the term-time, Jo saw them only for brief periods after they arrived home from school, though her regular Wednesday lessons had been resumed, but there were plans to start rehearsing a play during the Easter holidays.

And of course there was Patty. Patty was preparing for her wedding. Ken was now serving as a Lance Corporal in the Royal Engineers. Somewhere in England but likely to be posted abroad.

Chapter Seventeen

PATTY didn't wear a wedding dress. She was married hurriedly on a Tuesday morning in a grey suit and a pink hat with a veil. Ken, naturally was in battledress, his single stripe proudly displayed, his forage cap at a rakish angle on his shorn head. He had grown and broadened during his few months in the Army, was a boy no longer. Patty had persuaded him to let her have a perm, and luckily the tight waves suited her quite well. She wore dark red lipstick to match her corsage of carnations and Bea gave her a nice little reception in the staffroom. Chef made the cake. It was rather small, but it was recognisably a wedding cake and Patty was thrilled.

She spent the night before her wedding at the hotel, mainly because she intended to take a nice warm bath in the morning, impossible in the one inadequate bathroom shared between seven people in her parents' home. She and her father would be going to the church in a taxi, with Jo and Bea. Jo watched her packing her suitcase for the one night in a London hotel for which she and Ken had been saving. They thought they might go to the pictures in the evening.

Patty exuded happiness as she folded her new white locknit nightdress. Jo watched her pack the few things she needed, marvelling inwardly at Patty's air of confidence.

"Aren't you nervous?"

"About the wedding? 'Course not. They tell you what to say, and there won't be all that many people."

"No. I mean ..." Despite her closeness to Patty, Jo could

not voice her anxieties, her words trailed away. But the bride understood perfectly well.

"You mean about the wedding night and all that. No, course not."

"I would be," said Jo, conscious of wildly understating her fear and disgust of the whole thing, hoping for some sort of comfort from one who was willingly facing this trial.

Patty shook out the white nightie, looked at it thoughtfully, and refolded it more satisfactorily.

"I love Ken. When you love a person you want to be as close as you possibly can be. And perhaps I'll have a baby. Something of his to keep me happy till he gets back from the War."

She lowered the lid of the brown fibre suitcase and straightened her back. She looked for a long moment at Jo, who with downcast eyes was plaiting the fringe on the braid girdle of her school tunic.

"You're too young now . . ."

Normally any accusation of being too young would have enraged Jo as it would anyone else aged thirteen and a half, but said in such a matter of fact manner the words were robbed of offence.

". . . but you'll feel different one day. When you meet a nice boy who you really like."

Jo wished she could ask Patty what actually happened, if everyone did whatever Clive and Rosemarie had been doing. If that was true it made things better in one way, but worse, much worse, in another.

When Patty returned, two days later, to work at the St Andrew's, she appeared quite unchanged, but Jo felt shy in her presence. There were no more intimate chats in the kitchenette; they were not on a level any more. Instead of two friends, though with a marked difference in social status, their relationship had become that of an adult and a child.

It hadn't been exactly what he'd expected. He'd have a little office, he thought, and he'd be busy most of the time working out quantities of food and drink. He'd inspect camp kitchens, encourage the cooks, and if things got difficult he'd be driven round the countryside in a camouflaged saloon car, searching out farms and smallholdings, buying up whatever they had to offer, commandeering food in shops, going back to the base camp at night where his batman would have hot water ready, and have made up his bed. It was something like that, for a time, but the food got harder and harder to find and the base camp was being moved so often that there was hardly time to go to bed, but even then he didn't mind because he didn't want to think, and so welcomed being too busy and too tired. Then in the end when the order to retreat, though it wasn't put like that, came through, it was all chaotic, and hardly anyone knew which way to go, and they were machine-gunned and bombed and split up and lost and had dived into ditches heaven knows how many times, and in the end Clive, with three previously unknown soldiers, arrived on the beach at Dunkirk.

Clive lay painfully still in the sand, screened on all sides by dunes. With the sea mist and their khaki garments, he and the three men near him were, they hoped, barely visible from above.

The planes, having peppered the beach with machine-gun fire, disappeared inland. For the moment the sky was quiet. The small craft bobbed gently on the calm sea, while further out the fishing boats and ferries waited. Clive made an effort. He was exhausted, his back was torture from three days of unaccustomed exercise but he was uninjured, and he was an officer. It was his duty as well as his wish to see the others safely onto a boat of some sort.

"Off you go, lads, one more try. You'll be lucky this time." He dragged himself to his feet, speaking with as much energy and optimism as he could muster. He was desperately hungry but his hunger was as nothing to his thirst, he was dirty, unshaven, and his trousers were torn. He adjusted his tin hat.

Private Davis was wounded in the knee. He could not walk

unaided. And Lance Corporal Pratt, a bullet in his chest, had lost consciousness. Clive thought he had pneumonia as well. He hadn't long to go.

Clive addressed the third man. No more than a boy, he was short and slender. What on earth was he doing in the Army? He didn't look more than fifteen.

"You run for it and join on the shortest queue. You'll get in a boat alright."

The men were lining up at the edge of the sea, wading out to the little boats that had come dangerously across the channel to take them off the Dunkirk beach. The British Expeditionary Force was in full retreat, betrayed by out-of-date weapons and inadequate transport, but they would live, most of them, to fight another day.

"What about . . . ?" The boy hesitated, indicating the two wounded men.

"That's an order – run for it."

An order was an order, whatever the circumstances, stifling conscience, absolving from responsibility. Thankfully, Private Wilson ran for it.

"Now come on, make an effort. We musn't give in." Clive got Davis to his feet, despite his groans of agony.

"Bugger you, leave me alone. You go."

"I'm not bloody well—" Clive broke off. He had no breath to swear as he heaved the man to his feet. Had he done right to get rid of Wilson? The two of them could have joined hands and carried Davis across the sands fairly quickly. No, Wilson was uninjured, he had a chance.

"Put your arm round my shoulders, let me take your weight. Right, we're off."

They lurched and staggered out of the shelter of the dunes and at last reached the edge of the sea. Other men were doing the same, but not so many now, after three days. Some were limping westwards, for what reason Clive did not know. A dinghy, already dangerously low in the water, was within a few yards.

"No more," yelled the skipper, revving the outboard engine.

"This chap's wounded," shouted Clive from his dry throat. "Can't you make room for one?"

"Only if you want to sink us."

A man scrambled from among the packed bodies in the boat and began to wade ashore. "Get him in," he said. "I'll go along to the Mole. It's better anyway."

He helped to carry Davis, now fainting with pain, the last few yards, splashing through the shallow water, and somehow the occupants of the boat made room.

The man who had given up his place turned to Clive. "Come along, Sir. We'd best make for the Mole. There's no chance here now."

This was true. Nearby, a dozen or more men were waiting, queueing in an orderly fashion as though in a post office, to board a craft designed for five or six. At intervals along the shore, the same situation was repeated.

"What's the Mole?"

"Sort of pontoon. You can get straight on to one of the bigger boats, with luck."

"You go on. I've got to see to somebody."

But Bombardier Jarvis followed Clive up the beach to where Lance Corporal Pratt lay dead among the sandhills. Both inured to death, they wasted no time.

"Poor devil," said Clive. "I thought he'd have gone. I just had to make sure."

As they set out for the Mole the planes returned and this time they were bombers, diving repeatedly, aiming for the little boats and then for the larger ones further out. Clive with his companion ran back to the dunes, faster than he would have imagined possible in his exhausted condition, and crouched until the Stukas departed. Most of the inshore boats had disappeared, though neither Clive nor the other commented on this.

They wrung out their clothing as best they could and trudged for an hour along the sands, every now and then racing for

231

shelter as German planes appeared. Fear of being killed was not uppermost in Clive's mind. To satisfy his raging thirst he would have risked his life over and over again. But no such option was available, and at last the Mole, a wooden structure five feet wide and stretching out into the sea for upwards of half a mile, came into view. It was crowded with men slowly moving forward towards a fishing boat which lay alongside near the far end. They could see that there were gaps in the walkway, hastily bridged by rickety planks. Some of the men were carrying stretchers, from time to time forced to raise them to shoulder height so that they could see where they were placing their feet. All were tired, dirty, unshaven, and many had makeshift bandages stained with blood. They joined the waiting group where a naval officer in full uniform was counting men onto the Mole, businesslike and matter of fact, as though it was something he did every day.

Clive sat down on the sand. He was lightheaded from thirst and emptiness, his tin hat seemed to weigh a ton. He considered removing it, but decided that to do so would be setting a bad example. Now, for the first time since he had received the order to make for Dunkirk, rescue was in sight. Other men would be thinking of home, believing that there was after all a chance that they might again see wives and children, drink cups of tea or pints of beer, sleep in their own beds. There was none of this for Clive. The face at the door, with its expression of horror, he was now quite sure, had been Jo's face. And though an article on child psychology in a popular newspaper was all he had ever read on the subject, he knew this was no light matter. He'd tried to believe Rosemarie's fantasy about a fair-haired maidservant, but his daughter's subsequent behaviour, her eagerness to end the conversation when he had managed to speak to her on the phone, her brief stilted letters, could not be otherwise explained. And by now she must have told Beatrice. And the middle-aged voracious cow who'd got him into all this, well, he never wanted to see her again. She hadn't really loved him. What

232

had he ever seen in her? Only the fact that she was so unlikely a mistress, so dignified, so much an object of respect. What was he going back to? A damaged child who might never be able to lead a normal life because of what she had seen, a betrayed wife, and the woman who had brought it all about. And for this he must make the superhuman effort of getting to the end of the Mole, miles and miles away in the sea, and climbing into a boat, and staying alive, somehow until he reached . . . where? Who?

"Here you are mate. Drop of water." Somebody held a tin mug to his cracked lips. It was hard not to cry with gratitude.

The Mayor had been over-optimistic. Everything was changing. Troops from Dunkirk were disembarking at Culvergate, exhausted, wounded and dirty. The townspeople were supplying them with food and drink as they staggered, limped and were carried off the motley collection of boats. Asked for blankets, Bea sent every spare one in the hotel down to the harbour. Some wives and mothers had received postcards or telegrams, reassuring them that their loved ones were still in the land of the living. There was nothing from Clive, but Bea was confident. They were still coming off the boats and they had it on good authority that some had only just set out. He would be alright. He wasn't a fighting soldier, he was a catering officer. He'd have got away alright. Yet she was proud, with her husband taking part in this incredible adventure. She didn't say too much to Jo, only that she thought Daddy might be home soon, and they must both do everything they could, make things just as he wanted. Jo agreed, but the haunting picture came again. Perhaps what he wanted was Miss Wells, naked in her top-floor room.

That afternoon John Matthews walked into the foyer of the St Andrew's and asked to see Jo. Not knowing him, the receptionist did not send him up but telephoned the apartment asking Jo to come down. He stood, a lanky boy of fifteen in a school blazer that was too short in the sleeves. Jo was surprised to see him.

"Hallo, Jo."

233

"Hallo, John." She waited uncomfortably, wondering why he had come.

"So this is your private palace."

"It's not private. I'd much rather live in a house, like yours."

"I'd like to live in a house like mine too."

"You do live there."

"No. Eileen and I, and Beth are going up to our Gran's in Yorkshire tomorrow. Mum and Dad don't want to wait for the school to be evacuated."

"Oh. Don't you want to go?"

"What do you think? It will be ghastly. Depths of the country. All trees and things."

"Trees are alright."

"When you've seen one tree you've seen them all. I'm a townie. One of these days I'm going to live in London."

"There are lots of things you can go to in London." The pause lengthened, neither seemed to have any more to say. Jo wondered why he had come, then, "So I just thought I'd pop round and bid you farewell."

"Oh. Farewell, then. Thank you for coming."

"And it also crossed my mind that I might drop you a line occasionally, if that's alright."

Jo blushed. She felt her face grow hot. Staring at the floor she muttered, "OK. You can if you like."

"Anything from your father?"

"Not yet. But Mum says he'll be alright, he's a catering officer."

"Cheerio then. My mother will be expecting you on Wednesday. Air raids permitting."

John held out his hand and Jo placed hers in it. They shook hands firmly. Then he left, out through the swing doors down the steps and away, without looking back.

Jo stared after him. She wished she had risen to the occasion. She wished she had thought of something witty and sophisticated to say. She'd felt such an idiot, blushing and looking down. But the fact remained that he wanted to write to her. She'd be able to write witty, sophisticated replies. She could impress him that way. Funny how she'd always liked him from the first moment he had led her into what he called the 'torture-chamber'. It had never occurred to her that he might look on her as anything more than one of his mother's pupils. As she returned to the apartment she remembered Patty's words: 'If you really love a person . . .' For the first time she felt she might somehow, one day, leave behind the morass of guilt and revulsion that had so nearly engulfed her. As she went up the stairs, already planning what she would say in her first letter, her heart lightened. Bron's evil spell would, in the end fade away, leaving only a thin, dark sediment, though this would remain, carefully undisturbed, always.

Clive sipped the water, his dry throat seeming to have forgotten how to swallow. The naval officer turned towards him. There was room on the Mole now, he could climb up and join the tattered procession that limped slowly towards the waiting boat.

The mist had cleared and the calm water sparkled. No planes had passed over for nearly half an hour.

"On you get, sir." Bombardier Jarvis tried to guide him towards the step, but Clive moved aside and began to make his unsteady way up the sand.

Somebody called after him once or twice and then stopped. Reaching the dunes he staggered a little further, then he lay down.

And waited.